Secondary Attachments

Secondary Attachments

GREG HERRIGES

William Morrow and Company, Inc.
New York

Library of Congress Cataloging-in-Publication Data

Herriges, Greg.
  Secondary attachments.

  I. Title.
PS3558.E753S4 1986   813'.54   85-18769
ISBN 0-688-06171-0

Printed in the United States of America

First Edition

1 2 3 4 5 6 7 8 9 10

BOOK DESIGN BY MARY CREGAN

For Carmen and Jeremy, with love

Secondary Attachments

One

Shelly would never admit it to anybody, but she snores. I was lying in bed next to her, listening to her suck in air through her nostrils. I wondered how I could get across the bed to the alarm clock to find out what time it was. Looked to be about six. I could tell by the way the sun hit the blinds behind the bed, just lighting up the room enough so that you could get around without breaking your neck. If *I* had been the one to ask for the divorce, I could have listed her snoring as grounds. Mental cruelty, Your Honor. Seven years of listening to a 747 warming up on the runway.

This was the day the divorce would be finalized. The papers would come through, or something. I hadn't been needed at the hearings since she was the one suing me. Somehow that just didn't seem right; even in Algiers they give dope dealers a chance to defend themselves. But it was neater this way, my lawyer had told me. No histrionics. No bad scenes in the courtroom. Just a deposition that I had to read and sign. She got the house and I got the car. Even trade.

The house was a split-level job in Highland Park. The car was a 1977 Buick with rust and a bad muffler. The decree would state that Mr. Spector repeatedly refused to associate with Mrs. Spector in any social manner, and that his (my) behavior—which was characterized as that of a ten-year-old—caused her anxiety and embarrassment. There was something about pizza parties with sixteen-year-old hoodlums from the ghetto during which her grandmother's antique Hungarian vase had been shattered (it was a god-awful monstrosity; I had never liked it) (I think *I* was the one who knocked it over) (I think I did it on purpose) and mad forays like the time when I decided to paint the exterior of the house chartreuse without consulting her. It was all there, inaccurate for the most part.

9

I *had* told her that I was planning to paint the house, and the paint wasn't chartreuse. It was mockingbird yellow, or canary yellow, or something like that. Anyway, who cares? My lawyer, Herb Green, suggested that I not take the charges or testimony seriously—it was just in fulfillment of legal practices before the courts would give you a paper stating that the marriage was terminated. I took his advice and put the whole business out of my mind. It just seemed to me that if we weren't going to be married anymore, we kind of shouldn't sleep together, either.

I restacked my pillows behind me and socked them a few times to get them into shape. Polyester doesn't fluff. Seven years of housekeeping and we'd never bought decent pillows. That should tell you something. I sat up and laid my back against the pillows and felt the headboard cut into my back. Shelly began a new growl, broke off abruptly, and lay breathing quietly for a few moments. At twenty-nine she had pretty much kept her looks. A little heavier in the ass, maybe. I couldn't tell if that was a plus or a minus. It looked nice on her. She looked good to me, but in the way your sister might look good to you. Admired from a distance, the way you look at babies or perfect lawns.

"You awake?" This from my side.

I said, "No. I'm sleep-sitting. Don't wake me. I have a bad heart."

I reached over the side of the bed to the floor, groped for a cigarette, found one, and then let my hand blindly search for the matches.

Shelly said, "What time is it? Do you know?"

"The clock is on your side of the bed."

She leaned over, picked up the cheap electric clock that I'd bought at Ace Hardware after I'd moved out of the house, put the clock down, and returned to my side.

"Don't keep me in suspense, hey. What the hell time is it?" I said, finding the matches at last.

"You're asleep. It doesn't matter," she said, closing her eyes and drawing a deep sigh that might have meant something.

"If you deny a sleep-sitter a simple request, they sometimes act irrationally." I lighted my cigarette.

"Like that would be new for you."

"Sometimes they kill the person who pisses them off."

"If they have the strength," she said, poking me in the ribs with her fist, "and if I remember last night correctly, you don't have the strength."

"Everybody has a bad night from time to time."

"Hmmph."

"They do. Don't they? Aren't I entitled to a bad night?"

She sat up then, tried futilely to fluff her own polyester pillows (which were in worse shape than mine), and then said, "Hmmph," again. "You used up the bad night you were entitled to three years ago."

"Aren't they renewable?" I wondered what to do with my cigarette ashes.

"Oh, God, don't be clever in the morning."

"What does that mean?"

She wouldn't tell me.

It had taken seven years for our marriage to resemble leftover gravy. It had been hot, then it had been tepid, and we were currently in our room temperature state. Time to throw it out. I was surprised every time she made an attempt at foreplay. Foreplay was supposed to come before something. I was more turned on by my hand than by Shelly. My hand didn't scream when I made love to it. If her snoring was merely distracting, her lovemaking was positively debilitating. When I was in bed with Shelly, and if my eyes were closed, I often had visions of her climbing into a nice hot shower, only to find Tony Perkins waiting there. I wondered what the neighbors must have thought.

"He's doing it again, Harry. He's beating her within an inch of her life. That poor thing."

And of course, truth be known, the poor thing wasn't the one doing the screaming.

My poor thing.

I hadn't had time to line up my bathroom stuff in the modern but cheap medicine cabinet that was sort of a hallmark of my new high-rise apartment. Sundries. Whatever the hell you call that stuff. Shaving shit. I had Gillette Swivel razors in their little cardboard packages and Colgate shaving lather and Christian Dior after-shave and some generic antiperspirant and aspirin and Maalox all lined up on the sink top and the back of the toilet.

Was that me in the mirror?

Who's the guy with the swollen face and bloodshot eyes? How

come adults can't wake up and at least resemble the people they were when they hit the sack the night before? Must be one of the little extras that come with maturity. There's a word Shelly loved— *maturity.* She liked *responsible,* too. *Adult*—that word made her wet.

"Johnny? Do you have any orange juice?" Shelly's voice from the kitchen.

"I'm in the bathroom," I told her, lathering my face while rinsing off a new razor. The bottle of wine we'd shared the night before was making my head feel as though it had a new but permanent crease directly down the middle.

Shelly appeared at the bathroom door and watched me begin shaving. "Do you have any orange juice?"

"The frozen kind. The kind you have to mix with water."

"Yuch. I hate concentrate."

"It's all I've got," I said, turning to see her.

I dislike talking to the mirror. She was running around the apartment in just her bikini briefs. She looked good. My sister. My perfect lawn.

Apparently there was nothing better to do than to watch me shave from the doorway. That's where she stayed, at any rate. I measured my sideburns to see which was longer than the other. They never came out even. I wondered why that was.

"Who was the boy at the door last night? The one you didn't let in?"

"I don't know," I said, scraping my neck.

Shelly said, "What do you mean you don't know? Wasn't he one of your students or something?"

"No. I've never seen him before in my life."

She looked at the bathroom floor as though it were a crossword puzzle. "That's odd."

"Groupies," I said.

"Pardon me?"

"Groupies. From the book. I've had four since I moved in here. There was one little sixteen-year-old sweetheart of a waif I almost let in the other night. I watched her on the TV monitor until she gave up. She reminded me of you when you were back in high school."

"What do you mean? You mean, they know where you *live?*"

"Uh-huh."

"How do they find out?"

I rinsed my razor and noticed that I'd missed a little path of stubbles from my neck to my ear. "I don't know. I think I should get the building management to take my name down from the whatchamacall-it. The registry. Or change it. Come up with a secret name or something."

One of the little ironies of life that had at first amused me was the visits I'd get—nighttime visits—from a scant but consistent band of refugees who were determined to meet the author. I had published a novel the year before about a teen-ager who was troubled (if not out-and-out nuts), and since I'd moved into Chicago I'd been surprised to realize that I had a following. Then I'd been concerned. Then I'd been terrified. Many of the kids looked like they had escaped from centers for unwashed lunatics. Some of them sent me drugs in the mail. I never answered my door anymore; I simply watched the building TV security channel and waited until they went away. If they left notes, I tried not to read them. If they didn't break your heart with a story about cruel parents, the words were so misspelled that you had to wonder about the future of the world in the hands of the up-and-coming generation. The funny thing was, if a night went by and I didn't get a mystery visit from some punk, I felt lonely. I felt like I'd been abandoned. It was one of those nights that I had toyed with the idea of letting the little waif up. But I didn't. I just sadly watched her pick up her ratty knapsack and slink out of camera range.

Shelly left her post at the door, swayed over to sink vicinity, and sat down on the closed toilet seat. "Today's the day."

Today's the day. Jesus.

"Aren't you at least a little sentimental about it?" she wanted to know.

"If I think about it," I said, and then I fought for the right words so that I wouldn't be misunderstood, "yeah, then I get sentimental. I try not to. Think about it, I mean."

"We had some good times." She was lost in the floor tiles again, speaking as if to the laundry hamper. "There *were* some good times." She reached out and touched my waist with her hand. "Why don't you see somebody, Johnny? Why don't you make an appointment and just try it once?"

Good times. Swell times. My high school sweetheart, grown up and turned real estate agent. Responsible, adult Shelly. Who ever warned her that she would grow up alone?

"Let me get this straight. We're talking shrink, right?"

"Psychiatrist, psychologist, counselor, doctor. Take your pick."

"And then I'll just go in there like a good boy and say, 'Hi, Doc. I'm here 'cause my ex-wife sent me and I can't get it up. Have you got a pill for that?' and he'll give me a shot and I'll get an erection and we can get married again."

"Christ. You're impossible. I really feel sorry for you."

"Don't. I'd probably just paint the house red or something if we ever got back together, and then you'd have to go out and get another lawyer."

Shelly said, "Really sorry for you. You'll just never grow up." Then she got off the john, swayed into the hallway, and mumbled something about me being permanently set on high school. What a waste.

Nobody ever warned her.

When I was dressed and had had coffee, and when Shelly was taking her turn in the bathroom, I picked up an old battered and underlined copy of *The Human Comedy*, by William Saroyan. It happened to be a favorite of mine, and the language was easy enough for the thirty or so delinquents enrolled in my English I class. I grabbed a jacket from the still unorganized coat closet and stopped by the bathroom door. Shelly was putting on her makeup, examining herself closely in the mirror.

"Lock up, will you?" I said, looking for my car keys.

"Is that all? The day of our divorce and all you can say is 'Lock up'?"

I did not know what else to say.

"Congratulations?"

Shelly stepped away from the mirror and came over and put her arms around me.

"Nothing all that much has changed," she said. "We'll live through it, I mean. We can be friends."

"Sure."

It occurred to me that you had an odd relationship when it didn't make any difference if you were married or divorced.

"I'll tell you what let's do." Shelly backed away from me and looked actually excited about making new plans together.

"What?"

"Let's have a drink at Sweetwater's tonight, after the papers come through."

Shelly could take a funeral and turn it into something to celebrate about.

Goddamn drink.

"Okay." I don't know why I agreed. It just seemed petty to refuse a last request. Water under the bridge, and all of that.

"Say about eight-thirty? I'm showing a house on Fullerton at seven and I can meet you at the bar at eight-thirty. Give me fifteen minutes' leeway."

I said, "I'll be the one with the divorced look in my eyes."

When I was nearly out the door, I remembered something. It wasn't a matter of common civility so much—that same civility that was coloring almost every word we said to each other lately. It was more like gratitude. After having read Shelly's testimony and feeling about myself pretty much the way I felt about Muammar Qaddafi, it was kind of funny to think I'd been let off easy.

"Hey, I forgot to tell you. Thanks for not mentioning about that year, in the testimony and all."

Shelly was back to the mirror by now, carefully inventing new eyebrows.

"What year?"

"You know. When we were first married, and I didn't talk."

"Jesus," she said. She said it like it was the only thing you *could* say about that year. I guess it was. "I'd forgotten."

"Thanks anyway."

I was out the door then. The corridor in my building had two burned-out lights and no windows. It was like walking in an amusement-park fun house, not knowing what to expect. The elevator took me to the garage. I found two new dents on my car door and I didn't care. At least they matched.

Time for work.

Let's go. Steer the battered Buick carefully down Hampden Court, avoiding the potholes (you can't avoid Chicago potholes—you just think you can because you're part of a generally optimistic species). At the age of twenty-nine, I had spent my entire adult life in a high school. Not any high school. This was a one-of-a-kind high school, set in the heart of Chicago's Puerto Rican community, which advertises itself with tenement buildings and three thousand used-tire shops.

On Diversey Parkway now. Notice the people lined up, waiting to board the already sardine-tight bus. Tired-looking people. Dirty-looking people. Billboards in Spanish. Basic Spanish. A lady (a lady with too much lipstick) is sensuously caressing a bottle of Bayer aspirin. Beneath her in block letters it says, ME QUIDO CON BAYER. This means that she takes care of herself with the product. I'll bet she does.

Take a look out the passenger window at the twelve-year-old girl who is dressed in dime store clothes. See the fat man in a dirty T-shirt, leering at her as she carries her brown bag lunch to school? Isn't that nice? Now try to put the cheap dress and the crummy-looking sack lunch out of your mind. Go on, try it. Try not hoping that the fat guy gets run over.

Iglesias. Storefront churches. These were once upon a time delis, when the neighborhood was Jewish and Saul Bellow was still attending Tuley High School. Was there ever such a time? From Jewish to Puerto Rican—with a slight intermission to go Ukrainian.

Church of Christ the Redeemer. *Cristo,* as he is commonly known. Bumper stickers on old Dodge Chargers that ask if you've found the door to God, and you know you have a hard enough time finding the door to the bathroom, most mornings. Ah—exhaust smells from CTA buses, diesel trucks, and a few unidentifiable, repugnant aromas thrown in to create the spice of the ghetto.

Now down Western Avenue, where, believe it or not, there are at least half a dozen more used-tire shops and fast-food restaurants with no national affiliation. Walt's Shakes. Bunga's Place. I've never eaten at Bunga's Place in all these years. I wonder why that is.

Take a right down North Avenue. Disco Latino Record Shop. Jupiter. Why would they name a store after a planet? Up ahead, just past the intersection of California and North, is Humboldt Park. Rumor has it that when the neighborhood went solid Latin, they took the statues of Goethe and Pulaski out and transferred them to Lincoln and Grant parks. I think this may be true. They never replaced the goddamn things; they just removed them. Who would they put up a statue of? Geraldo Rivera? He's still alive. Which takes us to the predicament the school board found itself in when it was asked to name the new thirty-four-million-dollar high school structure in the middle of Humboldt Park after a famous but dead Puerto Rican. Roberto Clemente had already been used. So now we inch the ugly Buick carefully into the underground auto shop (the only semisafe place to park a car in the area) of *Freddie Prinze High School.*

I wish I were kidding you.

We haven't turned out one comedian yet, but a lot of the kids have found new and interesting ways to kill themselves, so there is some relevance to the name.

I was too tired to take the stairs from the basement of the school to the main office. I found my elevator key and waited outside of the kitchen. There were only six floors in the school, and I always wondered where the hell the elevator could get lost for ten minutes at a time. It smelled like they were cooking pizza for lunch. The kitchen staff regularly served pizza and baked potatoes. This was in case the kids weren't getting enough starch in their daily allotment of rice and beans at home. That's all those poor kids ever ate—*arroz con habichuelas*. I had heard that food stamps could not be used for paper products, and I spent a minute guessing what they used for toilet paper. That could explain where all the textbooks disappeared to every year.

When I got off the elevator on the second floor I stopped at the glass picture windows to survey the park. It was only a quarter to eight and already gang members were choosing up their turf for the day. Green-and-black-sweatered youths were holding down the patio. Cobras. The Spanish Cobras had adopted a paramilitary look of camouflage, which conversely made them the easiest to identify. Things had been heating up ever since an atypically warm spring vacation when two Latin Kings had been killed at close range by gunfire from a .22 caliber pistol. Everybody knew it was just the beginning.

I went to my mailbox in the main office and said good morning to the clerks behind the counter. Most of them never said anything back, but I was always polite to them. Be nice to people long enough and it will eventually drive them nuts.

In my mailbox was a crisply worded memo, hot from the principal's desk, concerning my lesson plans. He wanted to know where they were. I would've liked to know, too. I didn't keep lesson plans. I taught by instinct. Also from the principal's desk were three new ethnicity surveys, which, the paper-clipped dittoed instructions warned me, must be completed in homeroom and turned in to the main office by noon. High noon. As if I had nothing better to do with my time. My mail secured, I shuffled off to my office and wondered what I'd tell Dr. McCaskey, the principal. Dr. Theodore McCaskey. He was forty-eight and balding, had short white effeminate fingers, and never smiled. It was generally known that he still lived with his mother. I don't care what you say, that's taking devotion too far. I wondered what he did for sex. Probably used the curriculum guide as a stroke book.

I had two study sheets prepared on *The Human Comedy* and all I needed to do was run them off on a duplicating machine. The machine on my floor was broken, so I hopped the elevator to the history department on the sixth floor and was ready to roll off thirty copies when Mary Esther Sheenan walked in on me.

"That machine is solely for the use of history people."

Good morning to you, too, Mary.

I said, "Mary, I *am* a history person. I'm wild about the French Revolution. Great little device, the guillotine."

She clicked off the power switch of the duplicator, pulled out my master copy, and handed it back to me. "Use the English machine," she said.

"The English machine is broken."

"Fix it."

Then she pulled open the office door and held out her hand as if to escort me. As I left I said, "You really shouldn't be so accommodating. People will start to take advantage of you."

"Get out," she said.

At times you have to stop and think about what could turn a perfectly dreadful woman into an even more dreadful bitch. Mary supplied the contrast by which humanitarians were measured.

I checked my watch and saw that I had fifteen minutes until class time. I could stop in the breakfast room and have a cigarette. I trashed the idea of the study sheets. Fresh out of duplicators.

I thought to myself that I ought to get Shelly something for the Big Day. A free membership in a dating service or something. Maybe just a card. There ought to be a card for semi-amicable divorces.

HAPPY DIVORCE!
Now that you've had the best years of my life—
wanna try for the worst?

Two

The business club sold newspapers in the lobby of the school every morning in order to raise money for whatever a business club might need it for. Scholarships. Disposable syringes. I always thought it was a good idea because it happened to be convenient for me, and because it was one of the few examples you could find in that place of kids learning by doing. The kid on duty was a big black guy named Eddie. I liked Eddie. He was always tying his shoelaces.

"How's the news look today, buddy?" I asked him, tossing a quarter at him. He caught it in mid-flight.

"Looks okay to me," he said, pretending to study the front page. There was a model in a bathing suit with some caption underneath. "Best news I seen in some time." He went back to his shoes and I headed down the corridor to my office.

I thumbed quickly through a few pages and some kids walked by.

"Good morning, Mr. Spector."

I said good morning back to some little coed I'd never seen before and wondered how they all knew who you were if you didn't know who they were.

There was a crazy story in the paper about a brother-and-sister team who'd dug up their father's grave and pulled all his teeth out. Supposedly, they were under the mistaken impression that a secret bank account number had been inscribed on one of his fillings. They were caught when they brought the collection of teeth to a jeweler, requesting that he magnify each tooth in search of numbers. It was mornings like this that tended to indicate that Rod Serling's view of life wasn't all that far off the track.

Another story caught my eye as I was walking into my office. I threw my duplicator masters and my keys on my desk, folded the paper, and read about a teen-ager who had been killed by a street gang. The kid was sixteen and had been wearing a red-and-black jacket in front of his home, while walking his dog. Red and black were Spanish Lords colors. Apparently a car full of Lords happened by, and they resented the infringement on their trademark, so they offed him with a shotgun. The story said that he attended Freddie Prinze High School in Chicago.

Not anymore, he didn't.

I sat in my chair for some time and looked at the wall. The kid had just been walking his goddamn dog, for Christ's sake.

I tried to imagine Shelly going back to her maiden name. Greenbaum. She'd have to order new checks and sit for another driver's license picture.

I thought about what a good idea it would be for someone to open a lesson plan service, and then all you'd have to do would be to tell them your subject area and the dates you needed to cover.

Shelly Greenbaum. Huh.

I was still in my zombie pose when Tony walked in.

"What's up, Johnny?" he said. My kids call me Johnny. It cuts through the bullshit. It also infuriates the rest of the teachers.

I tossed the paper at him and tapped my finger on the story about the shooting.

"I know about this already," he said, reading the copy.

It was no big deal. Kids got killed in this neighborhood every day. Guys like Tony were just glad it wasn't them. Tony moved his lips while he read, and I studied him—his slouched posture, his toreador haircut jutting out into tight curls in the back. Tony made me sad. It was like just underneath the green, hooded sweatshirt was a hurt so big he couldn't for a minute think about it. I wondered what it might be, Tony's hurt, and since the possibilities seemed endless, I decided to handle it like he did. I ignored it.

I noticed, while watching him read, that he was wearing gym shoes with no shoelaces. The goddamn things were ready to fall off if he took one false step. I had a momentary fantasy about Eddie breaking one of his own laces and mugging Tony for *his*.

"Got dressed in a hurry today, huh?" I looked at his shoes and tilted my head toward them.

"Huh? Oh." He examined the hanging tongues as if they might

have been mocking him. "The sonofabitch. I'm gonna kill that sonofabitch one of these days."

Maybe Eddie *did* mug him, I thought.

"Who? Who are you going to kill?"

Tony pulled a chair up to my desk and extended one of his loose shoes into the area between us, as if the subject of discussion had to be on display. "Fernando, the goddamn security guard. You know Fernando?"

"Yeah. Why did he want your shoelaces?"

Fernando was a middle-aged school board employee who was assigned to the front door. He screened the students to keep the hardcore gang dropouts from entering and recruiting. He wasn't always diplomatic.

"Just 'cause my shoelaces were green and black, he took 'em. Thought they were colors."

"Well—as far as I know, green and black are still colors, right?"

"No, man." Tony took a deep breath, and for a moment his hurt seemed to bounce all over the office, right off the steel-paneled walls. "*Gang* colors. He thought I was representing."

"And of course you weren't." I looked at him eye to eye. The little bastard was bullshitting me and he knew that I knew.

"Look—I gotta wear laces to keep my shoes on, don't I?"

"Uh-huh."

"Well, don't I?"

"And they have to be green-and-black shoelaces or else your shoes will fall off."

Tony cracked up and slapped his hand on my desk. "Damn, Johnny! I swear to God they *came* that way when I bought them. Honest."

I smiled, and then I frowned so that he wouldn't see me smile, and then broke down and laughed with him. "You're a lying sonofabitch, is what you are. And liars go to hell, Tony. If God doesn't already know about this, I'm telling him. I'm gonna bust your ass."

"You don't believe me, right?"

There's a thing in the neighborhood about sticking with your original story no matter how many holes have been shot through it. I'd just got a bull's-eye. Tony was a Cobra. Green and black were Cobra colors. My impression, my gut instinct, was that he was one of the passive, reluctant members. A lot of the kids joined gangs just so the heavies wouldn't kill them on their way to school. Or while they walked their dogs.

"You know this kid, right?" Tony said, referring to the kid in the paper.

"I don't think so." I took the paper and read his name. David Hernandez. "Uh-uh. Doesn't ring a bell."

"Sure, you know. His nickname was Jughead. You had him a year ago in your English One class, remember? The kid who always came in late 'cause he worked nights, and he was the only one you never gave shit to about tardies, on account of he worked to support his mother."

The thought that Jughead was David Hernandez caught me by surprise and made me ache somewhere near the center of my stomach.

"Not Jughead. Not fucking Jughead."

Tony let his head drop so that his chin touched his chest. "The paper's got it all wrong, man. Friend of mine saw the whole thing. He was walking down Hirsch near Division Street—"

I asked, "Who? Jughead or your friend?"

"Jughead, man. He was coming home from the factory he works at."

"*Worked* at, you mean."

Tony said, "Yeah. He was just coming home from work when this black Chevy came around the corner real fast and these dudes slammed on the brakes and blew his fucking head off. Just like that. They honest-to-God blew his whole—"

"Enough, Tony. Enough."

The kid had been a student of mine and all I knew was that he worked hard and was called Jughead on the block. I wondered what they'd call him now.

Dead.

"They wanted him to join. He was the only one on the street who wasn't picked by either us—I mean the Cobras—or the Kings. If he woulda been one of our boys, they woulda left him alone."

I thought about this logic and coughed. "Yeah, well. I don't suppose anybody ever figured that if he didn't want to join either of the gangs, maybe they should've left him alone."

Tony shook his head. He was probably wondering why white people were so dumb. "It don't work like that."

"Doesn't," I corrected him.

"It sure doesn't," he agreed.

Then he pulled a Polaroid snapshot out of his back pocket and laid it on my desk in front of me. I was suddenly looking at one car of a CTA El train. In the vernacular, it had been *bombed*. Some street punk had invested fifteen or twenty bucks in spray-paint cans of orange, black, purple, and green and decorated it while it was asleep in the yards. This was common in New York, but had yet to come off in Chicago. The car pictured was covered with lightning strokes and two laughing heads. The artist's pseudonym—in orange lacquer—read FAST KID. Fast Kid, better known to me as Tony.

"Whad'ya think?" he asked, rubbing some pubescent beard growth on his chin while he leaned in close, obviously proud of his first piece of professional work.

"I think you're going to hell for sure, now."

Tony slapped my desk again. He liked to hit things. "No, man. Really, Johnny. Pretty good, huh?"

Actually it was a tremendous job. The goddamn train looked like it had been silk-screened, not bombed. Tony's skill as an artist was unquestionable. He was determined and disciplined. For some reason, though, he couldn't apply that determination or discipline to activities that were not against the law. Some alarm in my mind went off and suggested that I drop a few big-brotherly hints that he play by the rules, that he should not destroy property. That he should put this much effort into his art class, which he was failing.

"Have you ever thought about giving up all this glory and performing like a pro for your art teacher?"

Tony stood up and snatched the picture off my desk as though I'd just insulted his integrity.

"For that *bitch*? That white *bitch*?"

This made me curious. "Who's your art teacher?"

"Flannahan."

That white bitch, I thought.

I suggested that he, number one, ought not show the picture around too widely, and that, number two, he carry it someplace other than his back jeans pocket.

"I got plenty others," he said.

Then he wanted to know if I would keep it to show the rest of the family. The family, or La Familia, as they called themselves, were my favored students. My delinquents. The same ones that had helped me destroy Shelly's ugly antique vase. I told him that he'd better take care of that little business himself since it didn't seem appropriate.

"Okay then," he came back at me. "You got a cigarette?"

I looked at him. At moments like these I tended to question my influence on kids. What kind of teacher supplied smokes to sixteen-year-olds?

I two-fingered a Kool out of my shirt pocket and threw it at him. What the hell. I was immature and irrational—and if you don't believe me, I've got the divorce decree to prove it. It was signed by a judge. It *must* be true.

The first-period bell rang and I stood up, threw the newspaper in the wastebasket, picked up my attendance book, and was about to walk out the door when Tony told me why he couldn't make it to class during third period.

"I got this doctor's appointment."

"Good. While you're there, tell him you failed English to keep that appointment. He'll appreciate it."

"I honest-to-God do, Johnny. I'll bring a note."

"You're going to hell. I'm warning you."

I was clear at the other end of the hall, dodging sleepy students coming from the opposite direction, when he yelled at me, "Where the hell am I supposed to get shoelaces around here?"

I said, "Ask Eddie—the newspaper guy. He'll know."

The kids never showed up on time for the first period and I always felt a bit like a jailer waiting around for them in the doorway of my classroom, so I headed for the breakfast room. The breakfast room was on the fifth floor adjacent to one of the cafeterias where every morning hungry and tired-looking students would line up and wait—sometimes as long as half an hour—for individual cardboard servings of shredded wheat, or whatever the going breakfast cereal was. Frosted Ghetto Flakes. Many of the kids were bored and leaned against walls and said "shit" a lot.

"Your mother ain't shit," or "Are they givin' the same ol' shit again?" or "You lowdown wasted piece of fried shit."

They were mainly Puerto Rican or black; occasionally you could pick a Mexican kid out in the crowd. He'd be the scared-looking one with the straight black hair, seemingly lost and afraid to ask directions.

Inside the breakfast room teachers were sitting in not-so-even rows along two rectangular tables. The Lobotomy Club sat at the first of these, and it included mostly matrons from the home ec and phys ed departments, and a few emasculated specimens who I always pictured sitting home on Friday nights, knitting. If you listened closely you were certain that Jackie Gleason had taught them all English. "Yous guys."

The other table was the other table. You sat there if you were a substitute and didn't know anybody, or if you were *completely* burned out, like Megan Croner, who was ancient and couldn't remember anything that had happened to her in almost a decade. She talked to herself and people pretended not to notice. Or you sat there if you were one of the ranking bad boys, like myself and a friend of mine, Dave Volmer. I spotted Dave sitting—removed by a chair or two—near the burnout cases.

"Can I join you, or would you prefer to wait until Megan remembers who you are and includes you in her conversation?"

"Johnny. Sit down. We're a delinquent short on this end."

"That for me?" I asked. He had a spare cup of coffee next to his own on the table.

"Cost you a quarter to find out. What's new in Divorceland? Is the judge going to let you keep your Jockeys, or do they go with the house?"

Dave Volmer. Married twice, divorced twice. A kid from each marriage. At five-ten and 170 pounds, he looked like he took it all very well. The only damage was a loss of hairline. I figured out once what his child support payments were and counted him lucky if he could buy lunch without a personal loan.

"Listen—Johnny Spector's Jockeys are Johnny Spector's Jockeys. If she wants them, she'll have to pull them off herself."

"She will," Dave said, smiling. He lighted a fresh cigarette and handed one from the pack to me.

"No, thanks. I've got a first period."

I sorted out my morning stack of papers in front of me on the breakfast table. Dave noticed the unmistakable memo from McCaskey's desk.

"Notes from the principal. I didn't even know you two were close."

I said, "We're not. He's just dying to read my lesson plans."

"That's horseshit," he announced. Two or three gym teachers

caught his emphasis and left a blank in their conversation to see what else they could pick up from our end of the table.

"And I've got a racial survey—to be completed by high noon."

Dave looked it over and then sipped some more of his coffee. "That's horseshit of another color."

I liked talking to Dave. He was the only guy I knew who should have been absolutely miserable and wasn't.

"Dave, did you see the thing in the paper, the killing?"

"You mean the kid who used to go here?"

I nodded.

"Yeah. I saw it. Things are heating up, it seems."

"He was one of my students, and when I read his name, I didn't even know who he was. One of my other kids filled me in. Kind of makes you sick, doesn't it?"

Dave took a long hit from his Parliament cigarette and blew a cloud of blue smoke toward the row of fluorescents above us. "Kind of sort of. Listen, if you're depressed about it, you can always join the other table and talk about sump pumps or something. They don't even know about that shooting."

He wasn't kidding. A gleeful roar of laughter swept over the Lobotomy Club and you had to wonder what was so funny at that hour of the morning in this particular section of the city.

"His fly had been open the entire time!" It was Janice Newman, an English teacher. Open flies were precisely what she thought about most mornings.

"The papers come through today," I offered, not knowing what else to say to Dave. Sometimes I regretted that what we had most in common was divorce. He didn't seem to mind, though. It was like discussing space with an astronaut. There was always enough space.

"Congratulations," Dave said, lifting my arm and forcing me into a handshake. "A free man. May you go forth and fornicate."

I had finished half of my cup of coffee and had just noticed that it *did* taste like something, but I couldn't for the life of me figure out what.

"Did I ever tell you that at one time I didn't talk for a whole year?"

Dave looked at me over the top of his coffee cup, and judging from the way his eyes pulled tightly at the corners, I guessed that he was smiling. Then he put down his cup and swallowed. I watched his Adam's apple bounce up and down again.

"You want to talk about not talking?"

I checked my watch and figured I was about as late to class as I dared be. "Some other time, maybe. Thanks for the coffee."

Dave caught me by the shirt sleeve as I was standing up and said, "I'll be in my office if you want to talk. No fooling."

No fooling. He still thought he had to explain things to me, like when he was serious and when he wasn't. That was another thing I liked about him.

"I'll see if I can catch you later," I said.

"Listen, Johnny. It'll only hurt when you have to sign the check to the lawyer. If you want, I'll sign your name so you don't have to watch."

I said, "What a guy," and slapped him on the back. The matrons' table burst into hysterical, screeching chortles over something as I left, closing the door a little harder than necessary. I realized suddenly that there would be a funeral, and I kicked around the idea of sending Jughead off. It didn't seem to make much difference.

Even though I was ten or eleven minutes late, I only had seven students waiting for me in my English I class. At Freddie Prinze High School you didn't take attendance until the end of the period. Kind of like you don't count your chickens. In the last fifteen minutes of the period four or five kids would walk in and mutter something about the bus being late, or the alarm clock being broken. I passed out copies of *The Human Comedy* to everyone and watched their faces take on identical not-this-shit-again expressions.

"All right, boys and girls," I said.

"We're not boys and girls," a girl said. This was Damaris Rodriguez. Short, heavy, and illuminated by about a pound of eye shadow, ranging from magenta on one end to turquoise on the other. She looked like Hawkwoman and was hard to take before nine in the morning.

"I'm sorry to hear about your loss of sex, Damaris, but we're on the chapter entitled 'The Girl on the Corner.' "

"That's Sonia's mother on the corner."

Well. At least Jasper was awake. Jasper Johnson was a skinny black kid who was permanently horny. He deliberately sat behind Sonia Vazquez every day and watched her legs, or what he could see of them.

"You shut up, *maricón*," Sonia said.

Maricón translates loosely as *motherfucker*, or *bitch*, or *faggot*. No one seems to know for sure.

I had to hold their hands through any piece of literature we attempted. This meant reading aloud most of the time, and sweating through the broken syllabic monotone that characterizes nonreaders. I felt depressed as Hector, a short kid with a tight 'fro, stumbled over Saroyan's once-lively prose. No wonder they were bored shitless.

I took over the reading chores myself, looking up from my book occasionally to catch students with their heads on their arms, eyes closed, or looking out the window, or, in Jasper's case, leaning over Sonia to see what he could catch sight of in her blouse. I wished he would just jerk off before coming to school and get it over with.

"What do you think about that?" I said, rhetorically, when we had finished the chapter.

"Think about what?" Jasper asked. His book was closed on his desk.

I counted to ten and smiled. "About Mr. Spangler running up to the girl on the corner and kissing her."

One girl said she would have slapped his face.

Jasper said that if it had been him and she would have slapped his face, he would have kicked her ass.

"You wouldn't kick *my* ass, honey," Damaris volunteered, somehow thinking that she might have been the girl on the corner. Who knows? Maybe she was.

"You're missing the point," I said, wondering how far I should go with the lesson. I could stand on my head and hand them bits and pieces of philosophy and theory and theme and insight, I reasoned, and they might just look back at me with dead faces. Or I could just drop the whole matter.

I opted for explaining. It wasn't noon yet and I still had a tangible feeling of hope. Guide them kids, teacher.

"You see, it all has to do with innocence and beauty. Spangler wasn't being fresh—or maybe he was—but what he was doing was like honoring the girl's beauty. See?"

Oh, Lord. A sea of blank faces. And me without a life preserver.

"Look at it this way. What's the most beautiful thing you've ever seen?"

Nothing.

"None of you can think of the most beautiful thing you've ever seen?" I said, jumping around the front of the classroom like a heart attack victim, just to get their attention.

"I can," Jasper said.

"Good. What is it, buddy? What's the most beautiful thing you've ever seen?"

Jasper sat back and stretched his arms on either side of his desk. "Sonia's pussy."

Sonia turned around and hit him smack in the mouth, sending him off his chair, backward.

"Spic bitch!" he shouted, holding his mouth.

Jesus. You could almost hear Saroyan spinning around down there.

Three

During homeroom I found out that I had nineteen Puerto Rican students, four Mexicans, two blacks, and one white non-Hispanic. I had to convince the white kid that he was not Asian. He didn't know the difference.

I took the escalators back down to my office. Between the fourth and the third floors some girl in front of me almost poked out my eye while she was combing her hair. She didn't apologize.

I threw the racial survey forms on my desk and began trying to make some sense out of the results so that I could fill in the proper numbers on the master sheet. High noon. Then I discovered that I was also supposed to separate each grouping according to sex. This I did by guessing. I always had trouble with survey forms and frequently lied on them. No one ever complained. I pictured some busy little clerical worker in a government office jotting down figures that would never attest to anything significant, other than what he did for a living. He just jotted numbers.

Then I decided to make the white kid an Asian. What the hell. *He* thought he was one.

I sat at my desk, staring straight ahead at nothing, and fished for matches in my shirt pocket. They're never where you leave them. I opened a drawer, lifted forms and absence reports, and found a cheap lighter that I must've stuck in there four years earlier. It still worked. I took my first drag off the cigarette and a minute later there was a knock on my door. I wasn't in the mood for company.

When I opened the door I found a gape-mouthed boy who stood approximately five feet and two inches. His hair was black, curly, and badly in need of cutting. He was wearing old janitor's baggies and a wrinkled light-blue shirt with cactuses hand-painted in red and yellow. The cactuses had seen better days. He held out a yellow program sheet. This wasn't out of the ordinary; students frequently came to me in my office with new programs. However, he held the program sheet out to me upside down. I smelled trouble.

"*¡Hola!*" I said. "*¿Qué tal? ¿Cómo estas?*"

"*Bien, maestro. ¿Y tú?*" he said, in a sleepy Puerto Rican accent.

"*Bien.*" This was the extent of my Spanish. If we were going to communicate at all anymore, it would have to be in English.

I looked at his program—after I had turned it right side up—and found that there had been an error. The kid was scheduled into English I for a period that I didn't even teach it. I started to explain to the boy—Carlos; his name was Carlos Villavaso—that I didn't have an English I class for the period indicated. Then I had to stop in mid-sentence. There was something disarming about him. It was his eyes. You had to swim in them. And he grinned a lot, but it was a nice grin. Then I figured out what it was about his eyes. They seemed to have once belonged to either Curly Howard or Bambi.

"Would you like to sit down?" I asked him, wheeling an office chair his way.

He shook his head and continued to smile at me. The kid went around making you love him on sight. But I realized there was something wrong. Carlos wasn't your average student. The kid had problems. There was a short circuit in his coordination, a twisting of the head, the posture. A blankness in the gaze. I looked at the program sheet more carefully and saw that he had a third-grade reading level. English I students are required to have at least a sixth-grade reading level. (In Chicago it's okay to have sixth-grade abilities in the ninth grade. A lot of things are possible in Chicago.)

"Well, buddy, we've got a problem here."

Problems seemed to make him smile harder.

"Yes?"

"Yes. In the first place, I don't have an English One class at the time listed here. Mr. Bane must've made a mistake when he filled this out. He must've put my name instead of some other teacher's name. You've got the wrong guy."

He walked nearer to my side, looked down at the form with me, as if I'd just asked him for directions according to some complicated map, and then held his finger over the consecutive letters in my last name.

"*S-p-e-c-t-o-r.* You are Señor Spector, *sí?*"

Jesus. What was he trying to do to me? His confusion was so honest and his attempts at solving mysteries so inadequate that just explaining the obvious to him was akin to playing a devious trick. *Life has tricked you, Carlos,* I thought, *and everybody's in on the joke but you.*

I rolled the chair in front of him again and this time insisted. "Sit down, kid. Please. We gotta talk."

"Okay."

He sat there smiling at me and shifted a notebook and an elementary math book to his lap. I recognized the math book as a text from the Special Ed department. That was it. He was a Special Ed student, a label that could stick for life, depending upon the nature of the program. Some of these "special" kids even got different diplomas from the regular students, diplomas that would allow them to go confidently into the world and saw lumber or dig holes forever.

I puffed nervously on my cigarette and looked at him. I thought about how it would take him all of today just to get his program changed, and the next few years to understand what had gone wrong. It would compute like this: Mr. Spector doesn't want you. You're stupid. Another tree trunk blocking another one of the roads he stumbled down endlessly. On top of that, it was April. There were only eight weeks of school left, and no teacher at Freddie Prinze High was about to give a full semester's credit for eight weeks of work. The kid would attend school every day for the rest of the year and then not even get rewarded for it. There would be a neat, block-lettered F on his report card—and again he'd have to figure out what he'd done wrong to deserve to fail.

"Why are you coming to class so late in the year?" I asked, stubbing out my cigarette and trying to avoid his eyes so I could at least *sound* objective.

He looked at me as though I'd just told him the score for the Cubs' opener. He didn't say anything.

"Carlos? Could you tell me why you come to school first now, in April? Not September?"

He said, "Ohhhh." He caught on. "See, the officer. He come to my door. My onkle, he say, no, I don't go school. I work. The officer, he say, no—I got to go school. So I go school. So I get this paper and I ask lady in hall. She say Señor Spector, room two-fourteen." He then stood up, walked back out of the office into the hallway, looked at the room number above my office, and came in again and sat down. "This room two-fourteen."

It had taken the truant system almost seven months to catch up to him. I could only guess as to how many kids never even got found.

I thought about the Special Education teachers Carlos might get if I took him to Bane and straightened this little matter out. Abigail Drake. Don Freelander. Margaret Riley. They'd either turn him to hamburger or ignore him altogether.

No fucking way.

I took his program and signed him into my office during my free time. Then I handed it back to him and shook his hand.

"Glad to have you aboard."

"Sí. Aboard."

"Only this is a slightly unusual class. It's just you. Just you and me."

He looked around the office as if I'd hidden other students in filing cabinets or under the desk.

"Me, yust?"

I nodded and lighted another cigarette. "Take out a piece of paper and a pen. I've got your first assignment."

Immediately his notebook flew open and two very nervous little hands went about the tough task of disengaging two sheets of notebook paper.

"Relax, why don't you? Slow down, Carlos. There's no rush."

But the busy little hands struggled with the middle binder and at last freed the paper, which he evened out by tapping it on top of his notebook. He grabbed a pen from behind his ear. He stared at me as though I were about to give him the Holy Law or something.

I thought about a subject. I wondered if he was capable of writing a sentence. There was only one way to find out.

"You like movies, buddy?"

"Movies?"

"Yeah. You know. Movies. *Star Wars*. Uh, *Gremlins*. I don't know, *Casablanca*. You know. Movies."

"*Time Machine*," he said.

34

"Yeah? You know *The Time Machine?*"

He said *sí;* he did.

"Great. Write about *The Time Machine.* What happens in it. When did you see it?"

He scratched his head and looked somewhere near the corner of the ceiling. Then his eyes flashed wider. "Tomorrow."

"Tomorrow hasn't happened yet."

"Other tomorrow."

"You mean *yesterday.*"

"*Sí.*"

"Good, good. You just tell me all about *The Time Machine.* Okay?"

"Okay."

"Do it right now."

"Okay."

'Sallright. Close de door.

I let him use my desk, and I rolled the spare chair across the office so that I would stay out of his way. That's when La Familia showed up. Or most of La Familia.

"Johnny!" The arms around my neck—which came from behind, about as gently as a half nelson—belonged to Elsie Montanez. Elsie was seductive and sultry and her name reminded me of a cow.

She kept me in a headlock and I was slapped on the shoulder by a kid named Alfonzo. Alfonzo was six foot five and gorillaed his way through life intimidating people unintentionally.

"Wha'sup?" he said to me. *Wha'sup* was his favorite expression.

"Yeah—tell us what's up, Johnny." Elsie slid a hand across my ear a few times and I had the notion that there must be thousands of lonely sailors in the world looking for a girl just like her.

Tony slouched his way into my office next, with a kid named Pedro. Pedro had a devil's sneer and specialized in a kind of abstract humor that none of the others ever understood. If he couldn't get a laugh with his intellect, he let his face take over. He could make bizarre faces.

They all studied Carlos, the stranger in the group. It took Pedro less than ten seconds to realize that the kid was at a mental disadvantage.

"Who let Einstein in?" Pedro said. "Hey, kid. Can you spell *relativity?*"

Carlos looked up, and for the first time I saw what fear looked like in his eyes. Not attractive. Without understanding Pedro's question, he unmistakably recognized the intent.

I said, "These are some friends of mine, Carlos. Guys, this is Carlos, and he's a student who at the moment is writing about a movie. Leave him alone."

I gave Pedro a look so that he'd understand. He made a face back at me. He got the message.

Tony reached into his back pocket and said, "You guys wanna see somethin' beautiful?"

I thought vaguely of Saroyan's girl on the corner, and of Sonia's pussy.

Tony held out his snapshot of the CTA car and everyone gathered around him like they were about to discuss football plays. Elsie released me, looked at the picture, and then told me that one of our regulars, a girl named Wanda, wasn't in school. She was worried about her and wondered could I maybe call her house and see if she was sick.

"You don't think she's sick, I get a feeling," I said.

"I'm afraid about her."

I asked her what that was supposed to mean.

"Her father's pissed at her on account of her boyfriend. I know she ain't supposed to see him no more—and then she doesn't come to school, so I think you better call."

I had to call my absentees anyway, so I figured why not. My stomach began to growl. I hadn't eaten anything since dinner with Shelly. The Last Supper.

I escorted all of them except Carlos out of the office and told them to see me later. Alfonzo held on to my sleeve. These kids always pull you by the sleeve, I thought.

"It's hot out there, man."

"So buy an air conditioner," I told him. He didn't think that was funny.

He said, "You know what I mean," poking me in the chest with his finger. "Between the Folks and the People. There's gonna be some action any day now, man."

The gangs had formed two mutually exclusive coalitions based on neighborhood geography. If you lived south of North Avenue—as did the Disciples, the Cobras, and the Imperial Gangsters—you were Folks. If you lived north—as did the Latin Kings, the Ghetto Brothers, the Spanish Lords, and the Unknowns—you were People. The distinction between Folks and People was taken dead-seriously on the streets, no matter how stupid it sounded to outsiders.

"Lay low," I told him. "You get Tony to tone down his act, too. He was representing with his shoelaces this morning. He's going to get his ass shot," I predicted.

"Man's gotta wear shoelaces, right, Johnny?" Alfonzo smirked somewhere about eight inches above me.

I said, "*You* know what I mean."

Absentees. I called five disconnected numbers, three wrong numbers, two numbers where no one spoke English, and I talked to Wanda's mother. Wanda had a cold, she said.

Wanda did not have a cold. Her mother was lying. In the background I could hear frantic shouting. One of the voices was clearly uncongested and unconditionally Wanda's. I'd have to look into this.

Dr. McCaskey stopped by and asked once more for my lesson plans.

"I'll have them for you tomorrow," I told him. "I'm making absentee calls at the moment."

He looked around my office, eyeing Carlos and the furniture as if he might want to expel the former and repossess the latter. We stared at each other for some time. He wrote something down on a little checklist and gave a meaningful snort and left.

Lesson plans. Honest to Christ.

Carlos finished his paper, folded it in half, lengthwise, handed it to me, and watched my face as though he expected me to grade it on the spot.

"Next time, buddy. We'll take a look at this next time." Then I ruffled his hair. In response, he shook my hand enthusiastically.

"Next time," he said.

"You betcha."

When he was gone I felt like cutting my throat, for some reason. Just to balance out the day.

That afternoon I taught approximately sixty students what a noun is. About six of them understood that a noun isn't something that you do. The rest didn't give a shit.

Shit is a noun.

On my way out of the building to my car I was thinking about a bottle of beer at home in my refrigerator, when I saw a girl walk by. She was carrying my book, my novel. I wondered if she'd got it out of the library, and what she thought of it. I then stopped and watched her cross the park. What was it about her? I knew what it was. She was the most beautiful girl I'd ever seen.

I was surprised at myself. She couldn't have been more than seventeen.

Four

A day at Freddie Prinze High School made you feel like a zombie when you got out. I didn't particularly attribute this to stress. There wasn't that much stress. Maybe it was stupidity. Or frustration. It could very well have been due to lousy air circulation in the building. In any case, I felt like a zombie when I got in my car and drove home. It was a big deal just to stay on my side of the yellow line once I was on North Avenue.

Folks and People. It was sort of like drawing a line between hoodlums and delinquents. All over the park gang members huddled in little groups like ants with nothing to do. Lots of big ghetto blasters playing cucaracha music—salsa. Conga drums, bongos, cowbells, and disco whistles. The factions danced, smoked joints, downed beers, checked out lovely señoritas, and glared each other into territorial imperatives. It was like watching pockets of leaky gasoline and waiting for someone to throw in the match.

When I got home I dumped my books and jacket on my living room couch and went in search of the lone beer in the refrigerator. It was hiding behind a bottle of Heinz ketchup that I must have bought a month before. The top was covered with coagulated crap. I should have thrown it out, but I didn't. I pulled out the beer bottle and then had to look in every kitchen drawer before I found the bottle opener. It hadn't been in a drawer at all. It had been magnetically stuck to the outside of the refrigerator door the whole time. This for convenience.

I once read somewhere—I think it was Steinbeck—that every bottle of beer has a mystery bubble hiding in it just waiting to grab your throat and make you choke. My mystery bubble caught me on the first gulp, and I coughed spasmodically once or twice, fighting with it. It won.

I walked around the apartment, trying to make it feel like home. It had, the first day I moved in, but since then Shelly's visits seemed to have had a cumulative effect, until it began to feel like the house I'd moved out of. It felt like the place was part hers. The suspicion that Shelly didn't know what a divorce was all about swept through me. I took another gulp of beer and mulled this over. Maybe she thought legal separations were solely confined to the world of paperwork. The whole idea was to not feel married anymore, or at least that was supposed to be the whole idea. I wondered if this was why husbands sometimes killed their wives.

Inside the bathroom, in a neat little row on the back of the toilet, were Shelly's fingernail polish, polish remover, lipstick, and deodorant. I had an impulse to gather all the tubes and bottles up, stick them in an envelope, and mail them to her lawyer, Brandt Levy. Brandt was an asshole. He spit when he talked to you. Little drops of saliva in the sunlight.

There was a knock at the door. I wondered if I should hide. I thought maybe one of the teen-age runaways had got through the building security, or that Shelly had sold the house on Fullerton already and wanted that drink now.

"Johnny? It's me. You in there?"

More knocking. It was Jack Henley.

I opened the door with the bottle in my hand. Jack immediately grabbed it away from me and took a swig. Then he choked. How about that. This bottle had *two* mystery bubbles.

Jack was a photographer I'd met through the school system. He at one time took photos of pimple-faced young graduates for a yearbook outfit, until he decided that there was more to life than acne. We'd been working on a project together for a Chicago newspaper—an article about the lives of street gang members. I'd first been excited about it because of my easy access to the kids and the danger involved, but the danger became too real. While interviewing the leaders of several gangs one day, driving around the city in my car (the only way they'd agree to it—none of them wanted to remain stationary for fear of becoming sitting ducks, targets for rival gang members), I'd been pulled over by a cop for making an illegal left turn. I didn't know that one of the leaders in the backseat was reloading his stolen .38 caliber Smith and Wesson. It had been a close call.

"Well?" Jack asked, when he'd finished coughing. "Don't you have anything to say about being published again?"

I took my beer back from him. "You mean they bought it?"

"Do I mean they bought it. Obviously someone hasn't checked his mail today. What's the matter with you, do you have something against income and fame?"

"They *did* buy it," I said.

"Of course they bought it. Aren't you excited? What's the matter with you?"

I suddenly felt sick and had to sit down. I thought about the huddled groups of gangsters in Humboldt Park and what Alfonzo and Tony had told me earlier—that things were hot. I was kind of like the guy with the match and Jack was telling me to throw it.

Oh, boy.

We walked down to a neighborhood bar on Diversey Parkway a few minutes later, at my urging. Before we'd left the building, I'd picked up my mail. The bar was a sub-street-level affair with only die-hard old drinkers and hackers leaning up against a dark-wood curved bar. A television with bad reception flickered over a shelf of shot glasses and I sorted my mail next to my beer. I found the check. It was for six hundred dollars. I felt better for a second.

Jack said, "You get a lot of mail."

"Yep. I sure do. Nothing you'd want to open in public, though."

"Whad'ya mean?"

There were bills from Saks Fifth Avenue, MasterCard, and Commonwealth Edison. There was a flier from J. C. Penney advertising barbecues. There was also a manila envelope from my publisher in New York. I put this one aside.

Jack said, "It's the divorce, isn't it?"

"What's the divorce?"

He slapped a hand on my back. "It's all right. I understand."

"What do you understand? I don't think you do."

"Look," he said, copping an I'm-your-best-friend-so-it's-okay-if-you-cry-on-my-shoulder attitude, "it's gonna be rough at first, but before you know it, you'll be on with the rest of your life. Sort of like measles, you know? Sooner or later you get better."

Measles. Jesus.

"Jack, do me a favor and shut up until you know what you're talking about."

I lifted my glass, but somehow didn't make it on the follow-through. Jack looked grim. It made me feel like an asshole, his looking like that.

What the hell. I slapped his shoulder and sipped my beer. "Look, we got problems, big buddy. Not you so much, but I do. *I be going to get the shit pulled out from under me, mama.*"

"I don't know what you're talking about," he said, staring me down. I'd rained on his parade.

I told him I'd explain in a second, and then said that he should open the manila envelope. He picked it up, tore the flap open, had some trouble with it, and then reached in and pulled out five or six little envelopes addressed to my publisher.

"Now, open one of those."

"What is this?"

"Fan mail."

Jack selected a letter written on sky-blue stationery. He sat silent for the next few moments, reading the letter. Then he looked up and said, "This woman wants to know if you enjoy mutual masturbation."

I drank some more of my beer.

Jack said, "Well—do you?"

"That sounds like my mail, all right. Read another."

He opened the least legibly addressed envelope and began reading again. He sipped his beer. He scratched his head.

"Johnny, I think you should take a look at this one."

He slid the letter over to me.

Dear Mr. Spector:

I bought your book and let me tell you what I think of you. You are a heathen and a disciple of Satan. You corrupt the minds of our nations youth with the poison garbage you call literature. Our comunity libary has banned your book and articles and their is right now a petition circulating at our youth group which we will send to your publishing company asking that they fire you and keep you from leading young people astray with your atheistic and Satanic poisonous garbage. You cannot turn your back on Jesus, Mr. Spector, without sealing your doom in hell forever. Christ is the answer and the way. We live in a free country that will not tolerate your Comunistic and atheistic views. You should be thrown in a pit and buried before you bury the lives of our children.

Amen,
Helen Mary Baker

I let the letter fall on the bar between our beer glasses.

Jack said, "You never told me you were a Communist."

"I just found out myself." I got the bartender's attention by waving my hand and ordered another round. "Things are getting pretty crazy. Sometimes at night I find joints slipped under my door. Quaaludes. Runaway teen-agers wait for me in the lobby. I watch them on TV."

"And the divorce doesn't bother you at all." Jack was watching my face to see if I was on the up-and-up.

"Oh, it bothers me. What bothers me more is that Shelly leaves her stuff all over the apartment. I think she's marking her turf."

Jack looked baffled. "You two still *sleep* together? I thought that was supposed to end when you moved out."

I said, "So did I. I'm always the last one to find out."

I looked around the bar at the sad cases studying the woodwork. I had to get out of there.

"C'mon. Let's go up to my sun deck and split a joint."

Jack asked me if the joint was one that had been left by the groupies. I said, "I have to do *something* with them, don't I?"

We walked back to Hampden Court and took the elevator to the roof. Twenty-four stories. A brunet rode up with us as far as the sixteenth floor, and when she got out I found myself thinking that she had the ugliest legs I'd ever seen on an attractive woman. They were knotty and blue-veined. Jack followed her with his eyes until she was out of sight, down the hall. Her legs didn't bother him.

It was windy on the roof. I'd gone through half a pack of matches trying to get the joint lighted until I gave up and handed the works to Jack. He had it going in one effort.

"You bastard," I said.

He wanted to know what the shit was that was about to be pulled

43

out from under me. I told him about the gang momentum at school and in the park and how one spark could set it off. He thought about this a minute and handed the joint to me.

"This is a piece of journalism. I don't see how telling the truth is wrong." He squinted at the western horizon, patches of green and concrete and brick. Puffy white mini-clouds.

"Yeah, well. That's good in theory. I don't think the principal or the police will see it like that."

Jack said, "Fuck 'em if they can't take a joke."

"Right."

He took the joint back between his thumb and index finger and drew in deeply, expanding his chest. "You worried about your job?"

"Am I worried about my job." I watched a lady walk a dog down Clark Street until the dog stopped and lifted its leg on a Cadillac. "Not in the way you mean, no," I said. "I'm not worried about being fired. I'll get heat from the administration 'cause it makes them nervous when someone goes public about anything close to home. But they can't can me. What I'm worried about right now is a girl who didn't come to school today and a boy who did. The boy is learning disabled or something, and the girl is probably nursing a black eye."

For some reason I flashed a little cartoon in my head of me writing. I was at the typewriter working on a best seller and Norman Mailer and John Updike kept calling me up, desperate to know how I handled writer's block. I told Mailer that tough guys don't whine. Updike— I didn't tell him anything; I just hung up. What can you tell Updike? In the bedroom Shelly was still screaming from the multiple orgasms that I'd inspired nearly an hour before.

Marijuana dreams. No wonder that stuff is illegal.

Jack was saying something, but I hadn't heard him.

"Pardon me?"

"I said, what went wrong with you and Shelly, anyway? I would've bet you two had it solid."

"Jack," I said, tossing the roach over the side of the building and watching it until it disappeared, "that was one of the problems. Things weren't solid on my end, if you know what I mean."

Jack looked confused and then said, "Ohhh. I didn't know you had that problem. Can't you go to a doctor or something?"

"It's psychological," I said. It made me feel better, somehow, to think it was only my mind that was in trouble. "Did I ever tell you that I didn't talk once for a whole year?"

Jack said I hadn't. Good, I thought. Somebody's going to finally hear the story.

"When Shelly and I first got married I was listening to a lot of Jimi Hendrix and Bob Dylan. I thought, hey, these guys know something I don't, so I experimented with acid. The first trip was great. I was at a friend's house and kept getting lost in different rooms. Then I tried it again. And again. My last trip left me speechless."

"For a whole year?" Jack asked, looking a little as though being on a high-rise roof with me might be a bad idea. He was probably thinking of Art Linkletter's daughter.

"Will you quit looking at me like that? I'm not going to jump, for Christ's sake."

Jack said, "You'd better not. I left my camera in the car. So go on. You didn't talk for a year."

The wind was rushing past my ears and I almost had to shout by then to be heard. "Yeah. Oh, I mean I said *some* stuff. Like 'When's dinner?' and stuff like that. But mostly I just went to my classes and took my exams and came home and watched the window a lot. I got into the sky. I used to have an obsession about watching it. On a cloudy day I'd feel like I'd been cheated. You know?"

Jack asked if that meant we'd had a lousy marriage for the whole seven years. I thought about that. It didn't seem like seven years at all. It seemed more like seven months.

"No. It was good, I think. It just got to the point where I didn't care about her houses and she didn't care about my students. Real estate and teaching. They don't mix."

Jack said, "Huh," which is what he said about most things.

A newspaper page flew by, riding a gust of wind. I wondered how that could happen, how something could start off on a sidewalk and work its way up twenty-four stories.

Jack said, "How long has it been since you, uh—"

"Don't ask. Besides, I know you. You'll call up Guinness and give 'em a new record."

But that wasn't what bothered me so much. I could live without that. I could even put up with not talking, if I had to. What had me worried was that lately I couldn't write. It had been three months since I'd written the article about street gangs. And then, nothing. Not one word. It made me feel like a bad oil field. My wells were running dry.

We watched the sky for a few more minutes and then a large object showed up over Lake Michigan.

"Is that the Goodyear Blimp?" Jack asked, his hand visored over his eyes.

It was just hovering, lost in the mist over the lake.

"It better be," I said, and slapped him on the back. "Let's go, hey. I've got to meet a lady for a drink."

Jack was gone and I was stoned and the apartment felt lonely. I sat on my bed with a few school folders. I noticed that Shelly had left a pair of earrings on my dresser. Goddamn it, I thought. Relationship debris.

The phone rang and snapped me out of a few indistinct daydreams. It was Shelly's secretary, Ellen. I'd never met Ellen, but I'd always liked her voice on the phone. She sounded like Joan Rivers.

"I'm supposed to remind you that you have a date for drinks at The Sweetwater Café with your wife at eight. She said to remind you—no blue jeans."

"I never drink blue jeans," I told her.

"Okay," she said. "Just remember. Wife at eight."

That was funny. Wife.

"For your information, Ellen, that's ex-wife."

There was a moment of silence on the other end. Then Ellen said, "Johnny, I had no idea."

"Yeah. A lot of people seem to have no idea. I got your message, though. Tell her I'll be there with bells on, if I can find any."

"Right."

Click.

I wondered how much the *Sun-Times* charged for a full-page divorce announcement.

I was feeling sleepy but it was only five o'clock, so instead of dropping off I went through my folders and found Carlos's summary of *The Time Machine.* I had to strain to focus my eyes.

46

The Time Mashine
by Carlos Vega "Villavaso"

The movie that I see, and I like it was the Time mashine coz there was a man who he want to go to the fuchure but no one beleeve him so he come back and tell them he awhent there. When he awhent there he beri suprise to find the people they were been eaten by More Lox. Then this girl she likes him and her name is Weaner and she gots locked in a tunnel and the man he goes back all cut up and broosed and no one still beleeve him. but he gots a flour which he brang back with him so he go back on the Time Mashine to be with Weaner.

the End. by Carlos Vega "Villavaso"

Weaner. Jesus.

I circled the misspelled words, shortened a few sentences, and then read it over. A lot of what his problem was had to do with the way he heard English. I wondered how learning disabled he really was. He could remember plot. He understood motivation. Okay—it was a basic understanding, but Carlos had a little spark there somewhere and I knew that I'd done the right thing by keeping him. I was so goddamned excited after reading his little essay that I wished I knew his phone number so that I could talk to him. I wanted to know what he thought of the "More Lox."

Then I awhent to sleep.

The phone rang again and woke me up. I had a hard time determining exactly where I was, or what day it was, or *who* I was.

"Yeah," I said, untangling the phone cord.

"Johnny—I gotta talk to you. I gotta talk to you *now.*"

"Who is this?"

"Alfonzo. Tall Boy."

Tall Boy was Alfonzo's street name. I looked around for the clock. It was on Shelly's side of the bed, though, and from the looks of things, I was in trouble with someone who was most likely waiting impatiently at Sweetwater's. The room was practically dark.

I said, "Alfonzo, tell me this—what time is it?"

"It's around eight, man."

Eight. Well, I'd blown that one.

"Johnny, listen. My brother, he's been shot. I gotta talk to you."

"Shot? Is he okay?"

"Some Kings shot him in the back, man. They shot my fuckin' brother in the *back*. He didn't even see them."

I rubbed my hand against my face. The kid sounded hysterical.

"Calm down, buddy. Calm down. Where are you?"

Alfonzo told me he was across the street from a Jack In The Box restaurant on Fullerton near Kimball. He said he wanted me to get there right away, and then he went on a speed rap about how he was going to take care of the guys who'd got his brother, how he was going to tear their eyes out, and I told him again to calm down, that I'd meet him at the Jack In The Box in ten minutes.

He didn't even tell me if his brother was still alive or not.

I caught every red light west of Ashland. Someone had driven a car up on the sidewalk and well into a storefront on Fullerton and California. The driver could not have survived. There was nothing left of the front of the car. A mob of about fifty people, mainly kids, was trying to get a glimpse through the back window of the ambulance. The video arcades must have been closed.

Alfonzo was sitting on a curb in the parking lot of the Jack In The Box. He looked worn and troubled. His eyes were red little slits.

"Howsa boy?" I said, when I got out of my car, and he stood up. If he had been a foot shorter, I would have put my arm around him. We went inside and I bought him a cheeseburger, fries, and a large Coke. We sat at a table that had onion ring crumbs on it near the back of the restaurant and I waited until he could look up and talk. He was swallowing a lot.

"He's a fuck-up, my brother. He's been dealin' coke and shit for a year now. Makes my mother crazy. One day he goes to church and says he'll straighten out. The next day he's back on the street sellin' shit. Breaks her heart. He's a fuck-up. But damn, Johnny. He's my brother."

I finally got the facts. Alfonzo's brother had been shot by a .22 caliber handgun. The bullet had pierced and collapsed a lung. He was in stable condition at Northwest Hospital. At least he wasn't dead. It was a good thing he wasn't. There's only so much comfort in a cheeseburger.

I said, "So he ripped off his supplier." That's what it boiled down to, as far as I could tell.

"He was *gonna* give 'em the money. In a day or two. I kept tellin' him, you don't do business with K's."

K's were Latin Kings. Alfonzo was missing the point.

"Look, buddy. What're you trying to make me do, give you a lecture? You're not dealing with the facts."

"I'm gonna deal a few facts to a few Kings."

I picked up a French fry and pictured Shelly on her third vodka and tonic, eyes trained on the door, waiting for my entrance. "Your brother blew it. He was dealing shit and didn't pay and now he's shot. They don't give you credit on the streets, you know that. It was a matter of time, is all. You couldn't pull him out of it. Your mother couldn't pull him out of it. Nobody but himself. How old is he?"

"Twenty-five."

Twenty-five and he still went home to Mommy when his drug deals fell through. The story was starting to make me a little sick.

"You put this behind you, Alfonzo. Stay out of it. Stick to school. Do your work. Don't fuck up. You keep hanging on the streets the way things are cooking right now and you'll be in the morgue in a week."

"I'm trying to keep my grades up, Johnny. You know that. I'm gonna be a computer operator."

"Fine. But I'm not sure that's the whole point."

At least he had ambition. I wondered how much explaining I should attempt under the circumstances. You get philosophical with a street kid and you could lose him forever. Computers. All right. Grow up and punch buttons. Beats selling heroin in the ghetto. But there was so much he was going to miss. I thought better of telling him how much.

"School's the point, ain't it?" he asked.

I looked over my cup of coffee at him and noticed that the regulars were lining up near the door. The regulars were wearing black and gold. Kings. I thought about who would get my life insurance now that I was divorced.

"Learning's the point, kid. Learning, not school. I'll go into it with you sometime, but right now the natives are restless. Don't turn around, but there are about six Crowns looking at us like we're on the dessert menu."

Alfonzo was good at nonchalance. I had the feeling that every time he went to a fast-food restaurant, someone was there to tell him not to turn around.

"Is there a rear entrance to this place?" I asked. The Kings were talking in Spanish and eyeing us and grinning wall-to-wall grins. They all needed a shave and clean shirts.

"No. How's your karate?"

I grabbed another French fry even though I wasn't hungry. "A little rusty around the chops. Tell me you're not carrying a gun or I'll faint."

Alfonzo shook his head. The one time I needed a gangster with a gun and he didn't have one.

I kept hoping that the manager of the place kept an eye out for predicaments like ours, but he was ringing up sales and looked a little out of shape himself. He was deliberately not noticing.

"As long as we stay here and don't turn around to look at them, I figure we're safe. We'll just act like we're talking and ignore them."

"Kings shot my brother, man," Alfonzo said, turning around to see if he recognized any of them.

I put my head in my hands and gave up hope at that point. Alfonzo was challenging six or seven of the most nonevolved apes I'd ever seen. I tried to think of a prayer. I only knew "Now I Lay Me Down to Sleep."

I tried it anyway.

Something pushed up against my leg. Then it happened again. Alfonzo was looking at me like I'd better play along, so I reached under the table and he slipped a knife in my hand. A switchblade. I didn't know how to work a switchblade, and it seemed like the wrong time to practice, so I just covered it in the palm of my hand and pretended to keep up my end of the conversation.

"They say it's going to be seventy-five tomorrow." I'd called the weather report that day.

As much as forecasts intrigued me, I had to give up the pretense. Three of the Kings had walked over to our table and an ugly guy with a beard that looked like a pubic forest put a dirty high-top sneaker on my booth seat.

"What's up?" I said, casually, as though I might have wanted to know where he'd bought his shoes.

"Your friend here is wearin' King colors."

He looked over at Alfonzo, who was doing his best to look unshaken. Two other guys had moved behind him. I fingered the knife to find the button that released the blade. The ugly guy, the leader, pointed to Alfonzo's sweatshirt. It was a black high-school athletic shirt emblazoned in gold with the number 57. Someone had forgotten to alert the manufacturer that the Latin Kings held the copyright to that particular color combination.

"Look, man," I said (the Great Teacher. Peace-keeper of the ghetto), "that's a high school shirt, you know? They make 'em like that for Freddie Prinze High. No offense."

"Those be King colors, bro'."

"He doesn't mean it like—"

"Shut up, honky."

I never did put much stock in the peaceful approach. Now I knew why.

Cro-Magnon man walked slowly over to Alfonzo and took some material from his shirt between his fingers. "What you be about?"

In the neighborhood that question translated as *What is your gang affiliation?*

"I asked you what you be about, punk."

I be about to shit in my pants, I thought. Alfonzo just stared stonily at the guy—but I knew it was only a matter of crossing enough lines, making enough threats. Regardless of the odds, street kids have a kamikaze attitude toward life. Alfonzo was merely waiting for the right moment.

"I don't be about nothing," Alfonzo answered. He was keeping his cool better than I had expected. I nodded my head at him, but he looked away.

"Why, then, you won't mind if we take back our colors, will ya? Huh?"

The guy produced a small blade, the flat type of razor device that you remove automobile city stickers with, and started cutting Alfonzo's T-shirt down the front with it. Alfonzo's hand shot up and caught the guy by the wrist. The two Kings behind him moved in then and held him down by the shoulders while the leader pointed the blade toward his throat.

"Freeze, Alfonzo," I told him, standing up. I was pushed back into my seat by yet another King. But Alfonzo froze. He took my advice. I heard his shirt rip clean through; a second later the two stationed behind him were removing the shirt like a jacket, leaving him bare-chested in the booth.

They tossed the shirt around like a basketball, back and forth across the restaurant, until the leader, who—I'd just noticed—had a tattoo on his arm that said BUG, told them to stash the shirt in the car. The smallest guy responded like a robot and took it outside and threw it in the window of a beat-up army-green Dodge, which was parked directly next to my car.

Alfonzo's eyes looked as though the balls might fly out of the sockets, but he made no move. He stared straight ahead.

"Get your asses outa here while you still got 'em," Bug said, shoving us out of the booth simultaneously. Alfonzo reared and squared off when he was shoved, but I grabbed him by one arm and pushed him toward the door.

"King love!" came the shout after us. "King love! King love!" Over and over again in unison. It sounded spooky.

I walked to the passenger door of my car, guiding Alfonzo. He was humiliated and shaking. I unlocked the door and pushed him into the front seat. I was standing right next to their car, on an angle to the restaurant window. I let my keys fall to the ground and bent to pick them up, making it look like an accident. A second later I circled around the front of the car in full view of the leering gang members inside, got in, and drove off.

Next to me, Alfonzo was making clicking sounds in his throat. I turned off of Fullerton onto Washtenaw and put the accelerator to the floor. I headed toward Humboldt Park. I found myself thinking about the girl I'd seen there after school. That's when it dawned on me that I was single again. It struck me as a strange order of thought.

Alfonzo said, "You can slow down, Johnny. They ain't gonna follow us."

"I know that," I said, ruffling his curly hair with my hand. "I slashed their goddamn front tire when I dropped my keys."

I sped down Washtenaw, through stoplights and around groups of kids playing handball in the street. Alfonzo put his arms around me, almost making me crash into a white Pacer. "You're beautiful, man," he said.

Yeah. Beautiful. If not stupid.

Five

I had weird dreams that night. In one sequence I was a different guy, a real depressed guy, and I knew my death was around the corner and I looked forward to it. Actually wanted to die. I wore big horn-rimmed glasses and sat around waiting for this heart attack I knew I was going to have, as though in death there was some kind of answer.

When the phone rang I jumped. Before I even answered it I knew it was Shelly. That didn't make me clairvoyant, necessarily. I lifted the receiver and said, "You left your earrings here, Shelly."

The best defense. It took her a second to respond.

"Johnny, I'm not even going to ask you what happened last night."

Good, I thought.

"I just wanted you to know that I was worried about you. I thought maybe you were in trouble." She was smoking on the other end. I could hear her exhale the smoke away from the mouthpiece. Shelly only smoked when she was nervous. "Why are you angry at me, Johnny? Why the hostility? I thought we could go through this thing, you know, *civilly.*"

"I'm really sorry about last night. I didn't have a chance to call. It was an emergency." I waited, but she just exhaled more smoke. She was making me want a cigarette, but they're never around when you want them. "A brother of a student was shot last night."

Shelly made a funny sound on the other end. Sounded like a windstorm. "Let me guess. A drug addict, right?"

"The brother is a drug addict, yes. It's pretty common in that neighborhood."

"I don't want to hear about it," she said.

"All right."

"I want you to know that while you left me stranded there at the bar every horny salesman in the world tried to buy me a drink. I know that it's hard for you to care about me because *I'm* not strung out on heroin."

"I'm sorry, Shel," I said. I tried to figure out if I was jealous about the other men coming on to her. I didn't think I was. "I really am sorry. But look at it this way—you got the divorce and the free drinks. All I've got are your earrings, and my ears aren't even pierced."

She said, "You can't hide behind jokes forever. Sooner or later you're going to have to grow up."

I didn't know what that meant. I guessed that if you stopped joking, you were grown up. It sounded like something you did just before you died.

"Shel?"

"I'm still here."

"Look, I'm late at the moment and I've got ten weeks of lesson plans to write before nine o'clock, so if you don't mind—"

"Get going," she said. She sounded disappointed and that made me uncomfortable. She really hadn't deserved to be stood up.

"You know," I said, "last night. It couldn't be helped."

She laughed lightly. She'd heard that one before. "I'm having some people over for drinks Friday night. I don't suppose you'd like to stop by."

Not actually, no, was the response that came to mind. But if you could assuage some guilt and get free drinks at the same time, why not? Two birds.

"I'll see what I can do," I said.

Shelly said she wouldn't hold her breath, and then hung up. I tried to remember when I had started to disappoint people so badly.

I got dressed in the living room while watching a local news program that came on right after *The Thought for the Day*. It was brought to you by Kellogg's and they ran a Rice Krispies commercial at the break. I had a box of Rice Krispies in the cupboard, so I got it, poured some in a bowl, and then filled it with milk. It had been so long since I'd had a breakfast cereal that I didn't know if you were supposed to use sugar or not. After the first taste I remembered. You needed sugar. I didn't have any. I noticed that the milk carton was leaking from a small hole in the side, and that made me think of Tylenol. I had visions of me driving to work and being overcome by cyanide poisoning. Death was becoming quite a topic with me. Just in case, I scribbled a little note on a piece of paper and taped it to the refrigerator. It said:

It was the milk.

I arrived at work still breathing, but late. I signed in at seven-fifty and went straight to my mailbox, where I found a government questionnaire to be given to all homeroom students. It was about parent employment. What employment? Someone in Washington must have lost the welfare sheets and was in the process of trying to piece them back together.

I had seven students waiting for me outside my classroom door. Two of the boys were practicing kung fu on each other. The rest of them were looking at the carpet as if at any second something worth seeing would happen down there.

I gave out ten vocabulary words, words like *tumult, justify, malign*. I was halfway down the list, reading the words aloud to them, when a girl asked me if they were English words. I told her they were.

"I never seen them words before," she said, scratching her head with her pencil.

"Well, now you *seen* them," I said. I looked at the door and there was Dr. McCaskey. Good morning.

"Mr. Spector, may I see you?" He seemed to have less hair today and he was not smiling. It occurred to me that I had never known him to smile. I put down the vocabulary list and stepped outside into the corridor.

"I was originally coming to ask you for your lesson plans, which I don't suppose you have anyway, when I got a call on the walkie-talkie. We've got a code blue, so keep your eyes open."

A code blue was a bomb threat. If you were on free time, you were expected to search the hallways for strange devices. If you had a class, I supposed you were to listen for ticking.

"I'll do what I can," I told him. "I really don't think any of those kids has a bomb."

"We call it a *code blue*, Mr. Spector. Please don't use that other word."

"No one heard me but you, Dr. McCaskey."

He looked down his spectacled nose at me, like an old schoolmarm who had just stumped me at a spelling bee.

"That's hardly the point, Mr. Spector. I'm not going to stand here and explain to you what it means to act professionally."

"I wouldn't expect you to."

"No. You wouldn't," he said, poking the bridge of his glasses back over the hump in his nose, and then walked off.

Every once in a while, after talking to Dr. McCaskey, I had to wonder if he was deliberately obtuse, or just plain stupid.

For the remainder of the period I tried to get the class through another chapter of *The Human Comedy*. The response was pretty much what I was used to. Jasper was still staring down Sonia's blouse. Damaris was staring out the window. One boy, for variety, was rocking in his chair with a Bible propped open before him. This was Enrique. Enrique was weird.

I was about to assign some homework when the fire alarm went off. The kids just sat there. It was a phenomenon I'd only seen at Freddie Prinze. These kids wouldn't get up if the building was on fire. I had to shout over the blare, "Get the hell out of here, now!"

I stood by the door as the students, some yawning, some gazing at the carpet, marched dutifully, though not promptly, out of the room and down the side stairwell. One little girl named Aida stopped in the doorway and tried to tell me something. All I heard was Enrique's name; the rest was lost behind the racket of the alarm and the shuffling in the hallway. I bent down and shouted in her ear, "Tell me later, honey. I can't hear a word you're saying."

She nodded and joined the mob in the stairwell.

I hated to think what would happen if we ever really had a fire in that school. It took so long to evacuate the building that the administration usually started to let students back in before many of them had made it outside. Over the outdoor intercom system and above the wailing of the fire engine sirens, Dr. McCaskey repeated over and over again that this was a false alarm, but to stay outside nonetheless until the bell rang.

A bomb threat and a false fire alarm and it wasn't even nine in the morning. It was beginning to feel a little like being at a carnival around there.

I circled the building at a good distance. Patches of gang members had used the opportunity to assemble along the borders of their predetermined turfs. Loud disco music spilled from a clearing between a row of maple trees. The guys danced and punched each other on the arm and whistled at girls. One group was sporting red-and-white bandanas. I didn't know which gang red and white symbolized. They looked like the Red Cross.

The festivities were called to an abrupt halt by the return bell, and I was sucked up in a flow of kids when I spotted Wanda. I said hello to her and asked if we could talk. She looked a little sheepish and had some difficulty looking me in the eye. When we were out of the crowd I noticed that she had several parallel scratches on one side of her face, which she'd tried to mask with makeup. The half circle under her left eye was a faint purple. She'd used makeup there, too.

"We kind of missed you yesterday," I said, for openers. You couldn't come out and say, *So who beat you up?*

"I hadda cold," she said. She was looking at her shoes—little pink plastic shoes.

"You must've blown your nose kind of hard, huh? I mean, it's not so easy to blacken your eye with Kleenex."

She paced the concrete in front of me. The entrances were still crowded with people, so I used my time to listen to her. Between the sniffles and the head shaking a story was taking shape. It was what I had expected.

Wanda's father drank. He also did not want her to see boys. She was a few weeks away from being eighteen and had never had a legitimate date. Freud would probably have raised an eyebrow at her case. Her mother was afraid of the old man, so she sided with him. What Wanda's parents had discovered two days before was that she had a boyfriend and had been seeing him secretly for a year. I had been aware of this. I had known it would leak out someday. I had also thought that her parents would be able to take the news by the time she was eighteen. Well, they had taken it, and then given it to her.

I said, "Did your father do this?" She nodded. "Are you okay?"

"I'm okay." She made a weak attempt at a smile. "I just hope he isn't drinkin' today. When he drinks, it's worse."

"What do you mean? You mean worse than *this*?"

It always amazed me that some parents could beat their own children. It seemed a little like cutting off your own arm.

"Shit, Johnny. This ain't nothin'. If he'd've been drinkin' you'd have to visit me in the funeral home."

I said, "It seems to me that your life shouldn't depend on how many drinks your father's had."

"It seems."

"You can't just go home and play Russian roulette with a drunk, Wanda."

A determined little glint shone in her eyes. At least the bastard hadn't killed her spirit, I thought.

"Oh, don't worry. We have a plan."

I asked her who the "we" was.

"Me and my boyfriend. We're gonna get married as soon as I'm eighteen."

I asked, "Elope?"

"Um-hmm. I talked to the father at St. Aloysius last night. Him and a sister they got there are gonna help us."

The crowd had thinned out by then. I put my arm around her and we walked back to the building together.

"That's a lousy reason to get married, honey. There ought to be some other reason. Believe me."

Wanda smiled a lovely smile and said they had *that* reason, too. "It'll just be a little sooner than we thought. If I wait till I'm twenty, I'll be dead."

You couldn't argue with that. I guessed that if my life depended on it, I might have been willing to marry Shelly again. Maybe.

I asked her if she thought she would be safe for two weeks. She said that if she pretended she wasn't seeing her boyfriend, then yes, she would be safe. I wasn't so sure. When she went off to her next class I stopped by the Youth Counseling service. I wasn't going to give her father a chance at an encore performance. She didn't have enough face left for that.

The Youth Counseling service was an independent organization that operated on the third floor. Two little rooms, lots of posters, and cubbyhole recesses for individual counseling and therapy. I knew one of the guys there—Marco Gonzalez. Marco was tall and lean and looked like Ricardo Montalban's younger brother. He was one of the few professional people in the school whom I could talk to without having to remember all the terms they'd taught us in Educational Foundations class back in college. I caught him digging through a mass of manila folders that were scattered inside a steel filing cabinet.

"Well—professor. What brings you to our little corner of the universe? Want to rent a nut case?"

I said, "No. Actually, I came to report one. I didn't know you guys rented them out. No wonder this place is filled with nuts."

Marco shut the cabinet without finding whatever it was he'd been looking for and took a pen out of his shirt pocket and picked up a referral form.

"What is it, Johnny? Student trouble?"

"This one comes under the heading of *parent* trouble. You guys deal with that, right?"

Marco nodded slowly. "Abuse?"

"The kid's face looks like they used it as a soccer ball."

Now Marco shook his head. "I'll give you the lowdown on this. If you want to file a legal complaint, you'll need the kid and photographs. The kid will have to be willing to swear out charges, and Johnny, that gets a little sticky. Nine times out of ten, if you can get the kid to agree, he chickens out before the hearing. Usually at about the time we place him in a youth center or a foster home."

It figured. The one way to help a kid was to make the situation unbearable.

I said, "Can't you just scare the bastard father into leaving her alone?"

"Oh—off the record? Just a little family intervention? Sure. Absolutely. You know, sometimes it's even better like that. We just say it came to our attention that she looks like she's been beaten and we came to investigate. Takes the responsibility off the kid's shoulders that way. Of course, the old man will deny it up and down, and even show us how she opened the door and hit herself with it. I had a guy like that last week. He demonstrated how his kid set herself on fire by accident."

"You're kidding."

"I am not. Kid's in the hospital. Second-degree burns over seventy-five percent of her body. She was pregnant, too. Notice I say *was.*"

"What does the kid say?"

"Well, Johnny—she may never *say* anything again."

Marco was a swell guy and I liked him, but he knew too many stories.

I said, "Can you do one of those numbers? Intervention? The

kid just needs time till she can make her own plans."

Marco smiled at me; his eyes looked tired and knowing. "She's going to elope?"

"I guess there are patterns to these things, huh? Either that or you're her boyfriend."

"Fill out the form and I'll get back to you in a few days."

The form had twenty yes-no-maybe profile questions. Questions like "Does the student have trouble relating to peers in large groups?" There were no questions about cuts and bruises, so I had to add my own statement at the bottom, under "Recommended action." I wondered if it would sound flip to write, "Hang him by his balls." I just wrote, "Family conference," and headed back to my office.

Carlos was waiting for me by the door, looking a little lost. When he saw me his face came to life, and for a moment he reminded me of a puppy I'd had a long time ago. My parents had it put to sleep—bladder problem or something. It was the humane thing to do. Just like it would be the humane thing to put Carlos in a Special Ed class, only I wasn't going to let them.

We sat down at my desk and I went over his paper with him. When I was through explaining the corrections, all he wanted to know was the grade.

"Forget the grade. We're not going to worry about grades, Carlos."

"No grade?"

"Nope. Just learning. There are only two grades, buddy. Either you get it, or you don't get it. Now, you want to try some more writing?"

"Again movie?"

I thought for a minute. "Tell you what. You write me a paragraph about your family."

Carlos looked deflated when he heard the topic. There you go. We were *both* learning. I had him first write the paragraph out on yellow second sheets, and then asked him to write each sentence alone on a separate piece of paper. I was going to break down his units of thought into complete sentences before we got fancy. Sort of hold the building blocks under the old microscope. Every time I corrected his spelling he'd say, "*Gracias*, Señor Spector." I finally told him to call me Johnny.

"*Sí*, Yohnny," he said.

Yohnny. Geez.

I was on my third cup of coffee when La Familia came by and made themselves at home. Alfonzo and Tony were both wearing white shoelaces. They each gave me a weak "Wha'sup?" and slunk into a corner, talking in low tones. Pedro sat on my desk next to Carlos and waited to pick at something.

"How's Einstein today? Is he on nuclear reactors yet?"

I told him, "No. He's on sentences. Get a dictionary from my shelf and show him how to look up the misspelled words."

Pedro's face dropped. "Me?"

"Yeah, you. It's your grade for the day. I don't want to see any misspellings or I'm failing you, wiseass."

Pedro parked his book bag on the floor and reluctantly searched my shelves for a *Webster's*.

Elsie popped in for a moment and sat on my lap. She had her hair held back by a green-and-black headband and had painted her nails in the same color combination. Well, the Cobras had to have girlfriends, didn't they?

"We have to stop meeting like this," I said.

"I know a lot of other places, Johnny."

I had no doubt about that. "Wanna stand up? You're cutting off my circulation."

She took the hint good-naturedly and flashed me a suggestive look when she stood up. Did *she* ever have the wrong guy.

I joined the others in a corner of the office while Pedro showed Carlos the difference between the words *when* and *went*. "It's not *awhent*, bean brain. It's *went.*" Carlos seemed pleased at being called bean brain. I think he liked the attention. So much for sensitivity.

The hot topic among Alfonzo, Tony, and Elsie was Wanda's face. I told them I'd seen it. They knew about her plan to get married. They talked about it as if it were a lunch date. Then Elsie said goodbye, and that she had to meet someone. Someone who would assuredly have a very wide smile for the rest of the day. When she was gone, Alfonzo and Tony remained unusually tight-lipped.

"How's your brother?" I asked Alfonzo.

"A little better. Doctors say he'll be there for about three weeks." I nodded.

They were certainly keeping their thoughts to themselves. It was only April and school went into June. It was going to be like keeping the seal on a pressure cooker until then.

"How're the streets?" I asked next.

Tony snorted. Alfonzo looked at the carpet.

"I ain't gonna shit you, Johnny," Tony said, propping himself against the wall. "The boys on our block are organizing and keeping tight. We get seen alone and the People are all over us. I almost got jumped last night on the way home."

I asked him what he'd been on his way home from. He produced another Polaroid snapshot. This one was of a train car covered with crazy palm trees. Little people were peeking out of the fronds at the top. It was quite Caribbean—a departure from his usual style.

"Very nice," I said.

"I had some help on this one."

"Yeah? I thought Xavier Cugat was too old to climb trains."

Tony said, "Who's Savior Nougat?"

"*Cugat.* Famous train-bomber."

I wrote passes to the lunchroom for everybody except Carlos. His essay was filled with very interesting little facts about home. Facts such as his uncle was his only relative. They lived in an apartment on North Avenue, and before coming back to school, Carlos had worked for this uncle by collecting used and discarded pop cans for recycling. I asked him if his uncle had ever given him a cut of the money. It was not surprising to learn that he hadn't. I also found out that Carlos had to walk to school every day.

"Don't you have a bus pass?"

"No, sir, Yohnny," he said. I could tell by the way he said it that he didn't even know what a bus pass was.

"Carlos, buddy. I want you to listen to me, okay?"

He trained his eyes on my mouth, as if seeing was part of hearing. That was worth noting. I'd have to have him tested for audio difficulty.

"I'm going to get you a piece of paper that will let you take the bus to school for like half-fare. You can save money by showing this piece of paper to the driver. Do you understand?"

"Yes, Yohnny. Take the bus."

I put my arm around his shoulder and he smiled. It goddamn near melted me every time he smiled like that. Made me feel like day-old oleo.

I had another bright idea on our way to the bus pass window on the second floor. Why not get the kid a part-time job so he could blow off his dependence on his uncle? Our next stop was Helen Delvecchio's office. Helen was the chairperson of the business department.

She was eating a ham sandwich on rye when we caught her at her desk. I introduced Carlos and asked if she could set him up with a paper route.

"You got those kids in the lobby that little job, right?"

Helen chewed and looked at Carlos as though he might have been contagious. "What are you, Robin Hood?" She went right on eating.

"Come on, Helen. You know that you could just pick up the phone and call the distributor and set him up." I hated to be patient with Helen. She was forty-four, spinsterish, and convinced that she was in a close race with the Post family, or the Du Ponts. Big fish, small pond. But she was my only bet right then. "The kid is good. He needs the money. Great little worker."

"Helluva worker," Carlos said, with every watt of his smile trained on Helen.

I said, "There. You see? An unsolicited testimonial. What more could you want?"

"Can he make change?" she asked.

"Can he make change? Can Joan Collins screw? Are you kidding?"

I honestly doubted that Carlos could make change—but I'd got that far and wasn't going to let a detail stop me.

Somewhere between her ham sandwich and her fruit cocktail Helen made the phone call and told us to go to the paper distributor on Clybourn after school, before three-thirty. I thanked her, grabbed one of her potato chips, and told Carlos to meet me at the main entrance after school.

Whew. It was only third period.

Tony and Alfonzo were in my English lit class. They both showed up late, smelling like they'd tried unsuccessfully to put out a fire in a marijuana patch. I was teaching *The Stranger*, by Albert Camus, and today I'd been lucky enough to score a print of the movie, the one with Marcello Mastroianni. It was in French.

"They got the fuckin' *words* on the bottom, man. This is supposed to be English class, ain't it? Can't ya get it in English?"

That was Miguel Mendoza. Miguel was bright, lazy, and a pain in the ass. What bothered me was that he had accurately summed up the sentiment of the others. While the projector whirled away I looked over the room and saw kids falling asleep on their arms. One or two at the most were watching. I'd spent three months trying to track down this particular film, and the bastards slept through it. That didn't exactly make my day.

How do you behave at your ex-wife's party? I asked myself, later. I was heading for Dave Volmer's office because of his standing invitation, and because I always talked to Dave when I was depressed. Besides, he had written the book on divorce protocol.

Dave had his feet on his desk between piles of folders and papers and forms. He was just staring out his window at the park. Humboldt Boulevard—a winding stretch of broken cement surrounded by green lawn and wind-blown litter. A sea of gum wrappers and cigarette packages.

"I understand they're giving away bad coffee here," I said, standing in his doorway.

"Johnny Spector," he greeted me, taking his feet off his desk, as though I might have been offended by his casualness. "I'm glad you're here. Your application to the Audy Home has been accepted. They'll have a cell for you in a few days."

I grabbed his coffee pot by the handle and poured some weak-looking stuff into a semi-used Styrofoam cup. The Audy Home was a youth detention center. He actually did have a letter from someone there on the top of a pile on his desk. I read it and said, "Well, if we can't graduate 'em, we might as well jail 'em, huh?"

"That kid's a lost cause. I did everything for him humanly possible. Got him in the classes with the right teachers. I think he had *you*, in fact. Juan Alicea."

"Doesn't ring any bells."

Dave put his feet back on his desk. He needed new soles. "Yeah, well. You're better off. I got him a job at an auto parts factory, part time. He was arrested for stealing carburetors or something. Dumb fuck. Programmed for failure."

I said, "I've heard of that program."

Dave looked at me with a cynical eyebrow lifted. "Jesus. You don't look any more single than you did yesterday."

I didn't know what he meant by this.

"You're still wearing your goddamn wedding band."

I looked down at my left hand. He was right. I'd been wearing it so long I'd forgotten there wasn't any point to it. I took it off and put it in my left jeans pocket. I shook my head and smiled.

"Habit, you know?"

"Heroin's a habit, too. None of them are any good. So? You surviving? You're not having any sentimental flashbacks when you pass by the kitchen sink or do your own laundry, are you?"

"Who does laundry?"

He had his arms folded behind his head, his chair tilted back against the wall. There was a small tear in his shirt underneath his right arm. The shirt must have been ten years old. I found myself silently thanking some greater power that I didn't have to pay child support.

"I hope you wore your bulletproof undershirt today," Dave said next, back to staring out his window.

I asked him what that was supposed to mean.

"Didn't you hear about Dan Finley's gym class?"

I hadn't heard anything at all about Dan Finley for so long that I was kind of shocked to learn he was still on the faculty.

"No."

"Some street gang invaded the athletic field during his second-period class. Dragged a kid right out of a baseball game and beat the shit out of him with bricks and clubs. Right in front of old Dan."

I said, "What did Dan do?"

"Nothing."

I sat and thought about this and wondered if it had been me in that situation whether I'd have done anything. So far I was only good at slashing tires. I had retarded street skills.

"How's the kid?" I asked.

"Who? Mine?"

"No. The kid who was beaten."

"Oh—he's at St. Mary's Hospital. Fractured skull. Now, want to know how my kid is?"

I said, "Sure," not knowing if he was serious or not.

"Which one?"

He hadn't been serious. He sat back in his chair with his bad shoes and his torn shirt and smiled at me. I didn't know how he took it all so well.

I smoked a cigarette with him in relative silence, staring out the window at the park. It did not seem like a bright move to put a thirty-four-million-dollar school in a virtual battlefield with all the natural accoutrements. Trees to hide behind. A lagoon to toss kids into. Miles of free turf. It was a stupid thing to do. Who had okayed this place?

I put out my cigarette and headed for the door. Before I left I said, "Say—you ought to know the answer to this one. If you happen to go to a party that your ex-wife is throwing, what do you bring?"

Dave smiled at me with what looked like mixed humor and disbelief.

"If you're smart? If you're smart you bring a gun."

"Yeah, but if you're dumb what do you bring?"

Dave shrugged. "I dunno. If you're dumb you probably bring a bottle of her favorite wine and hope it's gone bad."

"Thanks," I said, and left the office. I didn't know if I felt better or not.

At the end of the day I found Carlos exactly where I had told him to meet me. His strong point was following directions. Maybe this would get him by in life, I thought. In any case, it was a foundation to build upon. He didn't see me approach, and he flinched when I put my arm around his shoulders—until he saw it was me.

"How're you doing, partner?"

"I come like you say, Yohnny." He was very pleased about having remembered. He shuffled nervously from shoe to shoe. It was his version of treading water. I sort of saw him treading through life like that.

"We're going down to the auto shop, little buddy. I've got my car parked down there. Do you remember where we're going this afternoon?"

He smiled. He nodded.

"Can you tell me?" I asked, up against the smile again.

"To the paper man, for a yob."

A yob. He had remembered. I slapped him on the back and giggled with him on our way to the stairs to the basement. Then I heard someone say my name.

"Mr. Spector?"

I turned around and it was her. She. The lovely girl I'd seen in the park.

I said, "Yes?" and noticed that close up she was even more strikingly beautiful than I had imagined. She had reddish-brown hair, beyond shoulder length, and stood about five feet six inches tall. She was wearing a beige skirt and a red-and-green plaid blouse and I remember thinking that she looked oddly preppy and thoroughly out of place at Freddie Prinze High.

"I—uh, read your book. I don't know you or anything, but I—I just wanted to say I enjoyed it a lot."

She was blushing. She started to say something else, but turned away. Her embarrassment was one of the nicest compliments my writing had ever got me. I wanted to keep her around all day and watch her gush.

"Wait a minute," I said, and found myself touching her elbow. I took my hand away immediately. I hadn't meant to grab her or anything like that. She turned around and faced me with more poise, now that *I* wanted to talk to *her*. "What was your favorite part?"

She was slender and had a terrifically narrow waist. She was wearing a khaki belt around it, a khaki belt with a brass buckle. She was carrying my book again, and it was tucked between her arm and her hip. It struck me as a nice place to be. I saw that it was not a library edition. Then Carlos tugged my sleeve. He must have thought I'd forgotten about him.

"My favorite part was—oh! I liked the part where he's in the video arcade with his girlfriend. Remember that part?" she asked. Then she laughed and put her hand up to her mouth. "God. You're the author. I guess if anybody would remember it, it would be you."

Not necessarily. Just then I couldn't remember a hell of a lot about anything. Carlos tugged my sleeve again, and the girl looked at him.

"This is Carlos. He's a pal of mine. Aren't you, buddy?" He giggled and I put my arm around his shoulders again. He seemed to be as taken with the young lady as I was. "We're going to get him a job right now."

She said, "That's nice. It's nice to meet you, Carlos."

Carlos put his head against my side and sort of stumbled over his own feet. Jesus. We needed choreography or something.

"Well, I suppose I'd better let you go," the girl said. She was turning to leave when something apparently came to mind. "Oh. Would you mind—"

Shit, I thought. Don't chicken out now.

"Never mind."

"No, wait," I said, touching her elbow again. "What was it? Really. We aren't in a hurry or anything."

She took the book from its place at her side and extended it to me. "Would you mind signing it? I know it sounds silly—"

"It sounds wonderful. I'd like to."

She went through her purse and found a pen and handed it to me.

I opened the book to the inscription page and looked up at her. "I kind of don't know your name."

"Oh. I'm sorry. It's Marlyn, with a *y*."

I wrote:

> To Marlyn, with a *y*—
> I saw you in the park yesterday.
> I'm glad we met, and thank you
> for the kind review.
>
> Best always,
> Johnny Spector

When I was done I handed the book back to her with her pen. I'd almost kept the pen, really, but remembered to give it back when it was halfway to my shirt pocket. Twenty-nine and still giddy around beauty. God.

"Are you a senior?" I asked, which was a nicer way of asking, *Are you past the age of consent?*

"Yes."

There you go. Proof that there actually *is* a God. The argument was over.

"It's funny. I teach English Four and I've never seen you."

She said, "I'm in the advanced placement class—that's probably why."

She stood around, swinging from side to side a little. Her facial features were chiseled and her skin cream-complected. Strong jawbone. She looked like an Italian movie star. I don't know. Maybe it was because I'd just seen a foreign film that I made this comparison.

"What college are you going to next year?" I asked. Carlos was tugging my sleeve again, but I waited around for the answer.

"I don't think I'll be going to college. Too many problems. At home and all, I mean."

"Not going? You're in the AP class and you're not going to college?"

She shook her head and bit her bottom lip. Now, *that* was strange.

AP students were the top of the heap. What was the point of having been college prepped and then not going to college?

"Like I said—problems."

Carlos was now very close to breaking my arm, he was tugging at me so hard. I told him I'd be right with him and then turned back to Marlyn.

"Listen, would you mind coming to see me in my office tomorrow? I'd kind of like to hear the story."

"It's not much of a story," she said, more to the floor than to me.

"I'd still like to hear it if you have the time. Room two-fourteen. Maybe around ten o'clock?"

She swung her purse strap over her shoulder, gave me an interestingly flirtatious little smile and a cursory "Okay," and then melted into the crowd of exiting students.

Meeting Marlyn was something like stumbling upon a flower in an alley and not knowing what to make of it.

I took out the little piece of paper that Helen Delvecchio had given me: 2616 North Clybourn. I stuck it in my shirt pocket again, next to my cigarettes, and looked through the windshield, seeing, yet not quite seeing, the traffic in front of me. Carlos and I were on Division Street and I had to make a left on Ashland. For the next few minutes Marlyn's face played in the transparency of the windshield like a mental videotape. My stomach felt funny. If it hadn't been for my ulcer I would have considered the possibility of infatuation. Or sheer lust. Maybe I had peptic butterflies.

The newspaper distributor was located in an old warehouse that was dirty and looked typically *Chicago*. I don't know why it was, but dirt and Chicago always seemed like a duo to me. Inside, behind a caged window, I could see the back of a fattish man who was struggling with a wire-fastened bundle of daily papers. His underpants were sticking out over the top of his trousers.

"Excuse me," I said.

He spun around, a red face topped by yellow-gray hair. He was sucking on a burned-out stogie and managed to say, "Be with ya in a minute," without dripping too much saliva down his chin. The guy, like the building, was typically *Chicago*.

When he finished with the papers he took out a spotted handkerchief and dabbed the area just below what I now saw were two chins, not just one.

"What can I do for ya?"

I said, "Got a kid here who needs a job."

"No jobs, sorry," he answered, and then spat on the floor.

"I believe Helen Delvecchio called about this boy. She gave me the address and told me you'd have something for him."

From behind his wire cage the old guy gave Carlos the once-over. The examination made Carlos turn his head toward his shoes. He was being judged and he knew it.

"Straighten up, buddy," I told him.

He bravely lifted his head a little, but lowered it again when the man pulled his cigar stub out of his mouth and continued to stare at him.

"What's wrong with him?" he asked, looking at me like I was trying to sell him a bad used car.

"There's nothing wrong with him. He wants a job. That's all."

The old guy motioned me closer to the cage. If I had kept a Christmas card list, I would have scratched Helen Delvecchio's name from it on the spot.

"This kid retarded or something?" he whispered to me. I looked back at Carlos. He had his back turned to us.

"Look, mister. The kid isn't a Rhodes Scholar, okay? But he also isn't a hoodlum. He isn't asking for a handout. He's honest, he's got ambition, and he just wants you to give him the chance to sell a few goddamn papers. That shouldn't be too much to ask." I went over and grabbed Carlos by the arm and pulled him back to the cage so the guy could get a better look at him. "If he screws up, he expects to be fired. But at least give him a chance. He hasn't had many, you know?"

Then Carlos looked up at the guy with those eyes of his and the guy scratched the back of his neck a few times and nodded and shuffled. "Okay—" was all he said. He gave us some papers to fill out and I wished just then that the old codger would either light his cigar or break down and buy a new one.

Carlos and I shared a pizza later at my apartment. We were both sitting at my writing desk (the one I didn't write at anymore) and looking out at Clark Street, at the movement and people and pigeons.

One old bum with ripped pants and a dirty white beard was hanging on to a streetlamp and holding his hat out to pedestrians. It was easily the worst job of panhandling I'd ever seen. Carlos said, *"Mira, Yohnny,"* and pointed to two muscular young guys who'd had a fender-bender in the parking lot of a McDonald's. At the moment they were trying to out-macho each other with arm gestures.

"How much do I get back if I give you a dollar for a paper?" I asked him. He'd just shoved a green-pepper-covered slice of pizza into his mouth, whole.

"Seventy-five cent."

"Good. What if I give you a dollar and want two papers?"

Carlos looked puzzled as he chewed. "Why you want two paper?"

"Don't worry about it. I just want two. How much change do I get back?"

"Fifty cent," he said.

"Bien. Bien, meshuggener."

He had learned to give change and it had only taken half a pizza's worth of time to do it. Look out, Rockefeller. Here comes Carlos.

We sat watching the street jive for a few minutes more. There was a lady dressed in what looked like a sack causing some disturbance in the middle of the street. A cop car went right by her while she waved and shouted something to the world in general. I had no idea what you'd have to do in this town to get arrested.

Then the door buzzer went off. I wasn't expecting company. I picked up the remote-control channel selector and turned on the TV security channel. Surprise. It was the little sixteen-year-old waif again. She was wearing muddy sneakers and her hair hadn't been combed in the recent past. I ate another slice of pizza and waited for her to go away. She was a persistent little snot, I'll say that for her.

Carlos said, "She want to come in, Yohnny?"

"She's got the wrong apartment, buddy."

"Oh," he said.

As I continued to watch her I couldn't imagine what I must have been thinking a few nights before when I had been tempted to let her in. Then Marlyn's face drifted across my memory and I found myself comparing every woman I'd ever known to her.

Everybody lost.

Six

It was raining. While my first-period kids were either working or not working on their study sheets, I watched the park glisten and the clouds break slightly, leaving a luminous little streak of what would have been sunshine if it had only been a little brighter. Spring tended to break my heart, for some reason.

I thought about the dream I'd had the previous night. Spooky. In the dream I was that depressed guy again. I had those stupid horn-rimmed glasses, bad clothes, the whole bit, only this time I was married to a very dull woman who picked on me constantly. I kept trying to tell her that nothing mattered because I was going to die, but she wouldn't believe me. I just waited around to drop dead, and as in the first dream, I was looking forward to it. I had nothing to live for. Then I was in a car, driving to work. I checked my face in the rearview mirror. No face. It reminded me of an LSD trip I'd actually had back when I was twenty; every time I looked in a mirror, my face was gone. Anyway, I was driving when a big diesel truck began to roll over on my car. You could hear the metal crunch— sounded like big walnuts being cracked open. Then I smiled. The roof collapsed on top of me and I thought, Well, it's about time.

I felt a flutter of panic just thinking about it there in the classroom. I was glad when a kid tapped my shoulder and asked if it was okay to cross out her answer and start again.

"Sure. You can always start again," I told her.

I was alone in my office second period because I had taken Carlos to Dave Volmer for testing. I found myself looking through the previous year's yearbook in the "Juniors" section. I searched every row of tiny black-and-white photos, and was pretty sure that Marlyn hadn't sat for a picture, until I got to the V's. She was the sixth from the end—Marlyn Valentin. It's funny what kind of a difference a year makes. In the picture she looked like a kid.

I was going to be voted lecher of the year if I wasn't careful.

Then I closed the book and sat in my chair for some time, just thinking. I tried to get a handle on what was happening to me. Love? Infatuation? Animal lust? Or maybe a combination, like love with a little infatuation and a lot of animal lust? Whatever—it was everything that wasn't supposed to happen, but it felt *healthy*. It felt good. It was sort of like having someone stick pins in you and enjoying it. How could *that* be healthy? I wondered.

Maybe Shelly had been right. Maybe I was permanently set on *high school*. I looked at my sneakers, my blue jeans. I tried to imagine what it would be like to dress in a suit every day and make business deals and go to luncheons and play golf. That gave me the chills. When I imagined it I had nearly the same feeling I'd had in the dream. Nothingness.

My phone rang and it was Marco. I was glad for the diversion.

"Johnny? Am I interrupting anything?"

"Yes. A really bad fantasy. You have wonderful timing."

Marco said, "Oh, fantasies are good for you."

"Not this one," I said. A grown man and I still wore gym shoes to work.

"I've got the scoop on Mr. Hidalgo—Wanda's old man."

"You work fast," I said.

Marco said, "You should talk to my wife. Listen—I think he got the message loud and clear."

I tried to picture the little meeting they'd had, Marco straight-facing it and Mr. Hidalgo all pleasantries and small talk, as if nothing in the world was out of order. "Did he show you how she did it to herself with the door?"

"No. He said she'd fallen on the front steps."

"Gotta watch out for those banana peels," I said. I looked at my clock and noticed that if Marlyn had any intention of keeping our appointment, she was already ten minutes late. My stomach sank a little at the thought of being stood up.

"He was shaking like a leaf by the time I left. I told him it was pretty obvious that she'd been beaten. He said, 'No, no, no! Anybody beat my girl, I *keel* heem.' "

"Then we should look forward to his suicide?"

Marco harrumphed into the receiver. "No such luck. If idiots would just kill themselves, I'd be out of a job. Listen—just thought you'd like to know the results."

"I appreciate it," I told him, lighting a cigarette and watching the match burn all the way down to my thumb before I blew it out. "Having a quiet day up there?"

"Are you kidding me? Right now I'm waiting for a therapy session. This is a kid who killed another kid in the park last year—with a Coke bottle. Spent three months in Cook County and now he's back in school. Two weeks ago he raped his own mother."

"Do you make these stories up?" I asked. Marco had the market cornered on bizarre student information.

"I couldn't make this shit up if I tried."

"How come he's not in jail?"

"Johnny, it's his *mother*. She won't press charges. What kind of a mother charges her own son with rape?"

"What about the other thing—the murder?"

"Self-defense."

I said, "Are you up for sainthood yet? The reason I ask, if you need my vote, it's yours."

"I knew I could count on you," Marco said, and was off the line.

I held the receiver in my hand for a second and just stared at it. Then the goddamn fire alarm went off again. Time to play inner-city exodus.

Down the escalators, out to the park. Screaming teen-agers, blaring radios, and no sign of Marlyn. If I could have found the bastard who'd set off that alarm, I would have broken his knuckles.

The all-clear bell rang with about two thirds of the student population still pushing their way down the stairwells and escalators. I searched every face to see if I could find her. Out of luck. I stopped by my mailbox, picked up some papers without looking at them, and then resignedly headed back to my office.

She was waiting by the door, books clenched in both hands in front of her. Gray skirt, red blouse, red shoes. Her hair against the blouse looked a softer tone of brown, and it made her face appear almost angelic.

I said, "I was beginning to think I'd been stood up."

She smiled. "I had to take a makeup test for history."

I opened the office door and allowed her to enter first. Sir Walter

Spector. I arranged a chair for her at the side of my desk and sat down. My mind had gone completely blank. The worst part was trying not to stare, not to just watch her. She shyly crossed her legs and kept her books in her lap.

"I'm glad you showed up," I started. "I've been wanting to talk to you. About—you know. Not going to college and all."

"And you've been spying on me in the park."

She said it so matter-of-factly, I'd missed that it had been a joke. "What?" She'd thrown me off. I was overly serious in my comeback.

"What you wrote in the book—that you'd seen me in the park."

"Oh, that. Yeah. I did. You were just, you know. *Walk*ing. And I just saw you. That's all."

She looked at her lap. "Should I be flattered?"

Jesus. She was flirting with me. Not like Elsie did. Elsie would just reach out and grab your crotch if she thought she could save time. But Marlyn volleyed into my court like a self-assured, seasoned adult. Coquettish repartee. Kids must grow up in the fifth grade these days, I thought.

"Yeah. I guess you should be. I noticed that you were very pretty. I remembered the face."

This made her blush. Talking to her was like walking on a tight line of dental floss, strung from the top of Sears Tower. One false move.

I told her, after clearing my throat and getting down to business, that it was a shame she wouldn't be attending college and that I'd like to know why that was. She repeated the same line about family problems—that she just wouldn't be able to.

"What do you mean, *problems*? You supporting fourteen kids or something?"

She said, "No. Nothing like that." She rearranged her books on her lap and finally came to terms with her fidgeting hands by placing them squarely on top of a physics textbook. "My father—I live alone with him, 'cause my mother died a long time ago, and now he's moving back to PR. I wouldn't have anybody to live with while going to school, and down there I'll have to wait and apply to Inter-American University. I don't know. I might have to work and—I'll just have to see."

I pointed out to her that there were such things as grants, and that she could probably have her entire tuition covered, depending on her family's financial circumstances and her class rank. Then I asked her what her class rank was.

"Third."

"You're third in your class?"

She nodded. She ought to carry a license in order to use those eyes, I thought.

"Have you taken the ACT test yet?" I asked.

She hadn't.

I picked up the phone and called Dave Volmer and asked him when the next ACT was being given.

He said, "Why? Think you can improve your score?"

"It's for a student, Dave."

The ACT was being given on Saturday at Lane Technical High School, on Addison Street. I thanked him for the information and was about to hang up when he said, "You might want to stop up here for the forms if you want me to push the kid through. We can talk about what's-his-name, too. Carlos. I've got some interesting results for you."

I hung up and turned back to Marlyn. Her hands had been reactivated. She was literally wringing them, and this made me wonder if I was poking my nose into something that was entirely her own business. I guessed that that was exactly what I was doing.

"Hey, look. This really isn't my concern, you know? I mean, *I* can't decide what's best for you. I hardly even *know* you. But it just sort of seems that you ought to have the option to go to college in case you change your mind later. That was Mr. Volmer on the phone, by the way. He says he can push through your application for the ACT this Saturday if you want him to."

We had a difficult time meeting one another's eyes, and I found myself directing half of the conversation to my ashtray.

"You think I should do it, right?" she asked.

Yes, I thought. *I think you should do it with me as soon as possible.* I wondered if, given the right circumstances, the right bed, the right time, I'd be able to operate with her. It was just one of those male fantasies that men have more or less constantly, the kind that Marco said were good for you. It occurred to me that if you couldn't perform with Marlyn as a partner, someone should drag you off to a field somewhere and, as humanely as possible, blow your brains out.

"Mr. Spector?"

"Hmm?"

"You think I should take the test, don't you?" She shifted her weight and recrossed her legs. There was something in the way she did it that gave evidence of maturity beyond her age. She was a girl-woman or something, and the mixture was engaging.

"Uh-huh. Yes I do. But Marlyn—hey. Far be it from me to push this."

"Right. We've met once before and suddenly I'm getting the sales pitch of the century, but you're not pushing it."

That stung. She smiled again, though, and then, with her head tilted as though she was trying to read between the lines, she asked, "Why are you doing this?"

"Honestly?"

"Cross your heart and hope to die."

Lousy choice of words.

"You liked my book."

She tilted her head more. She wasn't buying it.

"You did like my book, didn't you?" I asked her.

"Yes, of course I did. But you must be awfully busy if you go through all this trouble for everybody who liked your book."

"I am. I'm a hell of a busy guy. Let's go see Volmer—what do you say?"

She said okay and got up and walked with me to Dave's office. I thought to myself, *She knows.*

Knows what?

That you're interested, stupid.

I told my mind to fuck off. The crazy idea that she'd set me up from the beginning arose. I wondered if you knew when you were in over your head in matters like these.

She knows.

"Shut up," I said, aloud to myself.

"Beg your pardon?" Marlyn said, once we were on the escalator.

"Huh? Oh—"

"You just said, 'Shut up.'"

"Yeah, I was, you know. Talking to myself. They say it's a sign of something, but I forget what."

"Insanity, I think," Marlyn said, and put her hand on mine while I was holding on to the escalator rails. Just for a second she did it, I suppose to let me know she was joking.

"Insanity sounds right," I told her.

Dave was drinking a cup of the world's worst coffee and was wearing a sweater with little balls all over it. He glanced up at me and was about to say something until he saw Marlyn. Then he stopped short and just looked at her and back at me.

"This the ACT student?"

"Dave, I'd like you to meet Marlyn Valentin."

Dave shook her hand and told her to sit down. I noticed that Marlyn had a rather startled but pleased expression on her face as she regarded me from the side of Dave's desk.

"Fill out these forms, honey. I can get you in for tomorrow, but you'll have to get there on your own. The second form is just a fee waiver."

He gave her a pen, but she declined, going for her own pen in her purse. Her purse made me feel sorry for her for some reason. It was a little battered around the edges, like Dave's sweater.

Dave said, "Johnny, that Carlos kid you brought in. He's got problems."

"Who doesn't?" I looked around for an extra cup, found one, and masochistically loaded it with Dave's version of coffee.

"No, but I'm talking problems with a capital *P*. Some of it's a bit out of my backyard, so I'm recommending a speech and coordination therapist."

"We got one of those?"

"Um-hmm. Twice a week. She makes the rounds around the district. Mabel Blades."

The name sounded familiar. "What does she look like?" I asked.

"She looks pretty much like a Mabel Blades should look. Now, when she gets through with him, then we have a consultation. Mabel, me, you. We decide what kind of program is best for him. Right now it looks like a speech and audio learning disability. But I wouldn't rule out some organic damage of some sort—perhaps even petit mal. The goddamn kid almost had a seizure up here."

Poor Carlos. When they stack the cards against you, sometimes they use the whole deck.

I said, "He'll be all right, though?"

Dave absently looked at Marlyn's knees and then caught himself and turned to me. "What am I? A fortune-teller? If you mean, will he get better, I've heard of safer bets. We'll just see what we can do for him to help him around the turns, you know?"

"If that's the best we can do."

Dave said, "I'm afraid it is. Kid kind of special to you or something?"

"Kind of sort of—yeah."

Dave asked me where I'd found him in the first place. I told him, "I'm not sure. I think it was karma or something. Maybe it was God. If you were God, who would you send him to?"

"Mabel Blades."

Marlyn finished filling out the forms and we both got up and thanked Dave and left his office. I could feel him staring after us.

"Now, you know where Lane Tech is, right?" I asked her.

"That's going to be half the problem. I'll have to lie to my father, 'cause the way things are on the streets right now, he won't let me go."

"Well—" I thought. I considered. "Where there's a will. How about if I drive you?"

She looked surprised. It was time for third period and most everyone was out of the hallway by then. "If it's not too much trouble or anything. I don't want to put you out."

"Put me out. Go ahead."

"Okay. You sure it's okay?"

I said, "It's okay. Are you kidding? Anything for one of my readers."

She wrote down her address on a piece of notebook paper, and just before she put her name on the bottom, she said, "How'd you know my last name back there in Mr. Volmer's office?"

"You must've told me yesterday when I was signing your book."

"No, I didn't."

"You didn't? Huh. I'll be damned."

No truer words.

I took Sheridan Road into Highland Park that night. It's less congested than the expressway. And a much prettier ride. Next to me on the seat I had a bottle of Asti Spumante. With any luck, it had gone bad. I don't carry a gun.

I drove past the Bahai temple in Kenilworth, or just south of Kenilworth, in an area that used to be referred to as No-Man's-Land. Sounded like the right place to be. I was thinking about after school that day. After school I'd driven Carlos to the intersection of Western and Armitage for his first big day. The papers were unloaded from a *Sun-Times* truck that—before it came to a stop—had almost knocked down the traffic light at the corner. I showed Carlos how to stuff the supplements into each copy, and while I was doing so, I came across a little article about a sixteen-year-old boy who had been shot to death that afternoon in Humboldt Park. One member of the Unknowns was in custody. They didn't give the assailant's name. (No wonder they call them the Unknowns.) Carlos got the hang of selling the papers in no time. I stuck around for about an hour and watched him as he became more aggressive in his approach. He only made wrong change once, and the driver who'd asked for the paper was very nice about it. Before I left I told him I'd see him on Monday. He said, "*Gracias*, Yohnny." And then I hugged him, right on the corner. It was a great relief.

I kept the car tight to the center line around the Winnetka turns. It had been ages since I'd driven around there, and as I neared the green lawns and lengthy driveways of Glencoe, suburban depression wrapped around me like a damp gauzy blanket. Shaped shrubbery. Country clubs. What the hell was I doing there?

You know you're getting close to Highland Park when every other car on the road is a Porsche or a Ferrari. You could get a ticket just for driving an old Buick in that town. Possession of an unaesthetic vehicle. It's a city code.

When I got to our block—*Shelly's* block—I passed the house and drove just a little further. I wished I'd brought a joint with me. I took a left down Ravine Drive, circled the block, and then repeated the maneuver. Shelly's driveway had parked in it a blue BMW, a bronze Mercedes, a white Cadillac, and one car that made me feel a *little* more at home, at least—a brown Plymouth Horizon.

I pulled into the gravel drive and rested the car next to the Horizon. No sense in being conspicuous. I lighted a cigarette and sat smoking it in the front seat with the radio playing. The song was "Our Day Will Come," by Ruby and the Romantics. Well, our day had come, all right. And then it had gone. There was no reason to think that it would ever come back.

I grabbed the bottle of Asti and headed for the front door. I was still wearing the sneakers and the blue jeans, though at the last minute I'd conceded to putting on a beige cashmere jacket I'd bought with my first royalty check. My outfit seemed strangely reminiscent of the driveway situation. I walked in. Shelly rarely locked doors.

Inside the house voices were coming from the den, out back. I lighted another cigarette and made my way past my ex-couch and my ex–coffee table and my ex-stereo. I suddenly realized I needed a haircut.

In the den I found an assorted mix of people that I knew and people that I didn't know and people that I didn't *want* to know. Shelly was behind the bar spilling rum over the edge of a glass.

"Johnny. Why, you made it after all," she said, and then noticed the mess she'd made. "Oh, damn. The glass is leaking."

Randy Glick stood up and extended a hand to me. Randy and I had been friends since our freshman year in high school together. His girlfriend had been Shelly's best friend and we'd married these two, only now I wasn't married anymore and the discomfort level was close to being strident. Lots of memories there.

Randy said, "You're looking swell. I thought divorces were supposed to age people."

There it was. The ice had been broken.

"It's a myth," I said. "They just make you less of a virgin, is all. How are you, Randy?"

"He's *terrible*. He promised me a dinner at the 95th and now he's backing out." This from Janet, Randy's wife. Janet was a thin and pretty girl who whined if the weather was lousy.

"Business has got me buried," Randy said, holding out his hands, as if to add, *What're you gonna do?*

Out of the corner of my eye I spotted Brandt Levy, Shelly's attorney, sitting in what had once been my favorite recliner chair. Brandt was horsey and short and tended to wear white socks with business suits. I'd always wanted to step on Brandt the way you would a roach.

"Everybody's so *civil* here!"

I turned around. It was Mitzie Schwartz. Red hair. Breasts that made you think of Goodyear Blimps. Now I'd seen them all.

"Johnny, how is it that some people just hate each other forever after a divorce, and you and Shelly act like it didn't even happen?"

I had wanted to make my way to the bar and get a Scotch and soda, but Mitzie had me by the arm, and judging from her grip, she had no intention of letting me go in the near future.

I said, "I don't know, Mitzie. I guess some people know when the party's over, and the rest of us are—what did you call it?—civil."

I inched toward the bar with Mitzie on my arm the way one moves with a klutzy dance partner. I was close to the bottle of Scotch, but I couldn't reach a glass.

"I read that crazy book of yours," Mitzie said. I had the sudden impression that she was trying to climb up me. "It's so crazy! Did you really know a kid like that, or did you—"

"It's fiction, hon. Just fiction."

I had managed to reach a glass, but now a tall, blond, good-looking guy with an athletic build had monopolized the bottle of Scotch and I just stared at him. Shelly was at his side like a prom date. What have we here? I wondered.

"Oh, Johnny. Have you met Carl?" Shelly asked me, while the Adonis now poured neat little shots of vermouth into highball glasses and regarded me with blue eyes under a living carpet of hair.

"No, I don't think I have."

Shelly said, "Carl, this is Johnny. My ex. Johnny, this is—"

"Carl?" I said, and extended my hand. Carl proceeded to try to crush it with his grip. His handshake sort of said, *Go on—I dare you to call me a fag.*

"Glad to meet you," Carl said, from somewhere in his chest. I had a little inkling that his voice box was located between his pectorals, right next to his brain. "I've heard a lot about you."

"Well, I hope you don't believe any of it."

Carl didn't know a joke when he heard one. "No, all good. Everything Shelly has said about you is good."

"That's why we got the divorce, Carl. I was just too good for her."

It would take a crowbar to get him to smile.

When I'd finally got my Scotch and soda I milled around the gathering and shared inanities with everyone—with everyone except Brandt Levy, who repulsed me. I caught him sneering at me two or three times, but pretended not to notice. I heard a lot about golf scores and club parties and play openings and new books on success and how to think *money*, and I wanted to go back to the city on Dorothy's ruby slippers, if I could find them.

I met a couple named Leaker, or Bleaker, and they must have been attached at the hip. They went everywhere together. When he stood up, she stood up. They were both wild about sushi and said they knew the best place for it. So did I.

Then there was a tall, gaunt real-estate person named Reginald, who didn't seem to have a last name, or if he did, I've forgotten it. He wanted to know what my bracket was.

Jesus.

What a group.

As I was on my way to the bar, Mitzie showed up again and rubbed her knee along the inside of my leg.

I said, "I'm not itchy, but thanks."

"I just love your cake. You people are the most civil—"

"What cake?" I hadn't seen any cake and I certainly wasn't going to take responsibility for anyone else's.

"The 'Happy Divorce' cake. Haven't you seen it?"

"No."

"Well, it's right in the next room. Get with it, Johnny. This is *your* divorce party, too."

I had the feeling she wasn't kidding. "My what?"

"Divorce party. At least that's the way Shelly billed it when she invited me. I read about one once in some women's magazine, but I've never been to one until now."

"I hope you're kidding me, Mitzie," I said.

Sure enough. In the living room on a cart there was a HAPPY DI-VORCE, SHELLY AND JOHNNY cake. Pink letters. It was kind of nauseating, in a nauseating sort of way.

"Well of all the goddamn—"

"Like it, lover?" Shelly. She was carrying two bottles of Chardonnay and had paused to show off her cake.

I said, "You didn't mention anything about this being a divorce party, dear."

"Oh, what's the big deal? You hardly ever show up for anything anyway and I really didn't expect you to make it tonight."

Mitzie had found me again and put her arm around my waist. "I told you it was lovely. By the way, Shelly. I'm stealing Johnny away from you. We're going to do wild and illicit things as soon as we can slip away unnoticed."

Shelly's eyes hardened while she smiled at this last remark. "Be my guest, Mitzie. He's not spoken for anymore."

Mitzie's hand was playing in the rear pocket of my jeans under my sport coat as Shelly walked away. When she got to the den, though, I noticed that she turned around and gave Mitzie a look that might have had something to do with death. Or it could have been all the smoke. I don't know.

On my third attempt to lose Mitzie in the crowd I ran squarely up against Brandt Levy. In fact, my empty glass clinked against his full one and wet the bottom portion of his ugly green-and-red tie.

"Well—Mr. Johnny Spector," he said. He adjusted his horn-rimmed glasses by pushing the bridge up his nose with one finger. "I'll just add the expense of the tie on to your wife's divorce bill. I tried to get her to sue you for the total, but she's so damned gracious she wouldn't hear of it."

I said, "What's another dollar ninety-eight, Brandt?"

We were still nearly nose to nose. It sounds petty in retrospect, but I wasn't moving for him. Brandt's jaw tightened and his breathing came in quick snorts. Some guys just can't take getting their ugly ties insulted.

"My problem's only a tie. I didn't break up my marriage because I couldn't function. Know what I mean, Johnny?" He smirked, took a sip from his drink, and began to chew on an ice cube that slipped into his big mouth.

I said, "Brandt, I thought your law outfit was sharp till I saw what you didn't go after."

Brandt stopped smirking, stopped chewing. "Whad'ya mean?"

"Come upstairs and I'll show you. You won't believe it."

He looked at me with a puzzled little expression and then followed me through the living room and up the staircase. I took a left at the guest room, opened the door, and allowed him to enter first. I went in directly behind him and shut the door.

Brandt said, "What've ya got, some family heirloom?"

As he turned around to say this to me, I punched him in the gut with such force that the follow-through knocked him on his ass. He sat hunched on the floor, holding his lower stomach area like a little Buddha, and pursing his lips to suck in air.

"I don't like you, Brandt," I said, rubbing my knuckles. I'd cut my hand on his belt buckle.

I closed the door on my way out and found that my legs were quivering. I held the banister as I walked downstairs, feeling pretty much like a rubber band. I was nearly to the front door, attempting a sneak exit, when Mitzie and her knees found me. Shit, I thought. Some days you don't get a break.

"You leaving already, sweetheart?" she asked me.

"Well, Mitzie, yes. That's exactly what I thought I'd do."

She made a pouty little face and asked if I wouldn't wait right there until she got her coat. She needed a ride.

"I'm in something of a hurry, Mitz."

"But I only live a mile away, lover. Let me get my coat and I'll be right back."

I stood by the front door with my hands in my pockets and waited. At any minute I expected Brandt Levy to open the guest room door and come huffing and puffing down the stairs, but he must have lost more air than I had thought. Mitzie returned with her coat and there was still no sign of him.

"All ready."

For what? I wondered.

It didn't take long to find the answer to that question. While we parked in her driveway, instead of getting out of the car, Mitzie slid her hand into my pants. I had sort of known she'd get around to it sooner or later. She never just shook hands at the end of an evening.

"Can't you loosen that belt, Johnny? My hand is falling asleep."

"Jesus," I said. "Some guys have to do everything themselves."

"Not everything," she said.

The driveway was dark and surrounded by tall shrubbery, creating a little alcove away from the house by about fifty feet. It was a great house—colonial—and I saw only one light on in an upstairs bedroom. Just that one light and its shadows, penumbras. I wanted to ask her if her husband was home, but it would have ruined the mood.

I didn't have the heart to tell her she was wasting her time.

Seven

When I opened my eyes the sun was coming through the blinds in rows against the bedroom wall. Light bars. It hurt to look at them; they were so bright.

Mitzie Schwartz. Damn.

Somewhere in the middle of my shower I woke up. I didn't want to get out of the hot water. My back hurt. I wanted to be someone else in a different place and it didn't seem to matter who or where. Just not me. Not there.

I thought about the way Marlyn had put her hand on mine when we'd ridden the escalator together. There had to be another way to live other than on the line. I was always walking the edge and was damned sick of it. I wondered if this was why people retired and moved to Arizona.

The phone rang with Shelly-like precision at seven-thirty. I debated with myself whether to answer it or not. Was Shelly fucking this Carl guy? It didn't really matter.

"Hello?"

"You know, it's really better not to come at all if all you're going to do is sneak off somewhere in the middle of everything with that redheaded slut."

"Good morning, Shelly," I said.

How do you get divorced from a divorce? I was surprised that the American Bar Association hadn't come up with it yet.

"Did you hear what I said to you, Johnny? That was about the rudest thing possible. I always knew you were thoughtless, but lately you've been getting worse. I honestly *mean* it. Now you're totally rude."

"Well, that's why we're divorced, right? At least I'm showing growth. From thoughtless to rude, in one easy step."

"And with that *slut.*"

I said, "If you don't want sluts around, you shouldn't invite them to your parties. I noticed you weren't exactly sulking all by your lonesome either, for that matter."

That made her hesitate. "What *are* you talking about?"

Shelly was beginning to bore me. She was a walking edition of Trivial Pursuit, and you only won when you played with her if you were smart enough to quit playing.

"Listen, Shelly. I have an appointment. I have to go. Why don't you call up Brandt and figure out who to sue next."

"Brandt left early, too," she said. "As a matter of fact, he looked quite upset. Did you happen to say something to him to upset him?"

"No."

"Are you sure?"

"Yes. I'm sure. I didn't say a word. I punched him kind of hard, but I didn't say a word."

"You *what?*"

Everything you said, you had to say twice. "I punched him in the guest room. It was the height of my evening, believe me."

Shelly was hysterical on the other end. "You mean you ruined my party *and* hit my lawyer? Why?"

I said, "Why? Because I don't like him. I don't like cakes that say 'Happy Divorce,' either. And I don't like stupid conversations or people who want to know what my fucking income bracket is, either."

I heard the telltale signs of a match being lighted and then the inevitable first drag on the cigarette. The light bars were gone from the wall and I lifted the blinds to see what kind of a day I was facing. It looked a little overcast.

"Do you know what the smartest thing I ever did was?"

I said, "No, but if all you have to do is narrow down the choices, it shouldn't be too difficult to guess."

"Divorcing you."

"Goodbye, Shel."

I hung up. We'd fought less when we were married, for Christ's sake.

* * *

Marlyn's house was a two-story white frame job on North Francisco. It was leaned upon on both sides by two stone-faced two-flats that looked like shoulders. I parked the car, turned off the engine, and had a cigarette. I wasn't in the mood to go to the door and explain to her father that I was just taking her to a test. I searched both sides of the street out of ghetto reflex. There was a gutted apartment building across the street with large spray-painted IMPERIAL GANGSTER logos. No one was on the street, though, so I sat back and regarded the cut on my knuckles. The bastard had been wearing a Gucci belt buckle with what looked like Sears slacks. Pissing in the wind was what Brandt did best.

After five minutes or so I saw Marlyn's head appear in between the curtains in the first-story window. She was wearing a yellow barrette in her hair and held up two fingers, apparently to indicate how long she would be. Two minutes later she still hadn't come out, and I hoped she hadn't meant two *hours*.

Then another head appeared in the window. A balding man with salt-and-pepper-colored hair at his temples and a line-thin mustache stared brazenly, first at me, and then at my car, and then he disappeared from view. A moment later the front door opened and Marlyn said something to the hallway before she closed the door. She had a new purse slung over her shoulder, a tan one, and she was wearing a beige Windbreaker and a brown corduroy skirt. It registered with me that I'd never once seen her in a pair of jeans. Maybe I'd been mistaking her skirts for sophistication.

"Hi" was all she said when she climbed in and sat down next to me. She smoothed her skirt and continued to do so long after it was necessary. Those busy hands.

"I take it your father isn't altogether sure about this."

"My father isn't altogether—period." She smelled of some perfume. Everybody ought to smell like that, I thought. I tried to remember what Shelly smelled like.

Liquid assets.

I drove away from the curb and headed toward Lane Tech, down North Avenue to Western and then over to Addison Street. I regretted having taken Mitzie Schwartz home. Ever since the sexual revolution had got underway I'd felt like a man without a country.

"Did you have breakfast yet?"

Marlyn shook her head. "No. I barely had time to set my hair."

"How about stopping for some doughnuts or something? It looks like we're going to be early."

"All right."

There was a Dunkin' Donuts at the intersection of Damen and Addison and it wasn't too far out of our way. We sat next to each other on two stools and everybody looked pale under the fluorescent lights. Marlyn ordered a coconut doughnut and a glass of milk, and I just had black coffee. I took out a cigarette and lighted it, but before I exhaled the first jet of smoke, Marlyn whisked the damn thing out of my mouth.

"Hey—"

"Smoking is disgusting," she said. Then she threw it onto the floor as if to touch it were to contract cancer of the fingers. Then she stepped on it.

I said, "Yeah, well—maybe it is. Smart-mouthed young ladies aren't at the top of my list, either." I pulled out another cigarette and lighted it. This time I guarded it with my right hand in case she had any plans to dash it out. I watched her as I exhaled the first puff. She was drinking her milk. I had never been out with a girl who drank milk. Shelly preferred Bloody Marys.

"They're *your* lungs," Marlyn said, wiping off a white mustache with her napkin.

"That's right. Let's keep that in mind. They're also my cigarettes. You're just lucky I haven't got a thing against coconut or you'd be eating that doughnut on the floor."

She smiled, and for the second time in two days I found her hand on mine. She patted my cut knuckle twice before she let go. I was out with a girl who held hands and drank milk. I felt like Andy Hardy.

On the way to Lane Tech, Marlyn asked me about the test, the ACT test. It had been years since I'd taken it and I didn't recall how long it was, or if it was better to leave the answer sheet blank for the questions you couldn't answer.

"I'm not terribly sure," I said, rolling down my window a little, "if you're supposed to guess or not. I think you are." I tried to remember the rules, but it was no use. "Do what you think is best."

"Thanks a lot. What would I have done without all this help?"

"And I thought you were such a sweet girl when I first met you."

Marlyn caught a few loose strands of hair and tucked them behind her ear. "I am. I'm very sweet. You just don't know me, is all. Listen, I read that book and you should talk about *sweet*. You've got a filthy mind."

"Don't ever forget it," I said.

I parked the car across the street from Lane on Addison and walked with her to the front entrance. We followed cardboard Day-Glo signs to the auditorium. There were rows of tables set up, and students were to hand in their registration cards at the correct alphabetical listing. I waited while she got in line, and I watched the other students. They all looked so young. I checked Marlyn as a point of reference. In her bearing, her facial expression, her dress, she was light-years ahead of the other kids. I tried to imagine how that happened to someone, how she had got her adult admission ticket into life much earlier than the others. She must have known a lot of adults. Either that or she was suffering from some sort of maturity syndrome. I was still daydreaming about her when she returned.

"I've got to go now. Thanks a lot, Mr. Spector—for the ride and everything."

Mr. Spector. Mr. Spector was my father.

"Call me Johnny, why don't you?"

She said, "I feel funny calling you Johnny."

"Don't you like to feel funny?"

Kids were taking their seats for the test and the bustle was dying down and Marlyn just stood there.

"Look," I said. "I could wait and take you home. You have to get home somehow, don't you?"

"Yeah, but—"

"Well, okay then."

An old guy in a gray suit began to blow on a microphone to see if it was working. "Testing. One, two, three. Testing." Put a microphone in front of a dope and he'll always say the same thing.

Marlyn turned and looked at him and then faced me again. "No last-minute words of advice?"

I took one of her hands in mine and said, "Don't screw up."

"Oh, thanks."

"You'll do fine."

She looked at me with that milky expression of hers and kissed my cheek. Then she ran down to a seat in one of the back rows. I left the room, but caught a last glimpse of the back of her head before I let the door close.

During the test I walked Lane Tech's cavernous halls and read predictable bulletin boards and even sneaked a cigarette in a boys' room. It had been years since I'd smoked in a school washroom. It amazed me somewhat to find that the thrill was still there. It must be *really* exciting to smoke a joint in one.

No wonder teaching was beginning to bore me, I thought. I was on the wrong side of the fence. I tried to figure out how I'd got on that side. That made me think of college, and college made me think of Shelly, and Shelly made me think of the divorce, and I saw how easy it was to end up where you least expected to.

The test took hours. You can only read so many bulletin boards before biting your fingernails becomes an acceptable alternative. A *preferable* alternative. When the auditorium doors finally spilled open I found Marlyn in a swarm of students and grabbed her by the hand.

"Whew," she said, wiping her forehead with her blouse sleeve. "If this is what college is like, I think I'd be better off waiting tables."

I asked her how it had gone and she said she didn't have any idea. Then I invited her to lunch. She seemed surprised, the way she had when I'd first offered to drive her the day before. She checked her watch, said something about what she'd tell her father, and then accepted. The day felt lighter now, and I wracked my brain for restaurants.

On the expressway we got caught up in some long Jesus of a traffic jam. On our right was a gray bus filled with sailors all in white. I hadn't noticed them until they'd lowered the windows and began shouting. At first I thought they were trying to tell me that I had a flat tire. I realized soon enough that they couldn't have cared less about my tires. They were hooting and hollering at Marlyn to lift her skirt.

"You make friends so easily," I said.

"I'm so em*bar*rassed. Can't you get us out of here?"

"Not till somebody up front moves, no. Unless you'd like to leave the car here and walk, but then I think you'd have a pretty long line of sea guys following you. Wave at them, why don't you?"

Marlyn said, "*I'm* not waving at them. They're *crazy.*"

One sailor had squeezed half his torso out of a cramped square bus window and said, "Hey, pretty baby. I know a place you'd never be lonely no more."

I had mostly had it by then. I shouted back, "Yeah—your bunk-mate's bed, but that's where *you* sleep, so there wouldn't be any room."

I got the standard death and black-eye threats, and then the traffic opened up just in time and I got off the expressway on the next ramp. Ohio Street.

"What was wrong with those guys?" Marlyn asked.

"They're guys."

We ate at Boccaccio's. We both had the salad bar and I ordered pizza because their pizza wasn't bad. I was about to ask for a Scotch and soda, but Marlyn was having a Coke. Scotch was just too decadent to drink while I was with her. It would have been like snorting cocaine in front of Marie Osmond.

I watched her eyes take in her surroundings. She moved cautiously, spoke quietly, and I realized this was how she handled intimidation. She wanted to take everything in stride, and it was creating a little strain.

"I hardly ever come downtown," she said, after sipping her drink from a red-and-white-striped straw.

"How come? It's right in your backyard. Just hop a bus or an El and you could be at the Art Institute or Water Tower."

"My father, for one thing."

"He won't let you out?" I asked. I thought of the Hitler mustache in the window and pictured him closing a jail cell door and locking her in.

"He won't let me *breathe*. I had a hard time getting out today, even, once he saw you were a man."

"Does he think we're fooling around?"

Marlyn choked in mid-sip and started laughing. She had to hold her napkin to her mouth before she could gain control of herself.

How to deflate a guy's ego in nothing flat.

"I'm sorry." She wiped her mouth again and smiled at me. "He doesn't think at all, is the problem. Johnny? You really want me to call you *Johnny*?"

I nodded. "And what's so funny about what I asked you? I mean, what's such a scream about him thinking we might be—you know."

"Nothing. It isn't that. Hell, I'm *sure* that's what he thinks."

I said, "Oh, great."

"But he thinks that about everybody I'm ever with—if they're a man and everything. I just haven't heard that expression in a long time. It sounds like a black-and-white-movie expression from the fifties or something. *Fooling around.*"

"You make me feel like a relic."

Marlyn said, "What, you mean old?"

"I wouldn't go that far. Neolithic, maybe."

"Well, you don't seem old to me. How old are you?"

I deadpanned and said, "Forty-seven."

"You're not forty-seven."

"You only think so 'cause I shaved close today. Wait till my five o'clock shadow comes back."

I watched her eat and I talked to her and we had a pretty good time, all things considered. At one point in the conversation she told me that she worked at the Walgreen's on North and California, and that if she was to go to college, she wanted to become a nurse. She'd wanted to be a nurse since she was seven. I remembered that when I was seven I had wanted to be either Buck Rogers or Elvis Presley.

"You probably think that's silly, wanting to be a nurse."

"I do not."

She moved her hands smoothly across the tablecloth, palms down. "You look like you think it's a bad choice, then."

I said, "Well, I'd rather see you own the whole goddamn hospital, to tell you the truth. That's what happens when you get older. Your idealism matures into greed. I'm greedy for you. Do you have any experience with catheters, by the way?"

"With what?"

"Never mind. You'll find out."

Before the bill came we sat in silence for a while and I watched Marlyn's hands move over the tablecloth while she thought something to herself. Without planning to, I reached out and held one of them and folded my hand around it, and noticed that my skin was a good shade or two darker than hers. Her palms were wet and cold, and she closed her other hand around our joined ones and before long we had created a big hand orgy on the table. We sat like that and looked into each other's eyes.

I was almost thirty and divorced and in love again. With a Puerto

Rican eighteen-year-old. When the stars had got together to arrange my life's course, they must have laughed their asses off.

On the way back to the car we pretended to window-shop, still holding hands. At Marshall Field's window on Michigan Avenue we looked at one another by way of our reflections in the glass. Even though we were surrounded by shoppers I decided it was time to kiss her. It was a short kiss, as these things go, but one that led to a major discovery—Marlyn's tongue. It was right up there with Halley's comet and Franklin's kite and Monroe's tits.

"What are we doing?" she asked me.

"Fooling around."

We drove down Ogden Avenue and turned on Milwaukee a little later. The Saturday merchants had moved their racks onto the sidewalks. Pentecostal women, with hair down to their shoes and long black dresses that made them look like Latin pilgrims, shoved the wares around and occasionally yelled at their children. The children wore faded patched blue jeans and had black-blue hair and mournful brown eyes. Wash one up and you'd have a poster child for some cause. The clouds had broken somewhat and it felt good to be driving with the windows slightly open and the wind in your face. Marlyn's hair rode on the breeze, exposing her cheekbones. Some bones.

I thought about Wanda. I thought about her getting married and it made me nervous. Marlyn was sitting close to me in the front seat, at times resting her head on my shoulder. It occurred to me that there were a hell of a lot of loose ends to tie before I could sit back, before I had any right to enjoy the present situation. Someday I'm going to be on my deathbed, and instead of appreciating my last few minutes, I'll be worried about some little gangster getting shot, some little coed throwing her life away. And that brought to mind Tony and Alfonzo and Elsie. Fuck it, I thought. Bwana needs a rest.

"How about a sundae or a malt or something?" I asked Marlyn.

She said, "I'm a vanilla cone person."

She was in fact a lot like a vanilla cone, but it was better not to pursue that train of thought at the moment. I turned left on Diversey and headed for an ice cream shop I knew of. Marlyn turned on the radio and we listened to Bruce Springsteen singing "Dancing in the Dark."

"This is a different version," she said.

I listened. It had electronic disco drums. It had a girl chorus.

"So much for artistic integrity."

"What do you mean?"

I said, "He ruined the goddamn song."

She shrugged. "Oh, I don't know. I kind of like it."

And that summed it up. I wanted Bruce to be Elvis and she wanted him to be Boy George. Generations.

We stopped at Bresler's 33 Flavors (thirty of which no one needed). True to her word, Marlyn was a vanilla cone person. I suffered a malted. I'd had nothing stronger than a Coke all day and I was waiting for my nervous system to revolt against the lack of alcohol. I had visions of Heineken bottles dancing in my head.

Marlyn and I walked the neighborhood and found a leather shop we both liked. She looked at purses and the guys behind the counter looked at her. On one headless manikin I spotted a hot pair of tight black leather pants. I poked Marlyn.

"I know someone who'd look terrific in those."

She said, "They're not even your size."

We sat on a bench in a bricked square near a CTA station. On a piece of paper I wrote my phone number and handed it to her.

"In case you ever want to talk." I'd finished the malted and made funny sucking noises on my straw like a kid does.

She folded the piece of paper and tucked it in her purse. "Somebody at school told me you were married once."

"Once so far."

"You planning to get married again?" she asked.

"Who knows? If the right girl comes along, maybe. She'd have to be the right girl, though."

Marlyn asked, "How will you know if she's the right girl?"

"She'll be wearing those black pants we just saw in the leather store."

That earned for me her elbow in my ribs.

Then we walked back to the Buick. Jesus, it was battered. Driving it was a little like moving a piece of ugliness around the city. We were both at something of a loss for things to say on the ride back to her house. A fat woman pulled a child by the arm across the street in front of us. I had to hit the brakes to keep from running them down.

"Some parents you want to murder," I said. I watched as she yanked the kid up to the curb and scraped his ankle on the cement.

"Murder is a little strong, but I know the general feeling."

Images of the day played back in my mind and it seemed as though we'd been together forever. I played mental mathematics and figured out that she had been in the third grade when I'd started college. While I was reading Marx and Engels, she was spending afternoons with Bert and Ernie. I didn't know what to think about that.

Boy Springsteen.

Marlyn told me it was better to drop her off about a block away from her house. Her father might see her getting out of the car. I disagreed. The block she had to walk was like a training course for guerrilla warfare.

"I've lived here all my life. I walk home from school every day. Really. Don't worry about it."

I said, "Do you keep anything in your purse for protection? Hand grenades or anything?"

She shook her head. "The way I look at it is, if you don't worry, nothing will happen."

"*There's* a philosophy I wouldn't want to see tested."

I pulled the car over at Francisco and North and we both just sat and stared out the windshield. An old guy who was anything but hefty and who had a blue-green tattoo on his shriveled arm stepped out of a Laundromat with a dirty sack of wash balanced on his shoulder. If he had far to go, he wasn't going to make it.

Marlyn said, "Thank you. For everything today."

"I enjoyed it."

She hesitated. Her hand was on the door handle. "If we were to see each other again, and someone from the school saw us or found out, could you get in trouble?"

It depended on whether you consider castration trouble. I could always look into a life in opera. But that wasn't what I said. What I said was "Honey, I'm in trouble at that school all the time. I don't think it matters. Our lives are our lives, right?"

She looked unconvinced. I didn't blame her. *I* was unconvinced. It was not one of my better arguments.

"What are they going to do, make me wear a big red *A* on my jacket?" I said. "They can't do anything."

She kissed me quickly, hopped out of the car, and walked down Francisco at a businesslike pace. I watched her until she disappeared.

Then I started the car and drove down North Avenue.

If we were to see each other again.

Well, at least I'd know I wasn't dreaming when they fired me.

I thought about going home and didn't like the idea, so I drove toward Tony's house. Tony lived on Potomac in what was the gutter of the *barrio*. If the rest of the area was awful, Tony's block was a little strip of hell, mostly burned out by landlords who wanted their insurance money, and by stupid tenants who used kerosene heaters in the winter. I'd heard one story about a guy who'd barbecued on an old wooden porch. When the flames from the briquettes got out of hand, he grabbed a jar of gasoline and poured it over the fire to put it out. It must have been quite an act, but chances are he'll never be able to show it to you.

Rockwell and Potomac. Want any drugs? Curbside service. When I got out of my car I was approached by two guys who looked like they'd just auditioned for *Planet of the Apes* and cinched the job.

"Got that 'Bo."

I said, "I don't want any 'Bo." 'Bo was grass, shortened from *Colombo*, which was slang for Colombian. "I want Fast Kid. You seen him?"

One of the guys pointed to Tony's house across the street. "He be in his crib with Tall Boy."

"Thanks."

"How 'bout some snow, man?"

"Naw," I said. "Had all I wanted last winter."

He wasn't amused. Behind my back I heard him say, "Fuckin' honky."

I walked up the steps of a painted-brick two-flat. Red and white. It was in bad shape. I was about to knock on the door when I spotted Tony and Alfonzo and Elsie sitting on the bare boards of the porch, behind the railing.

"Is anybody invited, or is this not-for-honkies-only?"

"Johnny!" Tony said. He was obviously blitzed. "Get down, my man."

"What, you want me to dance?"

Alfonzo said, "He ain't kiddin', Johnny. He means *get down*, behind the railin'. Things're hot. Two carloads of Kings have been by so far, and they ain't shootin' jelly beans outa those things."

I stooped down below railing level. Elsie was smoking a joint and passed it to me. She held the smoke in her lungs and wasn't able to talk at the moment.

"No, thanks. I just had a malted and I'm driving."

Elsie blew the smoke out in one big blast. "Take one hit, Johnny," she said, still extending the joint to me.

I took it and said, "Okay, but if the dean at Harvard hears about this, there go your applications." I smoked a little bit of it and got high immediately. When in Rome. Ever since my acid days back in college all I had to do was *smell* grass and I'd get Timothy-Learyed. Instant cosmos. I was afraid that if I didn't talk fast I'd forget what I'd come there to say.

I noticed a bulge beneath the buckle of Alfonzo's jeans. "That better not be what I think it is," I said. I sat Indian style on the porch, because my legs were starting to fall asleep.

"Only two things it can be," Alfonzo said. "You wouldn't care for either of 'em."

It was a gun. An hour ago I'd been on Michigan Avenue having lunch in a semifashionable restaurant with a beautiful girl, and suddenly it was *At Home with Al Capone.*

I had dizzy little dreams of Marlyn's face, and when a breeze rustled the leaves of the decayed elms on the block I thought about her hair and the way it had blown in the car. That funny feeling started up in my stomach again. It wasn't my ulcer. I thought it was love. Love made me think of lawyers. I wondered how I'd be able to afford my lawyer's bill.

"Can we go someplace and talk?" I said. I checked their faces one by one. No one thought it was a hot idea.

Alfonzo said, "See that line? The one at the end of the block?"

There was a white spray-painted line covering the entire width of the street.

"Yeah. I see that line. What happens, if you smoke more of this stuff the line disappears?"

"No, man," Alfonzo interrupted. "That's the divider. No People cross from there to our turf, and no Folks cross it into theirs. All day long, Kings've been comin' over here, cappin' and representin'. If we let them get away with it, the neighborhood's theirs."

Capping meant shooting. *Representing* meant just that. Gangsters waved their colors at each other and shouted slogans, like a commercial between programs.

"I kind of hate to break this to you, folks, but two guys and one chicklette do not a gang make. Know what I mean?"

Tony stood up, put two fingers in his mouth, and let go a shrill whistle that felt like it went right through me. Down the block kids stood up from behind porch railings and waved and whistled back and then vanished under cover again. There must have been close to thirty of them. It reminded me of when I used to play cops and robbers when I was little. Only this game never stopped.

I said, "Don't you guys think you're getting a little old for all of this?"

Tony said, "Yeah. But if we don't organize, we won't get a chance to get old at all. Hey—no lectures, Johnny. I know all about grades and that stuff. I got the grades."

He got the grades.

"You know," I said, extending my legs in front of me on the porch, "I tried to tell Alfonzo about this the other night. He said the same thing you just did—about the grades, which you do *not* have, by the way. It's not just grades. You know what I mean?"

Tony said, "No."

"You guys got a lot to learn. When you get to be my age and everything, I'd like to think you aren't going to be hiding on front porches in the ghetto waiting for somebody to come by so you can shoot them."

"*You're* your age and look where *you* are," Alfonzo said.

"Come over here by me, Johnny," Elsie said. "I'll protect you."

I said, "Yeah, but who'll protect me from you? Like I was saying. Someday you guys could have a nice life, start understanding about things. Pass it along to your kids, make everything better."

Alfonzo pulled his gun out of his pants, opened the chamber, checked it, and closed it again. "Johnny, what're you talkin' about? You ain't got any kids. What're you gonna tell your kids if you ever do have any? This is a verb, this is a noun? That'll get 'em far, buddy."

"No—that's not what I'm talking about."

"Just what are you talkin' about?" Tony pulled a rock out of his front jeans pocket and began throwing it up and catching it in his palm.

I said, "I don't know exactly. It's not something I can pull out of my pocket and hand to you, like that rock. It's a feeling, don't you understand? Like instinct. It's awareness. Shit, it's a whole way of life. Like that book *The Stranger,* the one we're reading. Coming to terms with things."

"That book sucks, Jack," Tony said.

"Even the movie stank," Alfonzo butted in. "I only like when the Arab gets shot. Boom, boom, *boom!*"

Just then I heard something. I didn't know if I'd really heard it or if it was just a buzzing in my head. "You guys hear that?"

Tony and Alfonzo listened, then shook their heads.

"I thought I heard a car," I said. But then there was no sound.

A second or two later a black Oldsmobile came screeching down the street and swerved and stopped in the middle of the block. All four doors opened and about six guys with afros jumped out and gave some kind of arm signal.

"King love! King love! King love!"

In the next instant Cobras descended from their porches, surrounded the car, and threw rocks.

"Cobra love!"

Two pistol shots were fired and I looked around to see where Tony and Alfonzo had gone, and if either of them had been hit. I was alone on the porch with Elsie, who had crawled over beside me. "Stay down," she whispered, while she threw her arms around me.

The car tore off. There was a volley of shots and the street was filled with triumphant Cobras. No one had been hit. Guys were slapping each other's palms and dancing wildly. The whole thing looked like footage of a *National Geographic* show on primitive tribes in Borneo.

"This is just stupid," I said aloud, forgetting about Elsie.

"I think it's the smartest thing I've done all day," she said. She still had me down on the porch. I stood up, helped her to her feet, and walked down the steps to the street. Tony and Alfonzo were standing near my car.

"It's a good thing you stayed on the porch, Johnny," Alfonzo said. He was pointing to the windshield. There was a bullet hole right above the steering wheel.

"That woulda been close." Tony stuck a finger through the hole and removed a few flakes of blue safety glass.

Things were getting *too* close, as far as I was concerned.

Eight

When I woke up I had a headache. I was clear down at the other end of the bed. The blanket had been kicked to the side. I don't suppose I need to mention what kind of dreams I'd had. That guy with the glasses was becoming my alter ego and it pissed me off that I had nothing to say about it. He was sort of a suicidal Clark Kent. This time he (I) had been running, trying to get somewhere when a bus came out of the blue and ran him (me) down. The difference was, this time we tried to escape. I guess you could call that progress.

I lay there in bed for a while thinking about how I used to wake up on Sundays when I was a kid and my father would put Brylcream in my hair and help me into a pair of Bermuda shorts and take me to the club for golf. Usually I would just watch him and the other men play. I never could get my swing right. Who ever thought I'd wake up twenty-one years later missing a thing like that?

Brylcream. Jesus. I'd had a crew cut.

I staggered over to the Mr. Coffee machine and thought about Joe DiMaggio and wondered if he felt as shitty in the morning as I did. Poor Joe.

I went to the bathroom to shave. I managed to get shaving cream all over my goddamn face and then I couldn't find a disposable razor. Under the sink, in the little brown cabinet high-rises put there, I found three, and I didn't know which one was the good one. Process of elimination. The first one was as dull as a butter knife.

Then the door buzzer went off. Goddamn it, I thought.

I grabbed the remote control thing and turned to the monitor just in time to see Shelly. What was this? She wasn't alone. Behind her to the left was Mr. Adonis. Carl what's-his-name. I never did find out his last name. Carl Chest.

I pushed the intercom button and said, "I gave at the office."

"Johnny, Carl and I came down early for brunch and wondered if you'd like to join us."

That sounded like fun, all right.

"Sorry. I ate at the office, too."

I watched the monitor while they looked at each other. Carl was trying to pull her by the arm to leave. At least one of them knew when they weren't invited.

"Johnny? Johnny, let us up, then. I need those earrings."

She did not need those earrings. She just wanted me to see that she could get laid by attractive men if she wanted to. I pushed the door release and let them in. I wasn't going to argue about it.

Before they got to the apartment door I had time to put on a pair of jeans, wipe the lather off my face, and slip on a polo shirt. Awkward moments were becoming a thing with me.

When Shelly knocked I opened the door and said hello. I couldn't shake Carl's hand because I had strategically grabbed my coffee cup.

"How are you?" Shelly said. She kissed my cheek and then rubbed off some lipstick traces she'd left. "You haven't shaved."

"Yeah, I know. I keep getting these brunch invitations every time I try to."

"I hope we haven't come at a bad moment," Carl said. Even his voice sounded like it could be flexed.

"There's no one hiding naked in the closet, Carl, so I guess it's a good moment."

He straight-faced me. Goddamn.

Shelly had walked off to the bedroom, either to get her earrings or to see if I was telling the truth about no one being naked in the closet. I invited Carl into the living room. "Would you care for some coffee?" I said.

He waved an unsure hand, as though this was a quick visit, but Shelly yelled from the bedroom, "I would." Carl's hand gesture turned into a reluctant nod.

"Cream and sugar?"

"Sweet 'n Low," Shelly said, apparently for them both.

Calorie counters. It just so happened that I didn't have any Sweet 'n Low, so I gave them both sugar without telling them. The idea of slipping them a couple of calories appealed to me.

"This apartment is an absolute mess," Shelly said, as an entrance line. She slipped something into her pocket—some keys or something—and took her coffee from me and made herself at home on the couch with Carl. I felt like I should have asked them if they'd prefer to be alone.

"I'm kind of a bachelor now, Shel."

"That's no excuse. Oh, Carl read your book."

I almost said, "Carl *reads*?" But I didn't. Nipping snappy remarks is what makes me such a good host.

Carl nodded enthusiastically while he sipped his coffee.

"That's nice," I said. "Shel, you're getting wide around the hips. You really ought to watch your—"

"I am *not*! Carl—do *you* think so?"

Carl shook his head, but before he could deny it, Shelly was standing up to show off her slacks outfit. "It's these slacks that make me look like that. It's the look now. You wouldn't know. All *you* ever wear are blue jeans."

"They're all I can afford, after the divorce."

Shelly sat down, holding her cup poised in front of her, and ignored this last remark. "Anyway, Carl read your book. He had a lot of insight about it, too. Tell him, Carl."

"I really enjoyed it," Carl said.

Some insight. I did not want a ten o'clock book review. I didn't even want company. I was beginning to smell a motive somewhere.

"Carl majored in psychology in college before he got into real estate," Shelly butted in. "Tell him, Carl. Carl says that boy in the book is really a repressed *you* that you never let anyone see when you were a teen-ager, and so it had to come out."

Carl had not known me as a teen-ager. Carl was the kind of guy I'd hated when I was a teen-ager, and I could just barely tolerate that kind now. I wondered if coffee could disguise the taste of lighter fluid.

Carl shifted his coffee cup and saucer to his other hand. "It was nothing, really," he said, nervously, for him, "but I got the distinct impression that you hold a lot of adolescent resentment for the world. Things we normally get over when—oh, say, after college and we melt into the working force. Anyway, that's all I said."

Shelly said, "No, it isn't. You also said something about stunted emotional growth or something. The point is, Carl knows this doctor."

"Dr. Klein," Carl said.

"Yes. Dr. Klein, who's done wonders for a lot of motivation groups in business and all, and he gives everybody this new outlook on life."

"Well," I said, looking at Carl, "then I think you should go ahead and see him. You don't need to check with me."

"Not for him, sweetie. For *you.*" Shelly was grinning from ear to ear. Her caps had cost me twenty-five hundred dollars three years earlier. Now she could use them on me at times like these.

That's when the phone rang.

I reached over from my chair position and answered it.

"Hello?"

"Johnny? This is Marlyn."

In the background I could hear dishes and glasses being jostled. "How are you?" I said. Carl and Shelly were discussing something in low tones on the couch. Probably arguing over what size straitjacket I wore.

Marlyn said, "The reason I'm calling is, would you like to meet me for lunch?"

"You mean *there?*"

"Uh-huh. I'm at Walgreen's. I get off work in about an hour and a half and I thought we could talk or something."

She sounded nervous. I pictured us eating at Walgreen's together in front of the entire student body of Freddie Prinze High School. It was a little like being told you could have the bag of gold if you didn't mind swimming across the alligator-infested river first.

What the hell. I was emotionally retarded. What did I have to lose?

"Yeah, okay. Say about twelve, twelve-thirty?"

"That would be good," Marlyn said. I could hear some more commotion on the other end. She was telling someone she'd be right over.

"See you at twelve, babe." I threw in the *babe* for Shelly's benefit. It felt nice saying it.

After I'd hung up, Carl and Shelly were standing up to go. Carl said, "Thanks for the coffee."

"Thank you for the insight, Carl." I walked them to the door. "If I ever decide to do something stupid, like sell real estate, I'll look up your Dr. Klein."

Shelly said, "Let's go, Carl." And then they both walked out. For a moment there I'd caught a glint in Carl's eye that seemed to spell *fuck you*. Not only could the guy read, he could spell with his eyes.

It wasn't even noon and I'd been analyzed, invited to brunch, and invited to lunch. Some days are nothing but fun.

North Avenue looked like a slice of Sunday life imported from San Juan. All the men were dark and had mustaches and wore funny hats. As I walked down the block just east of California, an afro-headed youth whistled from a tenement window above me at a girl across the street.

"Where you be goin', babe?"

"To Nydia's," the girl shouted back.

Then he made very loud kissing sounds at her. I wondered how he could do that so loud. He sounded like a parrot. The girl was overweight by about forty pounds and had the worst case of acne I'd seen anywhere, including Clearasil commercials. Puberty in the ghetto.

Salsa music blared distortedly from bullhorn speakers attached to the outside of a record shop. A group of kids was pop-locking near the door of the place and I noticed a pastel-colored hair pick sticking out of each rear pocket. Pink, yellow, green. The street was cluttered with rusted cars—Pontiacs, Dodges—and every so often a Camaro with a jacked-up rear would screech by and challenge pedestrians who had been caught in the median strip. An alley cat lurched from a rotted wood doorway and rubbed against my leg. I felt strangely out of my element. The white interloper. But the image of Marlyn's face seemed to justify my being there.

I walked into Walgreen's and followed a fat woman in beaten sandals through the turnstile. Marlyn was sitting at the fountain on a stool. She was wearing a red Walgreen's employee smock and was sipping a Coke.

I sat down beside her and said, "If you buy me a drink, I can be had."

"That's my line. You're supposed to say, 'What's a girl like you doing in a dump like this?' "

"I know what you're doing in this dump. Want to come back to *my* dump?"

Marlyn continued to sip her Coke right down to the crushed ice. "That's up there with *fooling around*. You sure you're a writer?"

The girl doing the soda jerking behind the counter was Mary Chavez. She had been in my English I class a few years earlier. Mary had a punk haircut, dyed rat or something. At odd times she would half-turn to us and pretend not to know who I was. Well, I'd known there would be alligators. I pictured job applications in my mind and counted my references.

"I'm taking off early today," Marlyn said, her hand on her chin, her elbow on the counter.

"Any particular reason?" I said. I thought maybe she had to work on a homework assignment.

"When a girl calls you to meet her and she has free time, you're supposed to take the hint."

Mary was putting together an ice cream sundae for a guy who looked like he was on the losing side of twenty-five or so, and she riveted her eyes on Marlyn and me for a split second, like a security camera in a bank.

Blink.

We ate an order of onion rings together and I had a Coke, and somewhere in the conversation a short, dark Puerto Rican man with burgundy polyester pants tapped Marlyn on the shoulder and said something to her in Spanish. I saw her face change somehow, but I couldn't grasp what it was that had happened. It lost its light, I think. She spoke back to him quickly, and halfheartedly introduced me to him as her teacher. I recognized the word *maestro*. I put my hand out to shake his, but he pretended not to notice. He put one foot up on the bottom rail of the counter, exposing red nylon socks. He was Pierre Cardin's worst nightmare. I sat there not understanding a word either of them had to say, and tried to show by my expression that I was pleasantly on hold, waiting to be included as soon as it was convenient.

When the short man walked away, Marlyn said nothing. She just stared at the plate of onion rings. The man turned around and looked at us when he was a good distance away, standing in the shaving accessories aisle. His face reminded me of a picture I'd once seen of Juan Perón. Maybe he could read minds, I thought. Maybe he knew what I thought of his dressing habits.

"Can we get out of here?" Marlyn asked me. She played with her straw and then dropped it into the glass.

"Yes. I'm just waiting for you. Don't you have to punch out or something?"

She nodded, got up, and went out back. This left me alone at the counter with a prematurely dissipated ice-cream addict and Mary, who was still behind the counter. Mary smiled at me as she dried her hands with a dish towel. The smile seemed to say that we were in on something together.

Brother.

Outside a cool April wind was stirring and the sun had put a glare on everything. Marlyn walked beside me and said nothing. Occasionally Latin people would turn their heads at us when they passed. I had the feeling my zipper was open.

"Who was that guy?"

"A friend of my father's," she said. She looked straight ahead.

I said, "Is that bad?"

"I can eat onion rings with a teacher if I want."

"Yeah, you can. But it's not exactly one of your constitutional rights or anything. Can he make trouble?"

She kicked at a pebble in her path and said, "He can if he wants, but it won't amount to anything. You just happened by and I sat down and talked to you." She kicked at a rock this time, sending it into the street with some force. "We can't always be looking over our shoulders, Johnny."

"I know. We might walk into something."

We spent the afternoon on the roof of my building. There were two or three other couples up there and we had all found respective corners to occupy. I'd brought a bottle of white wine. I don't remember which kind. We drank a little and talked, and I heard her story. She was on a roll.

Marlyn had been born in Chicago in 1967. She was an only child. Her father and mother had emigrated from Puerto Rico in 1962 and started a small grocery on Western Avenue. He still owned it. She'd made one trip to the island when she was seven to visit her maternal grandmother. The only thing she could recall about the trip was her grandmother's rooster, which used to chase her around the yard. That and mosquito netting, which she'd had to sleep under. It struck her as living inside a bandage.

Her mother had got pregnant for the second time in early 1974 and died trying to give birth. The baby had also been lost; there were complications and she'd had only a midwife present. From the description, it sounded like toxemia. Because the neighborhood was in flux at the time, Marlyn had attended an all-black grammar school. Her third-grade teacher, a Mrs. Higgins, hated her. Marlyn attributed this to her ethnicity. Once, Mrs. Higgins had made her stand in a corner even though she had to go to the bathroom. Marlyn ended up urinating on the floor and was ridiculed for it for months afterward.

I saw all this in my mind like a black-and-white newsreel with Marlyn's voice dubbed in. I liked the part about the rooster.

"How did you feel when your mother died?" I asked.

She said, "Are your parents still living?"

"Only my mother."

"Well, how did you feel when your father died?"

That had the makings of a resourceful answer. She seemed strong, standing there, speaking to the city skyline. It occurred to me that if you grew up in the ghetto, you developed a kind of teen-age stoicism.

"You were what—seven when she died?"

"Yes."

"That's young, kid. How did you manage?"

"I made up friends. I stayed at home. My dad's mother came to live with us for a few years, and I liked her okay. She couldn't speak English, though, and she'd always get lost on buses. She was the kind of woman who always thought she was right, even when she wasn't. A lot of times we'd be waiting at a bus stop and my grandmother would pull me on a bus and I'd say, 'Grandma, this is the wrong bus,' and she'd think I was smart-mouthing her. She never listened. We ended up on the south side many times and then we'd have to call my father and he'd come and get us.

"But most of the time, if I was by myself at home or something, and if I was sure that no one could hear me, I'd take out this picture of my mother, one with her under a tree in Puerto Rico. Her hair was combed straight back, and she had on a blue print dress and her eyes kind of looked—I don't know—super*natural*. I'd talk to it, the picture. I knew she could hear me. I had to put the picture away after a while. It got to the point where all I'd have to do is look at it and I'd miss her so much I couldn't stand it. I still have it packed in a box with other stuff from when I was young."

She wasn't drinking her wine. Her glass was still almost full. I poured some more into my glass and set the bottle down carefully on the roof's concrete surface. The other couples had all gone in and we were left alone up there like a couple of wayward pigeons.

"Do you know I bought the yearbook last year just so I could have a picture of you?" Marlyn pitched this one at me out of left field.

"You knew who I was?"

"Everybody at Freddie Prinze knows who you are."

"How much does the yearbook cost?" I asked her.

"Ten dollars."

"I would've sold you a picture for half that price."

Marlyn left her post at the edge of the building and faced me. I had not known that this thing with us had been unilateral at one time. I wondered how it had started.

"Tell me something about yourself," she said.

"I'm hungry."

"I mean about your life. You never talk about it."

I said, "Well, if you don't have anything nice to say—"

Then she insisted. She asked me how long I'd been married. "Was it a long time?"

"Seven years. Yes, it was a long time."

"Why did you get divorced?"

"The way I get it," I said, while lighting a cigarette and guarding the match from the wind, "I'm still a kid and the rest of the world grew up when I wasn't looking."

"Was she nice?"

I thought about this. There had been so many Shellys since I'd first known her that I didn't know which one the question applied to. One of them had been nice at one time, I think.

"She was a lot like someone's sister, you know? She was okay at picnics and movies, but you always felt like taking her home afterward."

Marlyn put her head against my chest. She just leaned it there. She said, "I gave you my life story and you just gave me two snapshots."

"I didn't give you any snapshots."

"You got a mother and a father and two grandmothers and a rooster out of me, and all I got was a picnic and a movie. You make it sound like she wasn't even there."

"She wasn't, most of the time."

* * *

Later on, when we were in the apartment, we ordered Chinese food from the Far East restaurant. Or the Far Out restaurant. Or the Far Flung restaurant. One of those. We ate the stuff on my bed and we watched TV—*Knight Rider*. I like shows that have things that talk that shouldn't. When I was a kid I liked *Mr. Ed* for the same reason.

I'd ordered about seven times more food than we could finish. Chinese menus confuse the hell out of me. We had subgum and egg foo young and different squiggly noodles that looked like they'd washed ashore after a typhoon and dried in the sand. I was questioned about Shelly several more times and I realized that women like their rivals to be good and dead before they step into the ring to take their place.

Somewhere between the beginning of the show and the end it happened. It started when she put her head back on a pillow and I rested my head on her stomach. From my viewpoint I was in a wrinkled skirt landscape, interrupted by three or four inches of thigh, and then knees. Lovely knees. We embraced. I ran my hand up and down her legs. She had such soft skin. We undressed while we were kissing. There were cartons of food all over the bed, and it had been so impromptu we hadn't bothered to remove them. I kicked a few over and wondered if she was a virgin. She did not act like a virgin. She also did not scream. I could hear her breathe and when her mouth was near my ear it was like listening to somebody say things in a dream. Just sounds, mainly, but it was like the breathing sounds meant something that you couldn't put into words if you tried. And with Marlyn you didn't think of making love as a sex contest in which each partner tries to outdo the other. She made me think of the ocean. Possibly because of her name, but more probably because of the way she touched. I couldn't hold back very long with her, and when I climaxed, the sound track of a Chevrolet commercial became audible in the background, slowly breaking the spell.

And when I think of the money I might have spent going to a sex therapist . . .

"Johnny?"

"Hmm?" I was still holding her and my arms had long since lost sensation. They were asleep.

"I didn't know Chinese food could do *that.*"

I said, "Yeah. The only problem is, you get horny again in fifteen minutes."

There was no neat way to clean the bed. I finally resorted to rolling up the sheets and dumping them into the hamper. I went to get new sheets from the linen closet. There were none there.

"Don't you keep your sheets in the linen closet?" Marlyn said. She was wearing my bathrobe. I was still naked and felt kind of silly standing in the hallway, half-erect.

"I don't know."

"You don't know where your sheets are?"

I tried to remember what I had done with them. I found them a few minutes later on the top shelf in the walk-in closet in the bedroom. "Here they are," I said, pulling them down.

"You keep your sheets with your clothes?"

"Yeah, but don't ask me where my sweaters are."

We watched some dumb movie and kissed a lot and had strawberry ice cream because I didn't have any vanilla. Then we tried to take a shower together, but only succeeded in making love in the bathtub. I don't know how we managed to do it. It was a very small tub. I said, "We'll never get clean if we keep taking showers together."

"We'll always have food on our sheets if we keep eating together," Marlyn said, when we were drying each other off.

"Slobs in love."

Marlyn turned sharply toward me. "I'm glad you said that word, Johnny."

"What? *Slobs?*"

She whipped me with her towel and walked back to the bedroom.

I didn't want to take her home. It was a little as if the governor had called and canceled my reprieve. We concocted a story for her father during the ride down Diversey—one that had something to do with studying at her friend's house, Mary's house. It was exactly the kind of story most fathers wouldn't buy. Who studies?

The Parkway Theater was showing *The Natural,* with Robert Redford. A vitamin shop had a special on vitamin E. I stored that bit of information away for later. I might need it, I thought. As we got to the factory side of the parkway, there were no more neon signs to read. What there was, was people. Lots of them. Night people.

Lonely people waiting at bus stops. One guy was smoking a cigarette in front of a church that had been converted into a live theater. He stood under a murky orange streetlamp and paced within the perimeter of the glow. Marlyn leaned against my shoulder and I put my arm around her. She felt warm and soft and smelled like a girl.

"I feel like I'm living two lives," she said.

"Only two, huh? You're just starting, then."

"Starting what?"

"Life. It's one of those lessons that they don't prepare you for in the Board of Education curriculum guide."

She thought this over. "You know what it's like?" Marlyn asked me, propping herself up somewhat so we could have momentary eye contact when I wasn't watching the road.

"Yeah. I know what it's like. It's like being dropped out of an airplane and wondering if anyone remembered to pack your parachute."

"Mr. Gloom. For me it's like waiting for something to happen, and then when it's happening you don't realize it until you're on the other side. Like—have you ever stayed up all night?"

"More times than I should've."

"I did that once. My father and I were on a trip to Wisconsin with an aunt and a little cousin of mine, and I watched TV all night and then I took a walk down by this lake. I don't remember the name of the lake. It was an Indian name. Anyway, the sky started to get lighter, and by the horizon it turned blue and orange and then the sun started to show, but it was so bright I couldn't look at it. So I waited a while before I looked back at it. They say you can go blind during eclipses and stuff, so I didn't want to look right at the sun. And when I *did* look back at it, it was up over the lake and practically in the middle of the sky and everything. I'd missed it. I missed seeing the sunrise, but I lived right through it. That's what I feel like now, I think."

We rode on in silence. Marlyn had the soul of a poet; she made me think of a female Dylan Thomas. She'd have to watch herself around alcohol when she got older.

I said, "How old did you say you were?"

"I turned eighteen last week."

Eighteen. I was eighteen once, for about a minute.

The ghetto swallowed us up in no time. It was like crossing an invisible line between trendy restaurants and a war zone. Turn left at Hades. It was around this time that I told Marlyn that I thought I loved her. I said it as though I'd reported that my palms were sweaty. They were, too. We were right in front of L. Fish Furniture, with burglar bars drawn across its plate glass windows.

Marlyn said, "Now I'll have to remember this place every time I think of the first time you told me that."

She did not say it back. There's no quicker way to feel like an idiot than to tell someone you think you love her, and then not get a response.

I dropped her off a few houses away from hers. I had the headlights off and the darkness was palpable. You could run up against it and it would knock you down. She kissed me goodbye and got out.

"I don't want to go, Johnny," she said, and then ran to her front steps.

Well. I supposed that would do.

Nine

The next two days seemed like one.

When I got to school McCaskey was waiting for me at the sign-in sheets like a scorned parent who'd just had it up to *here.*

"Mr. Spector, can I see you a moment?"

I initialed the sign-in sheet, said "Sure," and then drew the general conclusion that he meant in private, in his office. I followed him through the tiny corridor off the main office into his inner sanctum. I wondered what I'd done this time to merit such an intimate meeting. Maybe he wanted me to fix him up with a senior coed.

His office was dark and featured lots of wood, and in the corner was a coffee maker. There was a Norman Rockwell print behind his desk. Taste was another area in which we differed.

"Please sit down," he said to me, removing his glasses to rub the red spots on either side of the bridge of his nose. I chose the chair closest to his desk. There was no ashtray, so I took it that I couldn't get away with smoking. He looked at me a moment without his glasses. The expression on his face seemed to indicate that he couldn't fathom how such an idiot had ever got into the field of education.

"Mr. Spector, I think it's important that you understand that I have a potentially explosive situation on my hands—the community. There are factions in turmoil here, and they are at the street level. They reach right up to the top community organizations and agencies. It is political turmoil and it is emotional turmoil. There isn't one part of this neighborhood untouched by discord. I wonder if you understand that."

I crossed my legs. I was wearing jeans and tennis shoes. Dr. McCaskey fixated on my shoes and then put his glasses back on.

"I've noticed the tension," I said. I did not know what else I was supposed to say. It occurred to me that if a community was going to explode, as he put it, it wasn't necessarily my job to make sure it didn't. My job was to teach.

"I received a call from a Reverend Medina, the pastor of one of your students. It was a complaint about a book that I believe you are currently teaching your English One students. May I ask which book you are reading in that class?"

"*The Human Comedy*, by William Saroyan. It's recommended in the curriculum guide."

I didn't like the way the conversation was going so far. I had the feeling that at any moment the flag was going to be referred to as subversive.

"And in this book, there is, I believe, a scene featuring prostitutes and a brothel. Is that correct?"

"No," I said. "That isn't correct. Saroyan never comes right out and says, you know, that it's a whorehouse or anything. I mean, you could take it that way. It could be."

"I see," McCaskey said. He pushed a pencil around his desk top and seemed to be lost in thought. He must have seen a Clarence Darrow movie at one time in his life and liked it an awful lot. I had the sudden impression that I should take the Fifth until assigned a public defender.

"The Reverend Medina was under the impression that you pointed out to your students that this was a brothel in the book, and that the women were common prostitutes. One boy in the class, an Enrique Sanchez, reported the incident to the reverend, and he in turn has voiced strong objections based on the immorality and general lack of appropriateness of such a book for fifteen-year-olds. I must say that I don't disagree with him. I don't think it's too much to ask that we avoid the subject of prostitutes in a basic rhetoric class. The Reverend Medina has suggested a book such as *The Story of My Life*, by Helen Keller if the purpose is to acquaint young people with modern literature. I'm sure you'll find the change easy and pragmatic—considering."

He picked up the pencil he had been talking to and studied it between two slightly tremorous pink hands. His hands looked as though they'd been scrubbed with steel wool.

I said, "Are you kidding?"

"Kidding about what?"

I uncrossed my legs and leaned over the top of his desk. I picked up a paper clip from a little container and began playing with it. "I don't know if you're telling me or asking me, first of all. And I don't know if you mean that I should just drop *The Human Comedy*, or—"

"That's exactly what I'm telling you to do. I think I've already underscored the extent of the turmoil in the community for you."

I found myself breathing hard and trying to fake that I wasn't upset. The old fool didn't know what he was talking about. *The Story of My Life* was an autobiography and *The Human Comedy* was a novel. The curriculum guide insisted that two novels be taught every semester.

"Dr. McCaskey, have you ever given any thought to the idea that we don't have to ask local ministers which books we can teach?"

"Why, no, Mr. Spector. I haven't."

"Well, it seems to me that it's a little like the master bricklayer asking the apprentice which bricks to use."

"I don't know what you're talking about, Mr. Spector. I just told you what I wanted you to do. It has nothing to do with bricks or apprentices. Change the book."

I could feel my face becoming hot. McCaskey gave me a signal that the meeting was over. He checked his watch and stood up, waiting for me to clear out. I sat tight. I said, "This is weird."

"I beg your pardon?"

"I just said, 'This is weird.' "

"What do you mean, weird?"

"Objecting to *The Human Comedy* is like finding fault with the national anthem. It's the most *decent* book we have in the stacks. Mickey Rooney played the goddamn lead part in the movie—"

"I'm late for an appointment," he said, and stood by the door of the office to see me out. I stood up reluctantly, looked around the place, and started for the doorway.

Enrique Sanchez. That little illiterate bastard. He'd just set local education back fifty years.

That morning in class I handed out the books. I did not replace *The Human Comedy*. Enrique sat at his desk and refused to open the little paperback. Instead, he had his Bible propped up, hiding his face. I still had a gallon of adrenaline in my system and nothing to do with it. I found myself giving an unscheduled quiz on "The Bethel Rooms."

I waited for Enrique to begin answering the questions. He didn't. I gave him ten minutes. Everybody else was scribbling away and looking through the novel for answers. I walked over to his desk and saw that he was somewhere in the Book of Mark. I closed the Bible, laid it down on his desk, and said, "I guess you've never heard the phrase, give to God what is God's, and to Spector what is Spector's."

He glared at me. Apparently he assumed that I'd already had my ass kicked by the administration, and I had. I kick back, is all.

"Start the quiz, buddy."

Enrique freaked. It started with a quaking around the shoulders, a quivering lip. Then he stood up and yelled at the top of his strange little voice, *"I am a soldier of Christ!"*

I said, "Okay. At ease."

He looked around the classroom at the other kids and lifted a finger at me, as though I were being singled out to be stoned. He said I was the antichrist, that I was going to burn in hell for eternity. He picked up his Bible next and paraded out of the room.

Funny, I thought. During his meltdown I'd noticed that his fly was open. Maybe I should have called in Janice Newman. She got a kick out of open flies.

Some of the kids stared after him and then looked back at me. I shrugged. Others were too busy searching for answers and hadn't the faintest idea what all the ruckus was about.

"Sumpin's wrong with that dude," Jasper pointed out, shrewdly. When Jasper had your number, you'd lost the bingo game of life. I wondered how long it would take before Freddie Prinze High had a weekly book-burning event.

During homeroom the faculty was informed over the intercom that there would be an after-school meeting to introduce us to motivational techniques and materials. It was a mildly amusing announcement. Most of the faculty saw it another way, however. A last-minute meeting was a violation of our union contract. I heard a few teachers grumble to that effect. Dennis Stewart, our union representative, called up the union headquarters to see how we should handle it. I didn't have anything to rush home for after school. What the hell, I thought. I'd go to the goddamn meeting.

I stopped in at the lunchroom for a quick smoke and my midmorning meditation. My mantra is *shit*. I just smoke and stare at the wall and repeat, *Shit, shit, shit,* until I feel better about life. Oddly enough, it works.

The lunchroom door opened and Marco Gonzalez popped in. "Hi, Johnny," he said, and began looking under tables.

"What's the matter, don't they feed you at home?"

Marco slapped me on the back. "Just rice and beans and all I can find. At the moment I'm supposed to be looking for a bomb. Do you have any bombs?"

I said, "Code blue again?"

"Um-hmm. Just received the threat in the main office. Where did you put it, Johnny? Under McCaskey's chair?"

"Nope. I *drive* my bomb. McCaskey's chair would be the first place I'd look, though, if I were you."

Marco smiled and sat down. He had a million little teeth and had probably been born with them all straight like that. "Fuck it, then," he said. "If we call off the search, he can be the first principal in space."

"He already is."

Marlyn came to mind suddenly. I thought about how nice it would be if we could wake up next to each other in the morning. Now, that would be nice.

Marco told me he'd talked to Dave Volmer about Carlos, and that Mabel Blades would be in to test him during his usual time with me. He wanted to know if that would be all right.

"Yeah. Tell Carlos to drop in and see me sometime today, though. Will you do that?"

Marco stood up, straightened the crease in his blue slacks, and stomped his foot on the ground so that his pants cuff came neatly to rest on top of one of his black oxfords. "Sure thing. I'll get Mabel's results to you as soon as possible."

I didn't want Mabel's results. I never knew what to make of those funny psychological terms they used. But I figured if they had to test him, get it the hell over with. Maybe it would be helpful. Who could tell?

Mabel Blades. Sounded like competition for Gillette.

At ten-thirty I found Carlos pacing in front of my office door; he was counting the linoleum tiles and walking around them in fenced-off little patterns.

"Howsa boy?" I asked, putting my arm on his shoulder.

"Yohnny, I sell lotsa papers Saturday, Sunday."

I said, "Atta boy. Pretty soon we're gonna see you on American Express commercials. . . . Hi. You might not know me without my papers—"

"Don leeve home weethout it," he finished for me. Carlos Malden.

I took him to Marco's office and left him with Mabel Blades, who had brought a number of scientific-looking tests with her. Marco introduced us. Mabel had orange hair and pancake makeup and wore a black hat. She must have slept in mothballs the night before.

Carlos grabbed me before I was out and made me bend down to ear level for him. He whispered, "Come see me sell papers today. After school."

"You do what the lady says and I'll help you sell a few. Okay?"

He flashed me the *okay* sign with his hand, and I left.

I went back to my office and was visited by Elsie, briefly, before she went out for her coffee break or whatever she did in the backseats of cars. Alfonzo tagged after her a few minutes later. They both stood around, chewing gum.

"Tell me about the streets," I said, while I finished filling out the attendance forms that are so vital to a clogged-up bureaucracy.

"You don't want to know, man," Alfonzo said.

"Tony won't be in today," Elsie told me, looking at the hair on the top of my head. "He's got a big job on some wall or something. I think you're gonna be bald someday, Johnny."

"The way things are going, probably tomorrow." I wrote a pass to the library for Alfonzo and pulled Elsie's hand out of my hair long enough to wish her a happy lunch.

I was writing phone numbers (mostly incorrect or disconnected phone numbers) next to the names of absentees when there was a knock at the door. Marlyn. She came in, closed the door behind her, and said, "Good morning."

I gave her a bear hug and lifted her off the ground and sat her on my desk.

"Good morning. You're beautiful."

She said, "If I find out you treat all your female students like this, you're in trouble."

"I'm an equal opportunity teacher. I date minorities."

"You date a minority of one, mister, or you'll be an equal opportunity corpse."

Latin blood.

I had a copy of Goethe's *The Sorrows of Young Werther* on my desk and Marlyn began to leaf through it. "This any good?"

"It's sort of stood the test of time. Want it?"

She asked, could she? and I told her to take it. She opened her book bag and placed it inside.

"Last night was wonderful," she said, as though last night existed by itself, cut off from time.

"You feel comfortable with this? I mean, can you handle it?"

She pushed back the hair from both temples with her hands and sighed. "It's different. I'm still learning."

"I know. Me, too."

"When I got home my father had the bright light and the glass of water waiting for me. I was reminded ten times that I'd been out past my curfew and that he's moving back to the island."

"*He's* moving back to the island?" That sounded funny. "What about *you?*"

Marlyn smiled uneasily. "I mean, *we're* moving back to the island. I was told there'd be a lot of changes made when we got there, and that Puerto Rico is not the United States. You know, parents."

I said, "Yeah. Parents."

"They're always reminding you that they gave you life, just when you're not so sure it's such a hot gift."

I lighted a cigarette and looked at her, took her all in. I thought, Where would I find another girl like this?

"You really planning on going? Giving up college?" And me? And my sex life? And my sanity? Well, at least me and my sex life.

She held my hand. She said, "Let's not talk about that right now, okay? Listen—I get off work at seven-thirty tonight. Come pick me up."

"We're going to be the latest gossip if we don't take it a little easier, sweetheart. Your father's going to read about us in the *Enquirer.*"

"No, he won't. He can't read English."

I said, "A picture tells a thousand nasty innuendos."

We worked out a meeting place in Humboldt Park. I was to remain in my car, parked near the benches on California. Johnny Bond.

Then Dave Volmer made an unexpected appearance. He opened the door so fast it barely gave Marlyn a chance to whisk her hand out of mine and to hop off the desk. I couldn't tell if he had noticed or not.

"Just the person I wanted to see." He said this to Marlyn, not to me. He seemed cool and unsurprised, so I breathed a bit easier.

"Mr. Spector here told me about your wanting to be a nurse, so I got together a few brochures and application forms for you. Your name is Valentin, right?"

"Yes," Marlyn said.

"Okay, Miss Valentin. From the looks of things, Loyola's your best bet. They've got a super nursing program and a lot of grant opportunities. Take these things and look them over. I'll send them in when you've completed them, and then you've got the option if they accept you. Okay?"

Marlyn took the packets and the forms, said thank you, and then excused herself from the office. "I have a physics quiz next period. I'll see you later Joh—Mr. Spector."

I waved and she was gone.

Dave stood over my desk and looked at me. He stared out the doorway into the corridor and then closed the door by kicking it.

Fuck. He knew.

He sat in the chair next to my desk, pulled a cigarette out of my pack of Kools, and lighted it. He blew the smoke upward while he examined the fluorescent fixtures in the ceiling.

"All I'm going to say is, if I notice, other people will notice."

I pulled a cigarette from the pack and he offered his for the light. I puffed a few times and then hunched over my desk. I gave him back his cigarette. There was an arresting grease stain on his tie. I said, "I suppose it won't do me any good to deny it, right?"

"I don't know. Do you want to deny it?"

I studied a poster of Oscar Wilde on my office wall. "It didn't do *him* much good," I said, pointing to the poster.

Dave said, "If you need a character witness, I'll be glad to say you're a character."

"She's beautiful, isn't she, Dave?"

He laughed and leaned back on his chair, expelling another cloud of smoke. "God, Spector. They're *always* beautiful. Famous last words."

I finished my cigarette, unable to keep my eyes from the stain on his tie. It told the whole story.

I taught that day as though I were on automatic pilot. I bullshitted about Camus and existentialism and was fairly sure that no one knew what the hell I was talking about. Whichever lobe of the brain does the creative stuff was filled with ex-wife memories and impressions of my night with Marlyn. When *I* had been in high school, teachers used to take their students on field trips. I don't think too many faculty members were having intimate affairs with eighteen-year-old coeds. I wondered if this made me immoral. It was sort of a chicken-or-the-egg question, and I let it somersault in my mind for a while.

Then an interesting thing happened. At the end of the school day, just before I was to head down to the auditorium to learn how to motivate kids, little Aida from my morning class met me while I was trying to find the key to lock my classroom door.

I said, "Hello, Aida. Something I can do for you?"

She looked a little nervous. She shifted her weight back and forth between two cute legs. "Mr. Spector, do you remember the day we had the first phony fire alarm?"

I thought back. "Yeah. I remember it. What about it?"

"Do you remember I wanted to talk to you, but you couldn't hear me 'cause of the alarm and stuff?"

"Right. Right, you did. You still want to talk about it?"

She covered up her mouth; she was laughing to herself. I had a paranoid flash about Marlyn. Maybe she knew, too.

"It's Enrique," she said.

"What's Enrique?"

"What I want to talk about."

"You got a crush on him or something?"

Aida took a step backward and held out her hand in denial. "No! I don't got a crush on him. That jerk? Are you kiddin'?"

"So what about Enrique?" I asked her.

"Sometimes—don't laugh. Sometimes—promise you won't laugh?"

I said, "Cross my heart and hope to spit."

"Okay, then. Sometimes when we're readin' the book—you know, the book."

"*The Human Comedy,*" I said.

She said, "Yeah. Well, Enrique—he don't read it. He gots his Bible open so you can't see what he's doin'. Know what I mean?"

"I know he doesn't read the novel. But what do you mean, what he's doing?"

Aida covered her mouth with her hands again and bent over, giggling to herself. Whatever it was, it had her in stitches.

"Okay," she said, between giggles. "While we're readin', Enrique is—I don't know how to say this right—he's doin' somethin' he shouldn't be doin'."

Uh-oh.

"He's—oh, God. He's pullin' his *pinga.*"

With that Aida went into full-blown hysterical laughing, doubled up at the waist and stomping her feet on the carpeted hallway floor.

"Pulling his *what?*" She had me going by then. When I asked her what it was he was pulling, she went off again. Then I asked her if she was sure about that, about his *pinga,* or if maybe she was imagining it, or guessing it. She held her ground, though.

"He had it out! Right under his stupid desk. Was it *gross*! Little bumps all over it. Yucch!"

Huh. Enrique, the soldier of Christ, was a *pinga*-puller.

It made my day.

Only half the faculty showed up for the unscheduled motivational meeting. I learned from Mary Esther Sheenan—the queen of the duplicating machine—that the union had advised us not to attend. It was a little late to do anything about it at that point, though. I sat by myself in a back row and sneaked a cigarette. Smoking wasn't allowed in the auditorium by order of God, or somebody.

The guest speaker was a schmaltzy salesman for an educational textbook company. He spoke like a farmer and wore striped suspenders and he'd found The Answer and he wanted to bring it to us (for a slight fee). The Answer was—*I can*! He brought out a little pencil holder that was in actuality an opened orange juice can covered by a piece of paper with an eye on it. Get it? *Eye Can.* He even had a big eye embroidered on his necktie. I listened to him for a few moments, but I didn't understand what the point was. He gave us a slide show and showed us a picture of a girl who he claimed had been on the wrong road. She used to hang out with the wrong crowd and may have even been drinking on school nights—though this wasn't a certainty. But now, since she discovered the Eye Can program, her life had turned around. He showed us a picture of her later, when she had a job working in a bookstore for three dollars an hour. Now she was a success.

End of show.

I walked out of the auditorium and took the elevator down to the auto shop. I could just picture our students enrolling in the Eye Can program. They could get little eye decals and stick them on their guns and switchblades. I thought about the pathetic girl who now worked in a bookstore. Jesus Christ. McCaskey had set a new low in lame presentations.

I caught up with Carlos at Armitage and Western. He was working the rush hour crowd, right out in the middle of the street. I parked in front of the Main Bank and watched him from the corner.

"Paper! Paper!" He reminded me of William Blake's chimney sweep. A warm sensation flowed over me while he performed his little job. Some parent ought to have been goddamned proud of him.

When he spotted me, he waited for the traffic to rush by and then crossed the street, back to his two stacks of papers.

"*Hola*, Yohnny!"

"*Hola*, Carlos. How's business?"

He dropped the papers from where he had them balanced on his shoulder. "Business good. People buy papers, ask me Cubs scores."

"Carlos, if you want to sell papers, lie about the scores."

He had a bunch of inserts on the sidewalk and I helped him stick them into the remaining newspapers. He had it down to a science. Funny how he was able to accomplish all this without some sales guy packaging it in a book and selling it to him.

"Tell me something, buddy," I said, when we had just about finished with the inserts. "Have you learned anything out here on the job?"

Teaching gets into your veins after a while. Sort of like cholesterol. You always find yourself asking some kid what he's learned.

Carlos said, "Oh, *sí*. *Sí*. Margie's Candies—over there. And right there," he pointed to a building across the street, "San Juan Travel. And Main Bank. And Oak Theater—it gots nood girls. *Brigitte's Whip* and *Hot Mamas*."

The crazy kid. He'd memorized all the goddamn business signs at the intersection. He wasn't kidding about *Brigitte's Whip*, either.

The four o'clock showing had already drawn a line of seedy-looking characters to the ticket window.

"That's fine," I told him. "What do you notice about people, though?"

Carlos looked off somewhere and then snapped back. "*Peeple?*"

"Yeah. You know. Have you learned anything about them? About how different people act?"

"Oh, *sí*. White *peep*le. They don smile."

The mouths of babes. Of course white people don't smile. They're all worried about paying off their divorces.

The concourse through Humboldt Park is lined with streetlamps that go on at sundown and create a huge picket-fence illusion. I parked the old Buick between two of these luminous pickets, near the benches that Marlyn had specified. I turned off the engine and leaned back in the driver's seat. A couple of old men with street-dude caps walked by. One of them was fetching a glob of phlegm so loudly that at first I had thought he was dying. Across the street I could see the Walgreen's neon sign flicker pink along the G. There was a steady exchange through the doors, people walking in and out. Almost all of them held small children by the hand. I thought about how many of those sweet little kids would grow up to be crime statistics, and if anyone would remember when they were just little things being held by the hand, smiling in the face of poverty and blighted buildings. Leave it to me to look for the end of the line in somebody's life. How about the end of *my* line? I thought. How would it look? In the back of my head I always had the grotesque fear that someday I'd find myself on a corner in shitty torn clothes asking some stranger for a dime. I don't know why I worried about this. It just seemed like something to watch out for.

I had a smoke and waited some more. Walking down the side of the road I saw two teen-age boys in distinctive black-and-green outfits. Camouflage pants and black hooded sweatshirts. The kid with tightly curled hair looked awfully familiar in the milky sundown light. I slumped in the car seat and eyed him from just above window level. He and his partner were talking and kicking rocks and walking toward the car.

Pedro. Old razor wit. I could just see me explaining to him what

I was doing in Humboldt Park at night, lying across the front seat of my car.

Yeah, I was just driving along and I got tired and this looked like a good place for a nap, you know?

But Pedro must have had a lot on his mind or was deeply caught up in his discussion. Amazingly, he walked right past the car and didn't even look inside. That was the nice thing about driving an ugly car. You tended to fit right in to the ghetto. Assimilation.

Soon after the near run-in with Pedro, Marlyn walked up to the passenger door and got in. She carried her red smock on her arm. She smelled wonderful, as usual. I got a big hug and a smile. There was something exciting about all of this, sneaking around, waiting, picking her up in the dark. I wondered if she felt the same way about it.

"Do you ever get real excited doing this? Secret meetings and us knowing and the rest of the world not knowing?" I said, starting the engine and driving away.

"Yes. Usually just before I get scared to death by it."

"Yeah? You get scared?"

"Don't you?" she said. She closed her window a little and turned back to me.

"Sometimes. What are you most scared of?"

"Your job. If you lost your job because of me, I'd never forgive myself."

"Yeah, well. I'm the adult around here, you know? I mean, I'm supposed to know better."

"What am I—in kindergarten?" Then she socked me in the arm. She was truly pissed off at me. "This isn't *Johnny Meets Shirley Temple*, you know."

"I know. I didn't mean that you aren't mature or anything. Did you ever consider taking up boxing, by the way?"

"Look," she said, unappeased, "if you think there aren't exceptions to the rules, then you think we're doing something wrong. Do you feel like it's wrong?"

I said, "No." She was sharp. Boy, was she sharp. "It's just the sneaking and everything. *You're* the one who said you were scared."

"Yeah, but *you're* the one who made it sound like I was a bimbo who didn't know what she was getting herself into. When you're in love and everything, none of the other stuff really matters—what other people would think. If it was just sex between us and I was a stupid kid or something, then it would be different."

"You in love?" I asked.

She calmed down then. She smiled. "You're just trying to make me say it."

"What's wrong with that?"

She gazed through the windshield. "Nothing. Nothing at all. Let me say it when I want to."

We budgeted our time. We got to my apartment at eight and figured we could stay until nine-thirty. Walgreen's closed at ten and she would tell her father she'd worked the whole shift.

We watched TV and ate raspberry sherbet. We must have had a gallon of it. I filled out the financial statements that her father was supposed to deal with. She wouldn't take them home to him because she knew what his attitude would be. I did my best with the questions and left blank spaces where the information required became too specific. She said not to worry—she'd take care of those. It was the first time I'd written fiction since my last book, and I kind of enjoyed it.

Then the inevitable happened. We were watching TV from the bed again. During a commercial I pulled her over on top of me. She was wearing a beige skirt and panty hose. I pulled up the skirt, slid the panty hose down, and made love to her on the spot. It was crazy. We kept our eyes open the entire time. We watched each other's face. I couldn't remember ever feeling as virile as I did when I was with Marlyn—not even back when I was a teen-ager and in love with the pages of *Playboy*. I could do anything when I was with her. Shelly wouldn't have known me. The only problem was climaxing. After being inside of Marlyn for a minute or two, I'd have to fight the inclination to come all at once. I did this by using an old trick I'd first heard about when I was in summer camp, one that my counselor had told me he used with his girlfriend. You just run pictures in your head of variously ugly people. You start with, oh, say someone like Phyllis Diller, and then run the gamut until you get to Ruth Buzzi. That trick only worked for me about 50 percent of the time, though.

"I love you, Johnny," Marlyn said, in her ocean whisper.

"You're just a sucker for raspberry sherbet, is all," I said. I hadn't climaxed yet. I was on Zasu Pitts in my mind, and running out of faces.

Marlyn said, "You can't be totally serious even when you make love to me."

"I'm being serious. After this I'm going to the freezer to see what chocolate mint ice cream will do to you."

I made my way through my catalog of ugly faces, went back to the top for a replay, but lost my concentration. I came. Marlyn kissed me and pushed the hair off my forehead, straight back.

"Go get it," she said.

"Get what?"

"The chocolate mint."

We made the same late-night ride back to her house that we'd taken the night before, only this time we had the giggles all the way. Everything was funny. We spotted two drag queens with blond wigs. They were having an argument that seemed to have something to do with a young boy of around nineteen who was leaning against a plate glass window of a gay bar. He looked bored. Then there was a sign that said WE FICKS FLAT TIRES. But the highlight of the ride came when we pulled up to a red light, right alongside of someone's grandmother. She was commandeering the biggest Harley-Davidson I'd ever seen. She had varicose veins and a leather jacket and big thick corrective lenses in her eyeglasses.

"Now," I said, tilting my head toward the old lady, "why isn't she home making cookies?"

Marlyn said, "Would you eat her cookies?" Which was a considerable point. When the light turned green, the old gal zipped into first and zoomed into the night.

The drop-off procedure was such that there was never time for a lingering goodbye. It was always a quick kiss and an "I'll see you." She ran up the steps and disappeared upon the dark porch as though she'd never been there. I kept the car stopped about fifty feet from her house to make sure she got there safely.

Before I pulled away I had a flashback directly related to that time of night. One year before, just past sunset, you would have found me closing the garage door and turning off the walking sprinkler. Rolling up the garden hose. I would have had a Scotch and water on the porch while watching the neighbors' yellow light through the leaves of a willow tree. I wondered if I was getting anywhere. Circuitous routes.

That night at home I fixed a Scotch and water and watched Clark Street from my apartment windows. It was an endless play of cars parking and leaving, lights blinking, and, in the distance, just about at Sheffield Avenue, the El worming its way around old buildings like a centipede. I watched the opening of the David Letterman show, but he looked depressed and Paul Shaffer sounded whiny, so I snapped off the set. It was too early to go to bed; I'd probably just have another nightmare, anyway. That left me facing my type-writer. I walked over to it and played with the power switch. Sipped some Scotch. Played with the switch again. If typewriters could talk, mine would have been calling me chicken.

Why not?

I sat down at the desk, took some paper from a drawer, and began:

"Wild Sex with a Puerto Rican Teen-ager"
by John Spector

Nope. Too blunt. I lighted a cigarette and sat and thought. More Scotch. A writing teacher in college once told me that the story that most needed to be written was always right under your nose. I flicked my ash, replaced the paper, and began again.

"The Worst Suspicions of Stanley Glickner"
by John Spector

His wife lay curled up under the blanket and quilt of their king-size bed, with her mouth opened slightly. Every morning Stanley would peek in at her just before beginning his daily task of shaving. The covers created little mountains and valleys around her and it was impossible for him to distinguish where at least half of her limbs were. The sun was just creeping over the horizon, and as it squeezed through the bedroom windows it added touches of orange to the wrinkles of the bed covers.

Stanley walked out of the room and closed the door quietly while scratching beneath his undershirt. He glanced in at his son, Barry, who also slept with his mouth open—in the bedroom across the hall. He didn't stop or linger; instead, he walked clum-sily to the bathroom and turned on the light.

He caught a glimpse of himself in the mirror just before he turned on the hot water faucet. He beamed a ridiculous grin for a second and then returned to his usual sober expression, which he wore like a dull gray necktie. As he began streaking his face with foamy cream in preparation for his morning ritual, he gazed deeply into his own mousy eyes. It had become Stanley's custom to involuntarily picture his death each morning, while shaving. Yesterday he had envisioned a heart attack that he imagined would take place at his office. In the mirror he had seen, or thought that he had seen, his last personal struggle. The pain had crept down his left arm, just as he'd heard heart attacks are wont to strike their victims. He'd seen himself fall from his chair and attempt to loosen his collar, beckoning to a fellow worker whose desk was situated nearby. But his effort had been in vain. The co-worker, absorbed in business, hadn't heeded the groans. Valiantly, Stanley Glickner had faced his last moments on earth alone.

And that was how it had happened. Yesterday, wrapped up in his vision, he had experienced death. It had been a spiritual feeling, a fantastic rush of oneness and belonging, when life seeped out.

He stared deeply at his own reflection, recalling the certainty with which he had expected to be stricken. But it never occurred. He had subsequently waited at his desk for the event, almost eagerly, the way a child feels the night before Christmas when sleep is nearly impossible. Even though the premonition had been stronger than any of the others, and even though he had pushed the papers that cluttered his desk out of his way and generally ignored the work that had piled up, it never occurred.

And so he was back at the sink on this particular morning, dragging his razor over his living face, still waiting, still staring. He rinsed the tiny hairs from his razor occasionally without looking or taking notice of the progress at hand. His wife had lately chastised him for not matching the length of his sideburns. On the left side of his face, the peninsula of hair was a good inch longer than its partner.

"I'm not a gloomy guy," he whispered to himself through lather-covered lips. "I have a good job, I love my wife, I have a normal kid—" he continued, as the next vision ensued.

A funny feeling welled up within him as he saw, far away and past the mirror, an auto on an expressway. It was a dark blue sedan with terminal rust spots, like his own. He saw himself at the wheel, driving home after a hard day at the office. He was tired and tried to loosen his tie as a big semitrailer in front of him slammed on the brakes, jackknifed, and rolled over. Stanley felt the panic and saw the futile attempts at swerving and shifting into low gear. In a flash, the dark blue vehicle collided with several cars and the fateful truck. Those seconds came to him slowed down into sprawling minutes of struggle and then surrender, as the feeling of warmth, of belonging, smoothed over him and life seeped out once more.

"It's beautiful," he uttered, cutting his cheek with a careless twist of the razor. The absurd little grin recurred, briefly.

"Stanley!" Mrs. Glickner bellowed from downstairs. "Breakfast is ready."

He smelled the breakfast links and toast and instantly snapped out of his reverie.

"Stanley, would you wake up Barry? He's been late for school twice this week."

He dutifully wiped the lather from his face and walked to his son's bedroom. The boy was fast asleep, snoring at an unbelievable pitch that echoed sinus problems. Stanley pushed the boy's shoulder repeatedly.

"Your mom says it's time to get up, slugger. C'mon. She's got breakfast and everything."

Barry turned around suddenly. He was still wearing his glasses, but his father didn't notice.

"Aw, Dad! I was a*sleep*!"

Nora Glickner was thirty-four years old and seldom did her nails anymore. She also seldom had her hair done, nor did she leave the house except for groceries or a rare jaunt to the post office to mail the bills. Her face betrayed the fact that she had conceded to the sameness of one day to the others. She cooked minimally, carrying her family from meal to meal on four or five recipes that she had got down to an art, though even the taste of these dishes took on a startling similarity to one another.

"Your sausages taste like your macaroni and cheese," Stanley told her, between sips of orange juice.

Nora was scraping the toast. "Look, Stanley. I don't want to hear it. Did you wake up Barry?"

"Um-hmm. He said he was asleep."

"No kidding, he was asleep. The sausages taste like macaroni, I hear," his wife mimicked.

"They do," he agreed. For a moment he became lost in the piping along the front of Nora's robe. She'd been wearing that robe for close to ten years, but Stanley had just noticed the red piping, and how it ran around the collar and down the sides. "Nora, if I were to, uh—if I were to—" he stammered, as he folded up his napkin. "If something were to happen to me—"

"Oh, God. No, Stanley. Tell me you haven't been having visions again."

"Uh-huh. Just now, in the mirror. Don't call them visions."

"Then what the hell are they if they're not visions?" she asked, raising her voice beyond her usual monotone.

"They're more like *suspicions*, or premonitions. I dunno. Feelings. Anyway, it's funny. I sort of think this is the one."

"I don't want to hear it."

"A car crash."

"I don't want to hear it!" she declared, emphatically.

Barry walked into the kitchen and sat down in his place between his mother and father, rubbing his eyes beneath his heavy corrective lenses. His glasses fell onto the table and he quickly retrieved them.

"Dad, what doesn't Mom wanna hear?"

"Nothing. Eat your macaroni."

"Huh?" The confused boy stared down at his sausage and toast.

Nora stood up and brought her plate to the sink. She ran the water, picked up a dish towel, and stared out the window into the front yard.

"Barry," she started, "tell your father what you told me last night after you finished your homework."

Barry smiled rarely, but at odd moments he beamed a ridiculous grin. He played with half a sausage, using his fork as a hockey stick. The improvised puck flew across the table and dropped to the floor.

"Aw, Mom. I'm *eating*!"

"Go ahead. Tell him," Nora insisted.

Barry looked up at his father and said, "Nothing. I just keep thinking that my arm is gonna get broke."

Stanley departed from his normal lunchtime routine that day. It had become his habit to catch a snack at a small restaurant called Mary's Beef, though her hash browns were quickly growing indistinguishable from her hamburgers. He walked instead to a temple in the vicinity of his office to keep an appointment he'd made that morning with a rabbi. Stanley was by no means *very* religious, though he fancied himself *slightly* religious at times, in his own peculiar way. His preoccupation with death was surely a sign of his awareness of the brevity and beauty of life, he liked to believe. This meeting, this impending talk with a rabbi was to his mind a sort of life insurance designed to clean up any loose philosophical ends. He believed without a doubt that he would find himself driving dangerously near to a semitrailer that afternoon on his way home.

Though it was a city temple not far from Chicago's Loop, it kept the atmosphere of a pastoral estate. The grounds were on the lavish side, and the path to the main entrance was surrounded by shrubbery and flowers.

"I'm not a gloomy guy," Stanley said to himself, as he began climbing the dozen or so stairs to the door. He noticed a gardener, a man with a tan cap and a gray mustache, staring at him. Stanley nodded. The old man simply continued to plant a rosebush, a job he went about with studied patience and care.

He met Rabbi Jacobson in his library and shook hands with him a bit longer than necessary. He went to glance at his wristwatch self-consciously only to find that he'd left it at home on his dresser.

"What can I do for you, Mr. Glickner?" Rabbi Jacobson asked, with gravity.

"Stanley."

"Hmm?" the rabbi inquired.

"Call me Stanley."

"All right, Stanley. What can I do for you?"

Stanley proceeded to narrate his morning suspicions to Rabbi

Jacobson, while pulling absently at a loose thread in his suit coat. He told the man of his certainty of death, of the spiritual feelings he anticipated at the last moments, and of the rushing completeness that followed. The rabbi listened with an intent expression and nodded frequently.

"Don't you think that's how it must be?" Stanley asked. "Don't you suppose it's fulfilling and peaceful?"

"I suspect, Mr. Glickner—"

"Stanley. Call me Stanley."

"All right, Stanley. I suspect it is something like that. However, I think you are letting life pass by with all this worry about the end. You are not enjoying the in-between."

"Oh, I'm not worried. I'm just certain," Stanley interrupted.

"Good. As long as you're not worried, why not enjoy? What can we know with certainty, I ask you? We know very little with *certainty*. This fetish of yours, this vision of your death is not bad in and of itself—so long as it doesn't interfere with your usefulness. So long as your family doesn't feel a burden as a result of your fascination with your final end. From what you tell me, this is not your first—uh—suspicion."

"Uh-uh. I was supposed to have a heart attack yesterday."

"But did you?"

"Uh-uh."

"That's my point, Mr. Glickner. Stanley. You're still here in one piece. Enough of this morbid talk. You are a *mensch*. Act like a *mensch*. You have your health, your family. No more of this gloominess."

"I'm not a gloomy guy," Stanley agreed.

"Of course you're not! When death comes, it will be as you say, I'm sure. A moment of meaning, of oneness. But so too can your life, Stanley Glicken, be a time of meaning."

"Glickner."

"Hmm?" the rabbi asked.

"Glickner. My last name is Glickner."

"Well, I've enjoyed talking with you, Stanley. Go out and breathe the air. Smell the flowers. This is a time of life."

Stanley thanked Rabbi Jacobson graciously, though briefly. As he walked outside he felt like a new man. He took a deep breath and smiled, not so ridiculously, as he skipped down the steps. He stood over the gardener and enjoyed the planting of the rosebush with the old man.

"That," said Stanley, "is a beautiful rosebush."

"Yes, it is, young man. It's a work of true beauty—but it sure is hell getting it to stand right."

Stanley continued to hover over the gardener as he watched him pat the earth into place with his bare hands.

"You know," Stanley began, "I came here thinking about death, and now all I can think of is life."

The old man struggled to his feet and wiped some sweat from his forehead with his sleeve.

"You talked to Rabbi Jacobson?"

"Uh-huh. I'm gonna start living today."

"That's good," said the old man. "Rabbi Jacobson is the finest."

"Yeah. Say, do you ever think about what death must be like?"

The gardener stuck a soiled finger in his mouth and released the air in a *plop!*—like the sound a cork makes when it's pulled from a bottle.

"Just like that," said the old man.

Stanley stared for a second. "Hmm. I was telling the rabbi that I think of it as a fulfillment. You know, like a signifi-cant—"

Plop! The gardener made the sound again and went off to plant another rosebush.

Stanley was too joyous to let the difference in opinion bother him. He nurtured something new in his heart as he strolled back to the office, a feeling of contentment and peace. The preeminence of life was everywhere. He found ugly women attrac-tive, and the obnoxious panhandlers who congregated on Rush Street were considerably less obnoxious—nearly tolerable, in fact. Every nuance of pleasantness was visible to him, and he praised the windfall that had led him to this new plateau. Rabbi Jacobson was indeed quite a man.

So animated was Stanley, that when Mrs. Orbison, the sad old receptionist for the insurance firm at which he worked, asked him for the three thousand and fifty-first time, "How's life, Stan-ley?" he kissed her.

"Life's beautiful, Mrs. Orbison. As beautiful as you are."

She stared after him and sniffed a little for telltale signs of alcohol.

Once seated at his desk, he pushed the remaining papers to the side and quickly punched the familiar number of his home phone.

"Hello?" Nora answered, sounding strangely distracted.

"Nora? Stanley. God, is it good to hear your voice!"

"Stanley, not now. Jesus, not now."

"Yes, *now*, Nora. You'll never in a million years guess what's happened to me. I feel so damn good I want to tell the world. I made an appointment today—"

Nora interrupted her exuberant husband. "Look, in case you're interested—"

"I am, I am! But listen, Nora. I made an appointment with a rabbi—Rabbi Jacobson, at Beth Or. He's changed my life. I told him about the death thing and he assured me that death *will* be important. It *will* be meaningful. But God, he opened my eyes to *life*. He made me realize about the in-between, the now. I never felt so good in all my life!" He sat back in his chair and placed his feet informally upon his desk. "I love you, Nora," he said, at last.

"Barry broke his arm at school today. Stanley? Did you hear me? You know that arm he's been having funny feelings about? Of course, *you* wouldn't know where he got *those* ideas, would you, Stanley?"

There was silence on the line for a second as Stanley stared transfixedly into space. Then Nora hung up. His smile faded as he sat motionless with the receiver suspended an inch or so from his ear. He slowly removed his feet from his desk and dropped the phone to the floor. Grabbing his briefcase, Stanley walked briskly out of the office, past the still-wary receptionist. He rang for an elevator and waited impatiently, pushing the "down" button several times. After what seemed like a lifetime, the doors opened and Stanley boarded. At the ground floor he beelined through the revolving door and ran toward LaSalle Street, to the garage where his car was parked.

It was precisely 2:13 P.M. when Stanley loosened his tie, rushed into the street, and was crushed by the LaSalle bus. One witness, an old woman who made the six o'clock news that night, said it was the dumbest thing she had ever seen. When the reporter asked her if she remembered any details, anything at all, the old woman stuck a gnarled finger in her mouth and released the air in a *plop!*

"That was it," she said. "He just went *plop!*"

I sat back, read the story, and smiled. I'd killed the bastard off, sort of like Walter Mitty in reverse. I guess everybody is responsible for running his own ghosts out of town.

I drank the melted ice in my glass and got up. My legs were asleep. It was four in the morning. It was four in the morning and I was exhausted—but I was able to write, to have sex. Great sex. (Although for me, any sex at all was great.) I pulled off my clothes and hit the sack. The sheets smelled like Marlyn.

Ten

At 4:15 A.M. the phone rang. Who—Shelly? I did not need psychiatric advice at that hour of the morning. What I needed was a Quaalude.

When I answered, an official- but tired-sounding man informed me that he was a police officer. I blinked myself awake enough to fear that this was the call that everyone dreaded getting in the middle of the night, the one that informed you that someone wonderful had been hacked to pieces by a maniac, or run over by a speeding car.

It wasn't.

"We got a kid down here who says we should call Mr. John Spector. A Tony Alvarez. Says you're his teacher at—uh, Prinze High School."

"Yeah. I am. He okay, or what?"

"He's okay. We picked him up for vandalism, destruction of property, and curfew violation. Want to bail him out?"

I said, "Curfew violation?"

"That's right. Tony isn't seventeen yet."

Now, first off, the charges sounded redundant. What is the distinction between vandalism and destruction of property? And if you've got the goods on a kid, it seemed a little frivolous to tag on the obvious—curfew violation. I didn't voice this opinion, however. I merely said, "What's the bail?"

"Five thousand dollars."

"Must be some piece of property."

"El car. We caught him spray-painting it. You gonna make his bail?" the cop asked.

"Where the hell am I supposed to find five thousand dollars at this time?"

He said, in a singsong voice, "We got bondsmen down here. Are you coming for the kid?"

I lay in bed and stared at the ceiling. Every bone in my body was telling me to stay put. I overruled them. I'd spent a night in jail once when I was a kid. My father had thought it a good lesson, but it wasn't. I shared a cell with a pyromaniac and an armed robber.

"I'll be there. Hey—where is *there*?"

"Twenty-sixth and California."

Christ.

I drove down to Twenty-sixth and California, which, by the way, is no hop, skip, and jump from Hampden Court. It's a goddamn schlepp. I hadn't had time to put on any socks, and all I was wearing was a navy sweatshirt and a pair of wrinkled blue jeans and some beat loafers. But the traffic was light and I found a good jazz station on the AM band. I listened to a sax solo that sounded like it was coming through a tin can. I felt like driving over to Tony's house and asking his parents what the hell their responsibility consisted of if I was the one who was always saving their kid.

In case you've ever wondered where all the muggers and robbers and low-life scum of the earth are at night when you've managed to avoid them after the theater or a party, I soon found the answer. They're at Twenty-sixth and California. Usually drunk. Or stoned. I talked to the sergeant, the same blithe tired guy who'd awakened me. He directed me to a bondsman. The bondsman took MasterCard, if you had one. I gave him mine and signed the forms. The cost was 10 percent—five hundred dollars. If this kept up, I'd be broke in no time. Tony was released in my custody after a lot more paperwork and some unnecessary waiting. The sergeant probably figured, as my father once had, that an extra hour in jail is good for a kid in trouble. That belief has its roots in the idea that you should give a crying baby a teaspoon of whiskey to shut him the hell up. Same thing.

Tony was beat and his hooded sweatshirt was slung over his shoulder when they escorted him out of the tank. He was given back a key chain and a ratty-looking wallet with a few bills in it. "What about my paints, man? They're *my* paints," he said to a bald cop.

"Hey," I said, grabbing him by the arm. "Let's not press our luck, whad'ya say."

Tony slumped off a little ahead of me and I could hear him mutter resentfully, "They're *my* fuckin' paints."

What we needed here was an attitude adjustment. The first thing he wanted to know when we were in my car was if I had a joint.

"I gotta clear my head" was the way he put it. "You got anythin' for the head?"

"For *your* head I've got a crowbar in the backseat. Now shut up and learn to say thank you when someone saves your ass in the middle of the night."

Tony chuckled. "How can I say thank you, man, if I'm supposed to shut up?"

"Just shut up, then," I said. I didn't know what to do with him. If you were indulgent, they listened a little. If you were authoritative, they listened not at all, but were still obnoxious. Somewhere along the line I'd lost that instinctive touch with teen-agers, and right now I was feeling the futility that meant you'd been initiated as a parent. I didn't want to be a parent.

I bought Tony an early breakfast at the all-night Golden Nugget on Diversey and Western. The syrup was watery and the bacon was skimpy. I had a few cigarettes with my black coffee and sat and tried to be understanding without being a sucker. It was like trying to take a dry shower. I *was* a sucker, plain and simple. Street kids appealed to me. Maybe I *should* see a psychiatrist, I thought. Then I remembered the willow tree and the neighbors' yellow light, and sanity suddenly lost its attraction.

"When are you gonna learn, buddy?" I said. I was puffing on a Kool and listening faintly to the Muzak in the restaurant. "You've got the talent, but you don't want to learn the lessons. You don't want to pay the dues or learn how to play it so you come out on top. It's like you've got this little dial in your head set on 'fucking up,' and you could change it to 'getting by,' but you won't. When are you gonna learn?"

Tony was eating fried eggs over easy, or over slimy, and lapping up the yolk with a piece of buttered toast. He drank some orange juice and wiped his mouth with his sleeve.

"Yes, Daddy."

I said, "Don't give me that shit."

"Then don't lecture to me, Johnny. You seen my work. I'm the best. What you want me to do, quit?"

"Well, at least you haven't lost your talent for missing the point."

Tony let his fork fall into his plate. He sank down in his chair and pulled a cigarette out of my pack on the table. Two meticulously groomed men behind me were talking about the merits of St. Thomas—the island, not the man.

"You tell me somethin', will ya? What's this *point* you're always talkin' about? I mean it, goddamn it, 'cause you're right. I don't get the fuckin' point." He took a quick drag on the cigarette and blew the smoke out of his nose. He looked like a resentful dragon.

"How many times do I have to tell you guys this stuff? Are we speaking the same language? The *point* is the truth. It's balance. It's learning. It's making something out of yourself and having the ability to see patterns and to adjust to situations. It's maturity. Want me to go on?"

"No. I don't know what you're talkin' about, man. That's a bunch of crap they taught you in Sunday school."

One of the guys behind me said, in an overarticulate manner, that St. Thomas was overrated, a tourist trap.

"I beg to differ with you," the other one said. There wasn't one conversation going on in that place that I wanted any part of.

"You just try living on my block, Johnny, and then tell me about your balance and makin' somethin' out of yourself and the rest of that shit, when half the world be gunnin' for you. You don't understand the streets, man. You go home to that goddamn high-rise every night and order in a nice dinner—and then you're gonna tell me about fuckin' maturity."

I'd had just about enough. No sleep, out five hundred bucks, and the little bastard never even said thank you. I'm always good for one last shot, though. I hope I never get to Las Vegas, because I can't walk away from a losing table.

"What—you think I was born in a goddamn high-rise, hotshot? Okay, it's feel-sorry-for-yourself time. Want to hear my story?"

He didn't particularly look like he wanted to.

"I was raised in Deerfield. Nice plush suburb, right? And then one night Daddy packs his bags and says, 'Goodbye, tiger,' right in the fucking middle of the night, like right now. I was eight. He never sent a check. He never called, and I had to watch while the goddamn house was auctioned off and every stick of furniture was taken away. When I was in high school I supported myself with a job in a motel and playing crummy joints as a musician. In college

I worked for a factory that turned out Dixie fucking cups, and most nights I didn't even have a half hour to study. I studied on the train, just before classes started. You want to talk hard luck, fine. But I didn't sit around on my ass complaining, either. I did something about it. You want to make the Latin Kings your excuse for becoming an overnight teen-age bum, well, go right ahead."

Tony threw his napkin in his plate and got up and walked out. I reasoned that he needed time to cool down. I sat and finished my coffee. I was thinking about my father. It hadn't all happened the way I'd painted it for Tony. All Dad did was divorce my mother, but I'd needed the Hollywood version just then. Most of my memories appeared in Technicolor.

I didn't have it in me to go home and shower and change. Instead, I drove to Humboldt Park and watched the eastern clouds and drank more black coffee that I'd got to go. I wondered if some people are born equipped to handle the lefts that life throws at them, and if some other people just take it on the chin and never fight back. It seemed plausible. Then the sun popped over the skyscrapers. Even the ghetto looks brand-new at sunrise.

I was the first teacher in the building. I grabbed my mail, retired to my office, and spent the next hour getting paperwork out of the way. Monthly absentee summaries. Lesson plans. Male-female enrollment surveys. What a bunch of shit. There ought to have been a form that asked how your students were coping, but the system doesn't run like that. Education is only the *name* of the game.

I was feeling that buzz that you feel when you haven't had any sleep and you keep on going. That silly feeling that you're only half there. Megan Croner, our resident burnout, must be very acquainted with that feeling, I thought. I waltzed through my first-period English I class, talking about life while kids fell asleep. It was somewhere in the second period when I heard a loud crashing and kids screaming and the fire alarm suddenly went off. I ran out of my office to see what the hell was going on. I wondered if this was the riot everyone was always speculating about.

I saw a stream of students running down the escalators and heading for the front door. By then, with the fire alarm going, it was nearly impossible to make your way upstairs, against the flow. And this was no ordinary false alarm. The kids were too animated, too wild. A few of the smaller, well-behaved kids were knocked down one escalator by a group of screaming rowdies.

Up on the third floor I saw a crowd of faculty members and assistant principals trying to control the onlooking kids. I moved closer. In the middle of the cafeteria, between scattered chairs and overturned tables, was Marci Lester, a math teacher. She was unconscious and had blood around one ear. The school nurse was bent over her and looked like she needed a drink.

"What the hell happened?" I asked Mike Bane, an assistant principal.

"The kids went wild," he said, holding his walkie-talkie to his ear. "Four or five of them beat up Marci and then led the lunchroom study hall in a goddamn walkout."

Marci Lester was around forty, black, frail, and a genuinely good teacher. She was one of the few that I knew who went about her job as though she believed in the kids. She gave parties for her homeroom. She picked up kids with no bus money and drove them to school. Now she was unconscious on the lunchroom floor with blood coming out of one ear.

"This is *it*," Bane said to the walls, shaking his head.

I didn't want to disagree with him, but this didn't seem like *it*. This seemed like just a distant preview of what *it* would be. A few minutes later they had Marci on a stretcher, and a few minutes after that an ambulance came for her and took her to St. Elizabeth's Hospital.

I spent the rest of the second period feeling as though I had to throw up. My ulcer was reminding me that we were still a team.

Third period. No Tony. He never came to school that day. I gave my lit class a test on *The Stranger*, and was called out of the room by Janice Newman. I had a phone call.

Most of the lit students were juniors and seniors, and I didn't see any reason why they couldn't take care of themselves for a few minutes. I picked up the phone in the English prep room and was greeted by someone who sounded faintly like Jimmy Carter.

"Mr. John Spector?" the voice said.

"Yes?"

"This is Father Don Perry, at St. Aloysius. I believe you have a student named Wanda Hidalgo."

"Look," I said, sitting down in the closest chair, "if you have any bad news for me, you ought to know I can't take any more right now."

He said no, he didn't have any bad news. I drew a minor sigh of relief until he got to the heart of the matter. That's when I determined that *bad news* was a purely subjective heading. He had all the plans worked out for Wanda's wedding and wanted to know if he could count on me to pick her up at her house and deliver her to the church on Friday.

"Oh, Jesus, father."

"I beg your pardon?"

I said, "I'm sorry. I've been up all night. You're sort of putting me on the spot here."

"Well, Mr. Spector. Wanda tells me you're acquainted with her situation at home. She's a battered child. Her father has been in jail twice for beating her mother as well." He held the receiver away while he coughed. It sounded like a horrible smoker's cough. "I'm not too terribly pleased about the way we're going about this, but the alternative, Mr. Spector, is worth avoiding."

"Isn't Friday kind of soon?" I asked.

"It's two days after her eighteenth birthday. Wanda was beaten again last Saturday."

The sonofabitch, I thought.

I took notes while the father gave me instructions. I was to pick Wanda up at five in the morning and deliver her to the convent where a Sister Eloise would prepare her for the wedding. The early hour was attributed to Mr. Hidalgo's rising schedule, which was usually around seven o'clock.

I can't say why I agreed to this plan. Part of it was that I didn't want to look into Wanda's eyes if I refused. The rest probably had something to do with the executive sound of Father Perry's voice. Turning him down was akin to telling a former president you had no desire to fight for your country.

After the conversation I sat in the chair in the prep room rubbing my eyes. Little mirages of my bed appeared to me. This boy needed some sleep.

Out in the hallway I could hear a small disturbance coming from my classroom. I stood up, walked into the hallway, and listened. There was a man in there screaming at the students. He sounded as though he was crazy—the tone of an administrator. Dr. McCaskey. I'd been gone from my room for two minutes and the jerk was raising hell about something. I looked up toward heaven, but all I could see were acoustic ceiling tiles.

Inside the classroom the kids were sitting at their desks, silent. McCaskey had Alfonzo by his shirt collar and was berating him in front of the other kids. "Delinquent—I'll have you thrown out of here—police," stuff like that. On Alfonzo's desk, next to his seldom-used notebook and a copy of Camus's *The Stranger*, was a half-finished bottle of Löwenbräu beer. The little bastard.

"What's going on in here?" I said, as I made my entrance. I'd thought about saying, *I'll have whatever you two are having*, but thought better of it. McCaskey was not noted for his sense of humor.

He dug in right away.

"Mr. Spector, may I inquire where you were during class time, and why I walked in here and found this . . . this *hoodlum*—"

"Careful," Alfonzo warned, quietly.

"—this *hoodlum* guzzling down a bottle of beer?"

I was still standing by the door. It seemed to me that there was a more diplomatic way to handle this. Simply take the bottle of beer away and write a student report and go about your business. With Marci Lester in the hospital, there were more important things to worry about. Not so curiously, I said none of this.

What I said was "I was called away to the phone."

"And you left your class unattended?"

"Essentially, yes."

I then received the same treatment Alfonzo had gotten. McCaskey was out of his mind. I stood near the door and listened as I was called, not every name in the book, but many of them—unprofessional, careless, incompetent, irresponsible, stupid.

Well, you pay your dues.

"I'll take care of this matter, Dr. McCaskey," I said. The students were looking at the imperious little man and myself. We must have seemed like poor seconds in a scene played in their own homes every night. What the hell. If you can't watch Mom and Dad fight, you might as well enjoy a good row between your teacher and the principal.

McCaskey said, "You will *not* take care of this matter. *I will.*"

"Okay. Fine. Have it your way. You take the hoodlum. But how about not calling me stupid in front of my students?" His head spun toward me as though it were on some kind of spring. A few kids started laughing. I took my position at my desk. "And as long as you're up, I'd kind of like you to show yourself to the door. I've got a class to teach."

A stunned McCaskey looked at me, standing stone-still. He was intent on turning this into a standoff. "Are you throwing me out of your classroom?"

"No. I'm not throwing you out. I'm asking you very politely to leave before I throw you out."

He said, "I'll *E-one* you for this, Spector."

"I don't care."

The kids were stomping their feet and whistling. McCaskey grabbed Alfonzo and marched out of the room. The catcalls grew louder and turned into applause.

I mentally estimated the balance in my money-market account and figured that I could always get a job as a proofreader. Either that or I could sell newspapers, like Carlos. Maybe we could get adjoining intersections. Then I thought about killing Alfonzo.

After a minute or so of the racket I told my students to shut up.

"Did you see that motherfucker hit the dirt?" Miguel asked. "Damn, Johnny. You somethin', dude!"

"Something like unemployed. Finish the test," I told him.

An E-1 was the beginning of the end. The first step in running a teacher out of the system.

I picked up the beer bottle and left the room. I walked to the washroom, found it empty, and polished off the rest of the beer in a toilet stall. Then I had a cigarette. I can't say that I felt better, but then again, I didn't feel any worse.

I had not seen Marlyn all day. I assumed our standing date was still on. After school, Dave Volmer caught up to me on the escalator and said, "Going my way?"

"Who are you, Bing Crosby?"

Dave said, "Nope. I'm Father Volmer, and if you're smart you'll have a beer with me. Are you smart?"

Just what I needed. Another priest.

I said, "Not necessarily. But the beer sounds good. Where do we go?"

"Follow me."

I was under the impression that we would get into our cars and drive somewhere, but Dave knew of a place in the neighborhood that was an old Ukrainian bar with lots of regulars cemented to their stools, speaking a language I'd never heard before. I guess it was Ukrainian. I had my money in my hand and caught the first round. I couldn't accept a free drink from a man who wore shoes that looked like his.

"If you don't mind me saying so, Johnny," Dave said, after his first gulp of some imported lager, "you look like unadulterated shit."

"Always trying to turn my head with compliments."

"No. It's true. Where'd you sleep last night, the park?"

"You've been following me."

"Who'd follow *you?*"

I caught a quick look at myself in the mirror behind the bar. He hadn't been lying. My hair was unwashed, my sweatshirt was wrinkled, and I was still running around in those beaten loafers with no socks. There were circles under my eyes.

"I was up all night," I said. I didn't know what made me feel like I had to apologize. Some people go through their entire lives looking like shit and never say, "I'm sorry."

On the second round Dave warmed up to his subject. "I was in McCaskey's office today."

I said, "Some people will go anywhere."

"I'm not kidding about this, Johnny. I think you ought to know that he's mounted a special campaign against you. He had a few counselors in there, and he asked us if we've had any trouble working with you lately. I think he's drawing up an E-one or an administrative transfer, with just you in mind."

"Who else was in there?"

Dave looked for a minute as though he were going to stand on ceremony and keep the identities to himself. Then he backed down, rested his beer bottle, and said, "Marco Gonzalez."

"I don't have to worry about Marco. Marco's cool. Who else?"

"Rita Gerrod."

"Uh-oh," I said. Rita Gerrod was a woman who disliked anyone who didn't wear a tie. "I'll bet she had a few choice words to say about me."

Dave winked and nodded.

"I'll bet I'm not going to hear them."

Dave said, "Let's just say she's removed you from her social calendar this year."

Someone played a song on the jukebox. I had never heard it before. Sounded like a cross between Lawrence Welk and Spike Jones. I looked at myself in the mirror again, and then at Dave, and then at two old Ukrainian women with gapped teeth who had taken to the floor to do something that looked like it was supposed to be a polka.

"Johnny, about Carlos."

Dave had finished his second beer and was turning serious on me.

"What about Carlos."

"I had a meeting with Mabel Blades today. There's no way we can keep him in a regular English class. He needs special attention. His program will be changed to EMH. I can give you a choice of who you think is the best teacher."

EMH was Emotionally and Mentally Handicapped. Zoo school. Carlos deserved better.

"*I'm* the best teacher. Don't give me that."

Dave looked at his empty glass. "Not for Carlos, you're not."

That was funny. I was the one who got him to write, got him a job and a bus pass, but I was the wrong teacher. I didn't understand this at all.

"Thanks for the little pep talk, Dave. I really appreciate it. You're a real buddy."

"Go home and get some sleep. It's been a tough day for you."

I did not want his sympathy.

"A real buddy," I said. I left a buck on the bar and walked out into the sunshine. The brightness hurt my eyes.

At home I took a shower. I let it run until all the hot water was gone. Then I let the cold water run. In my head Dean Martin was singing "Everybody Loves Somebody Sometime." Then I imagined Bob Dylan singing it. Then I turned off the cold water and heard the phone ringing. "Hold the fuck on," I yelled at it. It kept ringing. I finally picked up the receiver on the tenth ring.

"Johnny? Jack. Jack Henley."

"Jack," I said. "I just got out of the shower."

"Then keep a towel on. Listen, about the article."

I'd forgotten about the article. If allowing students to drink beer and reading about whores in class were not good enough reasons to get me fired, Jack had just reminded me of the capper.

"What about the article?"

Jack said, "As far as I get it, they're holding it till things simmer down in your neighborhood—I mean your *school's* neighborhood. The guy at the paper, the editor, he was none too specific. I wouldn't count on seeing your by-line for a while, though. Maybe even summer vacation."

On the surface, this was not wholly bad news. I wondered if someone at the paper had been in touch with either McCaskey or the district superintendent. Politics in Chicago frequently reached media level. Deals were cut. Did McCaskey know? That could explain a lot about the treatment I'd been getting.

"Well, Jack. We've been paid. Your pictures will be in the paper, so there's nothing really wrong, is there?"

"No. I . . . I just was sort of counting on a more timely release on this thing."

I said, "What do you mean? You mean you were hoping we could blow the neighborhood up with a story and get a lot of coverage?"

Jack cleared his throat. He sounded self-restrained. "No. We've been over that. I still maintain it's just journalism, Johnny. You're making it sound like the messenger should be shot."

"Maybe he will be."

"We don't invent the news. We just report it."

"Oh, shut up. I'm not a reporter."

"What are you, then?"

I said, "I'm a sleepy drunk. I'm going to bed."

Jack said he'd keep in touch and then I hung up. I found a cigar in a kitchen cabinet. I unwrapped it, lighted it, and took a few puffs. For the next half hour I think I just sat on the counter—still in just a towel—and watched the refrigerator until the cigar slowly burned itself out.

Eleven

"Do married couples make love every night?" Marlyn asked me, under the sheets, holding on to my waist. It was all I could do to keep my eyes open, by then. I was totally exhausted.

"Hmm? Oh. I don't know. Want me to ask a few?"

"No. Seriously. I was just wondering if married people are like this, or if it all stops when it's official. Wouldn't it be terrible if everything was beautiful, like it is now for you and me, and then, if we got married, we just ended up having dinner together and watching TV?"

That was a funny thought. The remnants of a large cheese-and-sausage pizza had been kicked off the bed onto the floor. I regarded the mess for a moment as I fluffed up my pillow that didn't fluff.

"That sounds pretty terrible, all right. The goddamn pizza's all over the floor."

"Forget about the pizza," she said, encircling my rib cage with her arms. "Do you think if we were to get married we'd still be— you know."

"Fucking?"

She slapped my chest with an open hand. "Don't say it like that."

"Okay," I said. "Screwing?"

She slapped me again, harder this time. "I'm leaving. If you're going to make it sound like that, then I'm leaving."

She started to get out of bed, but I pulled her back down by her hips. "I'm sorry," I said. "I was fooling. I'm delirious from lack of sleep. I don't think we'd . . . uh . . . do what we're doing, whatever it is, if it's not fucking or screwing, any less. No. Probably more. We'd have to go on a diet, though."

"You're impossible," Marlyn said, before collapsing on top of me.

Impossible. Where had I heard that before? What if there were only so many gestures a man and a woman could make together, only so many phrases they could repeat? There were times with Marlyn that I wished wouldn't sound so much like a replay from my days with Shelly. It made me feel strange. It made me feel like I was doomed to be cast in the same play for the rest of my life with different leading ladies.

That was a depressing thought. I shook it out of my head at once. That kind of thinking wouldn't get me anywhere.

I watched Marlyn lie next to me with her eyes closed. Her chest lifted the sheet when she breathed. Reddish-brown long hair. Creamy shoulders. She was truly beautiful. I tried to envision the future. Maybe someday she'd marry an equally beautiful young man and have beautiful kids, and on late summer evenings, under a full moon in her backyard, maybe she'd think of the teacher she'd had an affair with and wonder what had become of him.

This is what's commonly known as living outside of the situation. It is not recommended.

A while later, when I was nearly asleep in her arms, I heard her whispering to me. Her whisper was full of inflections and I glided up and down with every one. Sea whispers. She was saying, "I don't think I can live in Puerto Rico. I can't even imagine going there. To stay, I mean."

"Honey, we've got applications in to schools here. Let's not watch the kettle while it's trying to boil."

"My father will never agree to it, Johnny."

I found myself dozing for a second and snapped back. It was a lost battle. "He'll have to be told."

Marlyn said, "You don't understand. Latin people have their own ways of doing things."

I had the unnerving suspicion that I hadn't been told the whole story. I watched her some more while she stared out beyond the bedroom door at something I could not see.

Then the phone rang. We looked at each other.

"Odds are, it's not for me," Marlyn said, rising up and leaning on her elbow. "Aren't you going to answer it?"

"Every time I do, it's somebody else I'd rather not hear from."

I relented and answered it. I should have had the answering machine hooked up. I'd forgotten about it.

It was Elsie. Nine at night and she sounded scared to death. "There's gonna be a big fight tonight, Johnny. A big one. People have been in the neighborhood all day and Tony and Alfonzo say they're gonna kick ass. You gotta stop them. Hello?"

"I'm here," I said. Marlyn watched me; she was trying to read the story in my eyes. I broadcast as little information as possible. "Look, Elsie. This thing is kind of out of my hands. I bailed out Tony last night, and today I almost lost my job because Alfonzo tried to turn my lit class into a cocktail party."

She was talking a mile a second. "I know, I know, but they got guns and they got the boys organized and they're gonna get killed."

"Want me to call the cops?"

"No!" Elsie insisted. "Not the fuckin' cops, man!"

I switched the receiver to my other ear. Now just what was I supposed to do—drive over there and tell everybody to kiss and make up?

"Come to Tony's crib, Johnny. Talk to 'em. Make 'em stay inside." Some woman was screaming loudly in Spanish on Elsie's end. Elsie cupped her hand over the phone and for a few moments I only heard muffled noises. "I gotta go, Johnny."

I hung up and said, "We've got to get dressed, sweetheart. I think it's an emergency."

Marlyn said, "The Family again?" Then she made a little face and slowly got out of bed. Her skirt was folded over a chair by the dresser. Once again a flash of déjà vu took hold of me, making me think of Shelly.

I suddenly saw my life as a merry-go-round with little gangsters on it instead of horses. After tonight, I thought, the kids were on their own. Just this one last time.

Traffic was light and I was able to sail down Fullerton. Marlyn was keeping to herself. She sat unusually near the passenger window.

"Honey, I'm going to make you a promise," I said.

"Oh?"

"Um-hmm. I'll never do this again."

She looked at me the way teachers sometimes look at stupid children. "No, you probably won't. You may know how to teach English, but I don't think anybody knows too well how to keep gang kids from killing each other. If anybody knew, they would've done it by now."

I kept an eye on the speedometer and then remembered it had

broken a week earlier. I was going zero kind of quickly. "I know. You're right. I could get hurt," I said.

"You're so stupid sometimes."

I said, "What do you mean, stupid?"

"You could get *killed*."

"Say you love me."

Marlyn harrumphed at me and looked out her window.

"Don't you love me?"

"I'm not talking to you."

"If you were talking to me, would you say you loved me?"

She nodded. But she wasn't kidding. She really wasn't talking to me. She was the best not-talker I'd ever encountered.

Chicago, near where Fullerton meets the Kennedy Expressway, is a series of ugly viaducts and factories. I sped across Western Avenue. I was looking for cops. There were none. I wondered if cops were scared to drive around the Latin ghetto at night. I saw a girl in jeans walking down the sidewalk as though it were noon. Death wish. It dawned on me that if I were to open a rice and beans wholesale outlet around there, I'd be a millionaire in no time. Either a rice and beans outlet or an ammunition shop. Johnny's Rice and Beans and Ammo.

When I pulled up to Marlyn's house she already had her hand on the door handle.

"Wait," I said. "I'm going with you."

"My *father* will see you."

"It's better that your father sees me than you get attacked."

"You obviously don't know my father."

I walked her to her front steps, but before she could climb them, I held on to her arm a second. Beige jacket. Long legs. The prettiest face since—there was no one to compare her to. I said, "Maybe we could—" and then my voice fell. It was a beautiful night and I was with a beautiful girl eleven years younger than I and I was late to a gang fight.

"Maybe we could what?"

"Nothing. I've got to go." I kissed her cheek and ran back to the car. She looked at me from the porch and then went in the door.

I think I'd been about to ask her to live with me. I'd known her all of one week. Rebound. I wasn't sure you could legitimately call it a rebound if the first shot didn't even hit the backboard.

Insanity. That's what you could call it.

The corner of Rockwell and Potomac was dark. The kind of dark where you can't even measure the distance to the sidewalk. I asked myself why I wasn't home in bed. There was a girl running down the block who disappeared near some cars at the next intersection. I did not think she was jogging. What people did in *this* neighborhood to stay healthy was stay inside.

I had to knock loud and hard on Tony's front door before anyone let me in. When the door opened, it opened just wide enough for me to slip through. Inside I was faced by two kids I'd never seen before. Both were in janitor's baggies; one had an earring and a corny hat straight out of the forties, and the other had a bad case of acne topped by a new-wave haircut. Sidewalls above the ears. Tony popped out from behind the door and locked it. There was heavy cooking grease in the air, as though someone had French-fried a buffalo.

Tony said, "I want you to meet my mother."

It seemed to me that I had a few unpleasant words for a woman who would let her son paint trains at midnight, and who permitted her home to be turned into an armed camp. I followed Tony around plastic-covered living room furniture to the kitchen. If possible, the smell of grease became heavier.

There at the sink, her hair tied into a neat little bun, was a short fat lady with a tired smile and almost no teeth. She was washing a pan. When she saw me, she fluttered her hands over the sink, sending little water droplets in the air, and immediately dried them on her apron.

"Hel-lo," she said, in broken English.

Tony said something to her very rapidly in Spanish, and she nodded and smiled and she had even fewer teeth than I had first imagined.

"*Gracias, gracias,*" she said to me, along with some other stuff that I didn't understand. She was nearly bowing each time she said *gracias*.

"She says thanks for gettin' me outa the slammer," Tony explained.

She patted her son's back and said, "Goood boy. Goood boy."

I tilted my head and shook her hand. When she had my hand in

157

hers, she kissed it. She actually held it up to her mouth and kissed it. Not just once, either. I don't know how the pope puts up with that routine. You'd think he'd be downright embarrassed. I had the sudden impulse to spring for a pair of dentures for Mrs. Alvarez, or to buy her some flowers or something nice. These poor goddamn people, I thought.

Things got a lot less maudlin a few minutes later when Tony took me to his bedroom. The two punks who'd greeted me at the door were now sprawled across Tony's bed, and in the corner Alfonzo was sitting on the floor. Each one of the little bastards was loading a gun, or making sure that his gun was loaded by spinning the chamber.

"Somehow I get the feeling you guys aren't just collectors," I said.

Tony tucked his gun in the waist of his pants and said, "Elsie told me you were comin'. It's too late, man. It's gonna happen to-night."

"Wanna hold my gun?" Alfonzo said, from his position on the floor.

"I want to crack your head open. Why the hell did you bring a beer to class?"

"I was thirsty," he said. "That sonofabitch McCaskey suspended me."

"Yeah, well. That sonofabitch McCaskey is trying to fire me. What am I supposed to do, get a job in a bartending school?"

"He won't fire you, man." Alfonzo was spinning the chamber of one of the biggest handguns I'd ever seen. "You're too popular."

Whatever Alfonzo had a firm grasp on, it wasn't reality.

I said, "I guess I'll just notify my fan club and have them explain that to him."

One of the kids, the one with the weird haircut, was chewing bubble gum. He blew a bubble. It popped and stuck to his upper lip. "We gon' kill us some Kings, brother."

I took the only available corner on Tony's bed and sat down on it. So far, I was just listening.

Tony said, "We ain't gonna do nothin' till Elsie gets back with the word."

"Will somebody please tell me what's going on?" I said.

Tony paced his ratty, untacked carpet in front of me. "Elsie's out there talkin' to the People right now. She's friends with one of their chicks. Now, we're tryin' to make a deal for peace. Last I heard, they wanted the Cobras to leave the Folks or give up the block."

"Joinin' the People and givin' up is the same thing. They want us to surrender." This from Alfonzo. He was now rolling a joint on a Prince album cover. Prince's face was covered with little green flakes and seeds.

The bubble gum kid said, "Shit. I say we kill us some Kings."

I looked at him. I'd never seen such a dumb kid before. All he could do was chew gum and talk about killing people.

"Wait for Elsie," Tony said.

I stood up and walked across the room. I hadn't slept for so long that I couldn't remember when I *had* slept. I felt fifty years old. I slapped Tony on the back. "This the whole gang?" I said.

"Naw." He patted his gun nervously. "We got six more guys in a house on the other end of the block. We got the front and the back covered."

"I don't suppose it ever occurred to anybody that maybe this is unnecessary."

"Don't start with that stuff, Johnny." Tony was still pacing.

The bubble gum kid clicked and unclicked the hammer of his gun. "They be doin' this on all the blocks, man. One night here, the next night there. They tryin' to take over from the Folks. Only thing they understand is a bullet."

"Tell him to shut up," I said.

The kid had been about to blow a bubble, but looked at me funny instead.

"Shut up," Tony said.

The kid sulked and quit chewing.

If the school board needed any proof that I was a failure as a teacher, they needn't look for an E-1 rating, I thought. All they'd have to do is walk in that room and listen to that conversation and look at the punks and their guns. Unsolicited testimonials. I had no idea what to do next.

There was a knock at the front door. The kids dropped to the floor. They individually covered the bedroom and living room windows, while Tony peeked through the peephole in the door. A moment later the door was opened and in came Elsie, out of breath.

"What'd they say?" Tony asked.

She looked at me and came over and grabbed one of my arms. "Am I ever glad to see you," she said. She breathed hard a few times. "They want to talk peace. No guns. Three of them, three of you."

Alfonzo lurched into the hallway. He reminded me of a giraffe with an afro. And a joint. And a gun. He shook his head at Tony.

"How do we know *they* won't carry guns?" Tony asked Elsie, who—in turn—shrugged.

Elsie said, "You got some backup in that house. Call 'em and tell 'em to keep you covered. They want to meet on that corner, anyway."

Women, I thought. Blessed are the shrewd. Sixteen years old and she was their mother, strategist, and God knew what else.

We all sat down in the living room and looked at each other. Elsie sat next to me on the couch and Tony and Alfonzo both took chipped dark-wood dining chairs from a table and straddled them backward. The kid with the earring and the kid with the haircut both found places on the floor. Caste system.

"It's a trick," the haircut said. "I know it's a fuckin' trick."

"It might not be," Elsie said.

It went on like that for some time. Trick, no trick. Tony finally went to get the phone from an end table and called his boys down the block and talked things over with them. Then Mrs. Alvarez came in from the kitchen with a bowl of potato chips. She said something to me in Spanish.

Alfonzo said, "She wants to know what you'd like to drink, Johnny."

I wondered if it would be rude to ask a Puerto Rican lady for a beer.

"You didn't by any chance happen to save the rest of that six-pack?"

"*Una cerveza, por favor,*" Alfonzo relayed, and Mrs. Alvarez nodded and smiled and in a few seconds I had a beer. Blatz. I amused myself with the name and turned the can around in my hands. Elsie had started to rub the back of my neck with her hand.

"What do you say you don't do that, huh?" I asked, politely.

"White blood," Alfonzo said. "Boils easy."

It seemed to me that if you were in a gang you were always high or horny or angry. Or scared.

Tony came back from the phone and told Alfonzo to take it. Someone named Chilo wanted to talk to him. "We're gonna do it. Chilo says they'll keep us covered. I'll leave one of the boys here to cover our asses. Johnny and Elsie, you guys stay here till it's over."

Elsie said, "No guns. That's what they said—no guns."

"No guns?" Tony slapped his forehead. "Fuck *you,* no guns. One of us will take the little one and keep it hid. We ain't gonna shoot first, but I don't wanna be out there like a sittin' chicken."

"Duck," I said.

Tony said, "You can't duck bullets, man."

"I was talking about the expression. It's sitting *duck,* not sitting *chicken.*"

"Just what I need. An English teacher."

While the summit meeting progressed the TV was on and I found myself just exhausted enough to become engrossed in a Tom and Jerry cartoon. Jerry shoved a stick of dynamite into Tom's mouth as he came racing around a corner. There were very predictable results. Tom blew up, but he wasn't dead. It made me think that these kids' views of life and death could very well be rooted in cartoonland.

I sipped my beer and lighted a cigarette and noticed that there was no *Mr.* Alvarez. "Where's your father, Tony?"

Tony turned to me from his leaning position on the back of the dining chair. "I give up," he said. "Where is he?"

Alfonzo returned from the phone. He stared at all of us, took in the cartoon for a moment, and then said, "It's all set. We're gonna ask for a truce for the block. But we don't give it up. They don't accept it, boom. That's it."

In the little alcove between the kitchen and the living room I saw a shadow of someone standing in the doorway. Tony's mother. She was listening in. When nothing else was said, she came into the room, timorously. She looked as though she were about to apologize for being in her own house. Tony and Alfonzo and both of their junior partners stood up. They made a quick trip to the bedroom, ostensibly to drop off their guns. I was sipping my beer on the couch next to Elsie and I felt stupid. Elsie stood up, went over to Mrs. Alvarez, and put an arm around her and said something quietly in Spanish, but Mrs. Alvarez just shook her head and looked at me, pleadingly.

"You go weeth my boy," she managed, with her little distorted mouth.

There was a crescendo of music from the TV as Jerry whacked

Tom in the ass with a board that had a nail in it. Maybe selling real estate wasn't such a dumb idea after all.

The troops were gathered at the front door by then, and I stood up and walked over to them. Elsie and Mrs. Alvarez were huddled together, speaking quietly, when suddenly Mrs. Alvarez shouted, "No!"

Alfonzo said to Tony, "What's buggin' your OG?"

OG. I didn't know what OG stood for.

I said, "She wants me to go with you. I take it she's been listening in to all the fun and games tonight."

"Him?" the kid with the pimples and the stupid haircut said. "He's *white.*"

I looked at Tony. "You're going to have to screen your applicants more carefully in the future."

"Why does she want you to go?" Tony asked me.

"I don't know. She could be worried about her son, did you ever think of that? If I was worried about my son and I had to ask someone to go with him, and all I had to choose from was this group, I'd probably ask me, too."

Tony and Alfonzo exchanged blank looks and then stared at their trigger-happy assistants as though they were evaluating them silently. Mrs. Alvarez broke away from Elsie and walked over to me. It was more than I could do to look directly at her.

"Por favor, vaya con él."

Tony sighed. "You want to go, Johnny?"

"Kind of hard to say no, under the circumstances."

He nodded. He lowered his head and waved me along with him and Alfonzo. This sent the pimple-faced kid into hysterics.

"You got to be kiddin', man! What's he gonna do if they start cappin' at you? What's he gonna do—*talk* 'em to death?"

Mrs. Alvarez abruptly ran to the kitchen. When she came back she had an *alcapurria* wrapped in a little white-and-blue napkin. *Alcapurrias* are deep-fried, batter-encased ground beef. She handed it to me.

Tony said, "Oh, Jesus."

"Gracias, señora," I said, and she beamed back at me with wet sparkly eyes and those toothless gums of hers.

Outside, we walked calmly down the steps. Self-assured negotiators with a mission. And an *alcapurria.* I didn't particularly want it, but I couldn't just throw it away, either. I began to nibble on it as we walked like a three-man wall down the center of the street.

"What does OG mean?" I asked, with my mouth full.

Alfonzo said, "Old girl."

"Old goat," Tony corrected him.

I told him to be nice. He slapped me on the back and said if there was any trouble I should try to beat the People senseless with the *alcapurria*.

I stopped unexpectedly and pulled them both by the arms. "I want you guys to know something," I said. I felt like I was in the part of the war movie where the troops say it was nice knowing each other, before they get blown away by foreign machine-gun fire. "For two years I've been teaching you."

Tony said, "This ain't exactly the time for this."

"Yes, it is. And in those two years I've gotten you out of more jams than I can count. I don't seem to be getting any payback, you know? So I'm giving you my notice. I quit. This is the last time."

Alfonzo scratched his head. "This could be *all* our last times, Johnny. You sure pick funny times to quit, man."

"Hey—Johnny," Tony said. "This wouldn't happen to have nothin' to do with your new friend, would it?"

The street was quiet except for some occasional TV sounds floating through open windows. On either side of the street you could see little reflections from broken beer bottles on the concrete between parked and battered cars.

"Who? You mean Carlos?"

"No. I don't mean Carlos. The babe. One that looks like a model or some goddamn thing. *That* new friend."

It appeared that Marlyn and I hadn't been so discreet as we thought we'd been.

"I don't know what you're talking about."

"Oh, okay," Tony said. "I guess I'm wrong. I guess you guys are never together near North and Francisco. I musta seen two people who just *looked* like you."

"It's a big world," I said.

"Not as big as you think it is."

Well now. How about that, I thought.

As we got closer to the end of the block we slowed our pace. A streetlamp lighted up the intersection; I saw why the place had been chosen. In the distance you could hear a motorcycle cruising down

Western Avenue, changing gears and finally whirring out of range. Alfonzo indicated the house that supplied our cover with his thumb.

"When they show up, keep their backs to that crib," he ordered.

We stood under the lamp, casting long shadows behind us toward Tony's house. There was nothing to do but stand there. The street was empty. A German shepherd with an emaciated body and a hungry look sauntered past on the sidewalk and crossed the intersection diagonally. I chewed some of the *alcapurria* halfheartedly. My stomach began to growl.

Tony slapped my middle and said, "What'cha got in there, a squirrel?"

"I think this *alcapurria* is alive."

We stood there some longer and it crossed my mind what great targets we were if this was really a setup.

Bang, bang, bang.

Oops—a white boy. How'd he get in there?

I saw the door of a car open up ahead on the next block. Three big indistinct forms crawled out. I slapped Alfonzo's arm with the back of my hand, gulped down the rest of the *alcapurria,* and was about to throw away the napkin when I changed my mind. I couldn't seem to part with anything Mrs. Alvarez had given me. I stuck the napkin in my pocket and stood between the guys.

In the center of the intersection we came up against three rugged-looking apes—each of them older than Tony and his boys. They needed shaves. I got a sick feeling all through me when I recognized the one in the middle facing me. It was Bug, my friend from the Jack In The Box. He opened the proceedings.

"Well. White man. You got any idea how expensive tires be these days?"

I said, "Don't tell me you guys *buy* tires."

"You a funny man. Real funny."

Nobody said anything.

Bug lifted his arms. "We clean."

He was speaking figuratively. It was the only possible way he could have been clean.

Tony nodded. "We believe you. We're just here to listen."

A car drove down a side street near us. Two floating headlights and a bad muffler. Everybody watched it. The general suspicion, as far as I could read it, was that the Kings had their *own* cover. The car began to circle the block.

Bug said, "Since when do you guys let white men in the Cobras?"

"I'm not a Cobra."

"No? Then what you doin' here? Suburbs all full or somethin'?"

"I'm their teacher."

Tony held his hand to his head when I said that. I suppose I've said brighter things. Bringing your teacher to a gang confrontation was a little like taking your mother on your honeymoon.

"You *what*? Pablo—you hear that? This guy's their *teacher*."

Alfonzo put his hand up to cut the talk. "We're still listenin', only we ain't hearin' nothin'. Someone said somethin' about peace, so we're here for peace. You here for peace, or you just wanna bullshit all night?"

Bug made a move with his hand toward his pocket, but stopped short. "Watch yo' mouth," he said. He paced, staring at the pavement as though it had just kicked him. "Yeah. We wanna talk peace. We got a offer."

Bug's friends were sneering into the night.

Bug. It was pretty obvious where he'd picked up that name. His IQ was on an exact par with an ant's.

"People is People and Folks is Folks. This here line," he indicated with the toe of one of his sneakers, "is where the difference be. We been seein' a lot of Folks cross that line. You got snakes on this next block—Cobras. They get off the block or out of the Folks. Simple as that. We talkin' Turtle. You got a guy name o' Turtle. Big dude—"

Bug lifted his hand over his head to illustrate who he was talking about. Then from behind us there was the sharp crack of gunfire. One shot. Two. Another. Each one rang out as though whoever was pulling the trigger was counting the half seconds that punctuated the blasts. Tony and Alfonzo collapsed on either side of me. I was certain they'd been hit.

Bug lurched toward me, connecting with my shoulder. I thought he was just pushing me, at first. I caught him on the mouth with my right and knocked him over. He rolled backward, shot up, and ran into the night.

Tony grabbed me by my sweatshirt and pulled me low to the ground, where we crouched behind an old station wagon. From the house next to us, a fusillade rang out into the air. I saw a car drive away down the street. It had no lights and the tires screeched, burning rubber on the concrete.

I slowly became conscious of a wet burning sensation in my left shoulder. I touched it with an open palm and held my hand in front of me. It was covered with blood. Funny. I'd always thought that if you had been shot, you'd be in agony.

"He hit?" Alfonzo said, in a near whisper. "You hit, Johnny?"

I held my hand to my shoulder again. "I think I am."

Tony ripped my sweatshirt, beginning at the collar, and leaned me against the station wagon. A piece of door molding was right behind my head and it hurt to lay my weight against it. He touched the sore spot on my shoulder and I screamed.

"This is a slice. You been knifed, Johnny."

"Yeah?" I said.

"Can you walk?"

I did not know if I could walk. All at once I wanted to throw up. "I think so."

Tony took off his fatigue jacket. Then, ripping the rest of my sweatshirt into strips, he pressed them against the wound in my shoulder. I did the only sensible thing I could. I screamed again.

"Hold that here with your good hand," Tony told me. I did as he said. My arm was throbbing. He draped the fatigue jacket over my shoulders. I could smell the greasy smell that I'd first noticed in his house.

"You know who fired those shots, don't you?" Alfonzo said.

Tony blew some air between his teeth. "I know. I'm gonna tear him apart when I get back home."

I was piecing together what had happened. It must have been that idiot with the bubble gum. First Bug's hand had gone up in the air, then the shots had been fired.

Tony and Alfonzo lifted me to my feet and sort of half-ran and half-walked me to my car. Alfonzo put me in the backseat. Tony asked for the keys.

"Left pocket," I said. I wondered if I was dying. I didn't think so. But, I thought, if I died, I wouldn't have to pay my lawyer for the divorce. Always looking for the silver lining.

Alfonzo stayed in the backseat with me. He covered me with his own jacket. He held my hand, for God's sake. I said, "Thanks, but you're not my type."

"You gonna be okay, Johnny," he said.

"I know."

"I'm sorry about that beer today. You know? I don't want you to get fired or nothin'."

The little bastard. There was a heart there after all.

"Where are you taking me?"

Tony said, "St. Mary's. It's the closest."

"You can't take me to St. Mary's."

"Why not?"

"They'll know it was a gang fight. Your neighborhood is going to be covered with cops as soon as someone reports those shots. I'm a teacher. What am I going to tell them? That I'm a brand-new Cobra who passed the initiation?"

The plan went like this. We'd go to Columbus Hospital in my neighborhood. I'd tell whoever asked that I'd been mugged in Lincoln Park. Tony and Alfonzo had been with me because I tutored them in English. I was apparently stabbed for my money. We didn't get a good look at the mugger; it was dark.

Well. As far as stories go, it wasn't going to win me a Pulitzer.

At Columbus Hospital I was rushed in front of three or four people who sullenly watched the TV monitor. *Remington Steele.* Stephanie Zimbalist was driving a white Volkswagen convertible down a dirt road. That's as much of the program as I caught.

An intern and a nurse put something on my shoulder that made me scream once again.

The doctor said, "Does it hurt?"

"Does it hurt," I repeated. "Is it bleeding?"

"Yes."

"Then I suppose it hurts, right?"

He wasn't amused. He went about patting the wound with some gauze, and at one point I think he pulled it open so he could see how deep it was. I bit my tongue that time.

"How did this happen to you?"

"I was attacked."

The doctor looked at the nurse. The nurse was removing bloody gauze from the little stand near the bed I was on. I looked away at the first sign of red.

"This isn't as bad as it looks," the doctor said. He was a balding guy who was probably still in his twenties. He patched me up with much the same attitude a shoe salesman might display while measuring your foot. He was bored.

"Deep?" I asked.

"Naw. Just superficial. Well—maybe a little deeper than superficial, but I don't think you're gonna have to stay here."

Gonna. Who teaches English to doctors these days?

Before they let me go, I had to fill out some insurance papers. I was at a desk near the entrance trying to find my Blue Cross card in my wallet. Tony and Alfonzo were watching the conclusion of *Remington Steele* out in the lobby.

"I *told* you it was the guy who owned the goddamn wine place. I *told* you it was him," Tony was saying. They were unimpressed with my wound when they found out it wouldn't require stitches.

Two of Chicago's finest met me at the reception desk while I copied down my Social Security number on the hospital form.

"This the guy that was stabbed?" the older cop asked the receptionist. Alfonzo turned his head when he heard the cop. His instinctive paranoia of police clicked on; I could see it in his eyes.

I said, "How're you guys doing?"

"How're *you* doin'?" the older cop asked me.

"I've had better nights."

"I can see that. Did you get a look at who did this?"

"Uh . . . just a quick one."

"Any other witnesses?"

"Uh-huh. They're in the lobby solving a TV crime."

The police report took half an hour. We were asked for a description. Tony, in an attempt to sound legitimate, was contradicting me. When the cop wanted to know if the assailant had been white or black, I said, "White," and Tony said, "Black."

The cop put his clipboard on his lap and looked at us.

"Which is it?"

I said, "I guess he was kind of a light black guy."

The cop said, "Or a dark white guy, right?"

"It happened kind of fast, you know?"

"And the park was dark," Tony chimed in. Shut up, I thought.

The younger cop was talking to a nurse and leaning against a vending machine that would give you bad black coffee, bad coffee with just cream or just sugar, or both, or chicken soup.

"Height?" we were asked next.

I pretended to think this over. "He was, oh—close to six feet tall."

Tony said, "He looked bigger than that to me."

"I thought you didn't see him so good," the cop said. He was clicking his pen open and shut and staring at Tony.

"I didn't. But he was big, man."

"Heavy or thin?"

I said, "He was pretty heavy."

"But thin enough to run fast," Tony added. "It's a good thing for him, too, or we woulda been all over him."

The cop read the report back to us. "A light black guy or a dark white guy who was somewhere between six or seven feet tall, kind of on the thin-heavy side."

"Well," I said, adjusting the sling the doctor had given me, "a guy like that ought to stand out in a crowd."

I was released with the instructions to leave the bandage alone and not to get it wet. It would disintegrate by itself. I did not know how I was supposed to shower under those conditions. I drove Tony and Alfonzo back to my apartment building and parked the car in the garage.

Alfonzo said, "We can catch the Diversey bus home."

"Sorry for the way things turned out, Johnny," Tony said.

I didn't let them take a bus home. They would have had to walk through their own neighborhood past midnight. I walked with them up to Clark Street where I hailed a taxi and handed the driver a twenty-dollar bill in advance, in case they had any ideas about taking the bus and pocketing the cash.

I walked back to my building and was about to walk in the lobby door when I saw a teen-age boy sitting on the couch by the elevators. I did an about-face and headed for the garage entrance instead. I was starting to wish my publishing company had put a picture of Dave Volmer on the jacket of the book rather than one of myself.

"Mr. Spector?" the kid said, from behind me.

Well, what the hell, I thought. I turned around and faced him. He produced a copy of the book and a pen, and with my good hand

I scrawled my name across the front page. While I was writing, the kid told me about his dreams.

"I write for my school paper. I'm thinking of going into journalism."

"That's terrific," I said, trying to sound boosting. "Why don't you go home and get some sleep?"

"I will. I was wondering if you could give me some advice about getting published."

Now, this was a nice kid. He had bright blue eyes, short dark hair, and all the naïveté you could fit inside a five-foot seven-inch frame.

"Sure. What do you want to know?"

"How do you do it?"

How do you do it. In one easy lesson. Well, kid. Write until your heart falls out. Keep writing after it has fallen out. Throw away your rejection forms; don't save them. Keep writing after your ulcer exceeds the size of your head. Invest a small fortune in stamps and postage, and if you're lucky, someday someone will walk up to you when your arm is in a sling and—

I said, "Tell you what. Be determined. Read everything you can get your hands on. Then, gradually narrow down your reading taste. Don't ever let anyone make you doubt your own talent. It's all inspiration and discipline, you know? Write only what you believe in, and then rewrite it. And then rewrite that."

He said, "I don't like to rewrite."

"No one does, but it's the name of the game."

He looked disappointed. "Aren't there any short cuts?"

Kids.

"Short cuts? Oh, hell, yes. Find a small editor you can beat up."

I said good night and walked in the building lobby. He watched me until I got on the elevator. I waved and he waved back. The door closed and I suddenly realized I'd forgotten to tell him about booze. I supposed he'd find out soon enough, though.

The next day I arrived late to school and parked my car in the faculty lot. The auto shop was filled up. I was somewhere in the middle of teaching the difference between commas and semicolons when Mike Bane, walkie-talkie in hand, appeared at my classroom door.

"Johnny, you'd better come with me right now."

I said, "Wait a minute. I got reamed yesterday for leaving a class alone."

"Leave 'em. I've got something you ought to see."

The class was reading a sample paragraph on the overhead projector. I left them and walked with Bane to the windows of the cafeteria. Down below, in the faculty parking lot, a car was engulfed in flames. I watched as the fire burned its way to the gas tank and the trunk blew off.

"That yours, Johnny?"

A small group of onlookers had gathered at a relatively safe distance. It reminded me of the Fourth of July. When the fire fighters showed up, they were roundly booed by the crowd of kids.

I said, "Well, Mike. It was."

Twelve

I found a used Jeep at a dealership on Ashland Avenue. It met all of my requirements. It ran. I'd always wanted a Jeep. Maybe because of the army movies that had been popular when I was a kid. This one was two-toned—white with rust. It sort of made me look forward to winter. It was still only May.

I had that unsettled business of Wanda's wedding to attend to. I picked her up Friday morning at five, just as Father Perry had asked me to. I was a little surprised to hear birds chirping in the ghetto. If there was anything to *quality of life* in relation to choice real estate, the birds weren't in on it. They sounded just as happy on Augusta Avenue as they did on Dearborn.

I waited and had a cigarette. I was discreetly parked four doors down from Wanda's apartment building. My shoulder was sore from driving, but my arm was beginning to feel at home in the sling. I'd had to learn to do most of the work of shifting and steering with my right hand.

Bug. I wondered how he had managed so neatly to torch my car in broad daylight without being seen. It had to be Bug.

I heard clomping on wood and turned around to see Wanda carefully stepping down gray back-porch steps. She reached the ground level and walked through the alley carrying two pastel-colored suitcases and a dress in a plastic bag. It was a sad little picture. Wanda and everything she owned in the world.

I hopped out of the Jeep and helped her load her luggage and dress, and she said, "I *knew* you'd be here, Johnny."

Good old reliable Johnny.

On the way to the convent Wanda talked about how happy she was and how her fiancé had a good job and a nice apartment. I glanced at her and noticed a heavy layer of makeup intended to hide a fresh new black eye. And she was happy.

She said, "I'm so nervous I think I'm gonna ex*plode.*"

"I just cleaned the interior, sweetheart. If you have to explode, tell me so I can pull over and let you out."

A lady who did not look like a nun was waiting for us in front of the convent. She was tall and thin and had a ghost-white face and a sweet smile. Sister Eloise. Wanda nearly jumped into her arms when we stopped. I got the luggage out of the Jeep and took it to the foyer of the convent. On my way out, Wanda kissed my cheek.

"Don't I get any advice?"

Everybody was always asking me that. It was like answering a phone call for the wrong number.

I said, "Sure. Don't drop the ring."

Outside, Sister Eloise waited near the Jeep. She apparently had stayed there to thank me privately.

"It's a touchy situation," she said. "She's so young."

"They grow up fast around here. She'll be all right." That was more a spoken wish than a certainty on my part.

"Will you stay for coffee?"

I did not think I wanted to stay. The topics or conversation would be mighty limited.

"I'm afraid not. I should get to school. It's little missions like this one that keep me at war with the administration. I make up for it by marching a straight line."

I wasn't sure what I meant by that.

"Well, in this community straight lines don't make too much sense."

I said, "You know, sister, you're my kind of lady."

I hoped the flowers I'd ordered for Wanda's ceremony would arrive on time. The kid should at least have some nice flowers, I thought.

I did, in fact, march an exceptionally straight line for the next week. I turned in lesson plans—typed. I wrote absence reports so complete and neat they could have been sent to my publisher. When the false fire alarms continued, my class was out of the building in seconds. I explained away my sling as the result of a torn ligament. Only Marlyn didn't buy it, so I had to tell her the truth. The truth upset her, which is why I lied about it in the first place.

What unfolded between Marlyn and me was a three-part ongoing dialogue that started one evening when I took her to hear the Chicago

Symphony perform Rimsky-Korsakov's *Scheherazade.* She fell in love with it. Afterward we had dinner at Salvatore's, on Arlington Place. Old marble entranceway. Mahogany dinner tables and wall paneling. Expensive wine list. Waiters that appeared to have been cloned. Marlyn took my hand as we climbed the steps to the formal dining room.

"I'm used to eating in bed," she said, as two or three male patrons stared at her uninhibitedly.

"This will kind of be the same thing, only dessert will be a lot duller."

We took a walk later that evening, down Arlington, and she marveled at the manicured lawns and town houses and two-flats along the winding side street. She said, "Imagine living in one of these."

"Imagine it now, or in the future?"

"In the future, I guess. Not-too-distant future."

We picked a likely candidate for our fantasy. It was a black, two-story stone building with white shutters and trellises.

"What's it like?" I asked.

"Well, we're inside. I'm upstairs studying for my finals in nursing school. I'm going to pass with straight A's. I'm going to get a job at Children's Memorial. I want to be with kids."

"And young interns."

"Just kids."

"Where do I fit in?"

She pointed to the ground-floor window. It had a yellow light shining out of a gauzy curtained window. It made me think of hepatitis. Our house had a bad liver. "You're in there, working on a new book. Your phone number is unlisted."

"I always have an unlisted number."

"*This* one isn't even given to students. It never rings unless it's someone with good news."

"Are you sure it's *my* phone?"

She ignored me as one would a wise-assed kid. "And after you get off a bunch of good pages, you get tired and go to the kitchen and make us raspberry sherbet and wine. We eat in the dining room. Candles. If there's a leaky faucet, you fix it."

I said, "You just spoiled a hell of a nice little dream with your leaky faucet."

"Oh—that's part of the dream. What kind of husband can't fix a leaky faucet?"

Husband. I must have missed that part of the dream. We stared at the house and didn't say anything. She held my only available hand (I still had the damned sling) and we walked back to the Jeep while I watched her face in the night. There was something nice about being with someone who saw no difficulty in translating the dream into reality. There was also something scary about it.

That Sunday I took Marlyn to see the Stray Cats at the Rosemont Horizon. She had never been to a rock concert. It was a far cry from the Chicago Symphony. It had been years since I'd seen a live rock show. The music was nice, but the look of the audience made me feel as though I'd just crashed a grammar school birthday bash. They all seemed determined to shake their asses until they fell off.

Between numbers Marlyn cupped her hands around my ear and yelled, "I think I'll stick to the symphony."

I said, "You're an unusual kid."

"What?"

"I said, 'You're an unusual kid.'" I had to shout above the noise of the audience. A girl next to Marlyn passed her a joint and she politely refused it. Very unusual kid.

On the way home that night my ears were ringing and the Jeep was breezy and Marlyn kept to herself. She stared out the window at the fields, and then at O'Hare Airport, and then at a big airliner taking off almost directly above us.

"Do you wish I was more like them?" she asked, finally snapping out of wherever she'd been.

"Like whom?"

"Those kids we saw tonight."

I said, "Oh, yeah. Brain damage is a lot of fun."

"No, really."

"Somehow I can't see you bumping and grinding while you suck on a reefer."

I lighted a cigarette. The Jeep had no lighter and I had to fight the wind to do it with a cheap butane lighter that I could never seem to find a pocket for.

"Are we going to always be having an affair?"

"Jesus," I said. "I hope so."

"That's not what I mean. What I mean is, isn't it going to lead to anything? Like that town house we saw the other night?"

"Fix your faucets?"

She smiled. All those teeth. Spanish eyes.

Why were women always equating love with real estate?

I turned off at the next exit, the oasis over Route 90. Now it's a McDonald's, but then it was a Howard Johnson's. It wasn't the place I would have custom-ordered for the occasion. But it was convenient.

We took a table by the window. You could watch the traffic flow beneath you and actually see the people in their cars. We ordered sandwiches. I kept finding something to do with the saltshaker and my napkin.

"I've never known anyone who could make a marriage proposal sound like a plumbing contract," I told her.

"Well, at least we're talking about it, now."

"I kind of feel like a poor first to San Juan's second."

"That's got nothing to do with it," she said, a bit put out by the suggestion. I often felt like we were playing chess when we talked, and that she was two moves ahead of me.

"I'm eleven years older than you. I don't know if you're aware of this or not, but people get—they get *crummy*. When they get older they get crummier."

Marlyn nodded. "Uh-huh. They get lines in their faces and lose their hair. I promise I won't tease you about it."

"I'm not talking about physical stuff. Look—did you ever read *The Picture of Dorian Gray*?"

"You mean the guy with the portrait in his attic?"

"Yeah. You're really quite well read, you know that?"

"I saw the movie."

I said, "Well, it's the same, right? I feel like I've got this picture in my attic."

Marlyn laughed and grabbed my hand. "Johnny, you don't even have an attic."

"Yeah, but if I did, I'd have this goddamn picture in it. And it would look *awful*. You know?" For a teacher I sure had a hell of a time communicating, sometimes. "Honey, people's souls get lines in them, not just their faces. Jesus Christ. You're young and pretty and fresh, and I feel like I'm working on my third lifetime with all the crap from the first two stuffed in the closets."

Marlyn drank some of her water. The place had a great view, but I've had better service. I'd ordered the sandwiches twenty minutes earlier and they still hadn't arrived. It occurred to me that I was the only person in the world who could get stranded at an oasis.

"You make it sound like you're guilty for having lived longer than me."

"Longer than *I*," I corrected her. Automatic reflex.

"Longer than *I*, fine. That's crazy."

I said, "No, it's not. That's grammar."

"I meant that you feel guilty. I know what I'm doing. I'm not a kid, Johnny. Don't you want to marry me?"

A couple at the next table was listening interestedly to us. They wanted to see if I was truly the heel I appeared to be.

"How about we talk a little more quietly?"

Our waitress, a weathered girl who looked as alert as a junkie on a bad night, deposited two plates in front of us. The sandwiches were okay, but the pickles on the side looked as though they were plastic.

"Look," I said, "I think what we have here is a culture gap. Euro-Rican."

"I don't believe in culture gaps."

"Neither do I. That's what pisses me off so much when they pop up. Know me a year before you jump into marriage. If you can still stand me by then, and once you have a year of college under your belt, then I'll feel better about this. You've only known me a few weeks."

Marlyn unfolded her napkin and placed it on her lap. "I know you. I know I love you. I know you're not perfect."

"*Who's* not perfect?"

She told me to shut up and eat my sandwich.

That week at school it came to my attention that it was prom time. I had never paid much attention to prom before. The last time I had dated a high school senior, I *was* a high school senior.

To inner-city kids, prom was rated just under the second coming of Christ. It was an apex in their lives. Not many of those kids were going on to college, and some of the ones who did go on would drop out within two years and take jobs with the military or go on welfare and make babies for a livelihood. Prom was what it was all about. I had seen pictures of past proms and they always made me think of Cinderella. Banquet hall at the Ritz-Carlton. Seventy-five bucks per couple. The guys would usually rent tuxes with tails, or white tuxes with matching white top hats, gloves, and walking sticks. They did not think that this would make them look conspicuous.

Limousines. Anybody who was anybody would rent a limousine. Preferably one with a bar. Thirty-five dollars an hour, if you reserved one in advance.

The crowning glory was a hotel room. In the ghetto, it is assumed from the get-go that the girl will give it up after the dance, since the guy has gone broke for their mutual benefit. With flowers and incidentals, the average Freddie Prinze prom-goer (male) shells out close to four hundred dollars. To pay for it he must work a part-time job and save for nine months. Or he can sell drugs. Or he can borrow it from his parents. Or he can rob a liquor store.

I did not think that Marlyn and I should attend the prom. I asked her instead to have dinner with me at the 95th, in the John Hancock Center. I was surprised to learn that no one had even invited her to the prom. It must have been due to the *unreachable concept.* Guys are afraid to ask beautiful girls out because they assume a beautiful girl will turn them down. Macho guys especially adhere to this rule. A bruised ego to a gangster is the equivalent of an unloaded gun, or a Chevy that won't start.

I took Marlyn shopping for a dress at Saks. We'd had to leave directly after school because she was scheduled to work that night at six. She was wearing a red-and-white-striped button-down blouse with a matching red tie and a light-gray wool skirt. She looked like she had been *born* at Saks. I felt funny alongside her dressed in jeans and sneakers. The saleswoman who helped us tended to regard me as the chauffeur. She should have seen my Jeep.

Marlyn picked a lovely black-and-white dinner dress. Three hundred dollars. We got into a little whispered argument over the price; she wouldn't hear of me paying for it. But I insisted. The saleswoman looked surprised when I produced a charge card. She ran a lengthy security check on the account number. I had a passing desire to bludgeon her with her computer register.

After school on the afternoon of our dinner date, my phone rang constantly. I'd remembered to hook up the message taker and I listened as the calls came in.

Beep. "Johnny, this is Shelly. It's now five o'clock. Please call me at the office up until six." *Click.*

Beep. "Johnny, it's Shelly again. I want to talk to you. It's five-fifteen." *Click.*

I stepped out of the shower in time to hear this one:

Beep. "Goddamn it, Johnny. If you're home and just sitting there listening to these fucking messages, I'm going to wring your lousy neck." *Click.*

She didn't bother to leave the time.

I do not like to wear suits. Ties tend to chafe my neck. It's difficult to swallow when you wear a tie. I took a blue three-piece suit out of my closet. The last time I had worn it was to a preliminary divorce hearing. I should have had it cleaned afterward. It still smelled like lawyers.

At six o'clock the phone rang again. There was a *beep* and the sound of Alfonzo's voice and I picked it up before he finished.

"Hello, Alfonzo."

"Hey, Johnny. Listen, man. Can you spot me a twenty till Monday?"

"No."

He breathed a little fiercely into the receiver. "C'mon, dude. I can't count on nobody else but you."

"What do you need twenty dollars for?"

A snicker. "Oh, man. What is this, twenty questions?"

"No. It's twenty dollars. *My* twenty dollars. What do you want it for?"

"All right. I'm gonna be straight with you."

"That would be nice for a change."

"Some terrific 'Bo just came in and I can give you some if you'll spot me twenty bucks. Deal?"

"Fuck you, Alfonzo."

"Hey, man—"

I hung up.

Johnny Spector. Drug broker to the stars.

Picking up Marlyn for a formal date meant having to go to the door and meeting her father. A breakthrough. I stepped out of my Jeep in front of her house. I wondered if I should have had it washed. What would be the point of that? I thought. Clean rust? A Cadillac limo passed by and stopped in front of another run-down house. A young kid hopped out of the back. He was dressed in a tuxedo and walked nonchalantly to the door, where he was greeted not only by his date, but by her entire family. Three generations. They followed the two down the sidewalk right to the curb. They oohed and ahhed at the Cadillac. An old man reached out and touched a gleaming hubcap and nodded his head. The elegant couple got in and the limo drove away and the contingent remained on the dirt where a lawn should have been. The mother was crying.

Good God.

Marlyn's doorbell did not look as though it worked. I chose instead to knock. This was the first day I had not worn the sling. I used my left hand to knock in order to check the progress of my shoulder. Not much progress there. I felt a sharp twinge as I lifted my arm and then rubbed it with my good hand as the door opened.

Marlyn's father was a stoop-shouldered man with thinning hair and a tiny mustache—the feature I found so striking when I'd first seen him look out the window, a few weeks before. He did not seem to know who I was. Marlyn appeared in the hallway in her dress. She was beautiful.

Her father, who held a folded newspaper under his arm, looked at the two of us. I was introduced only as Johnny Spector. From the way he talked to me—or rather, the way he talked *at* me—I gathered that he thought I was a student.

"My daughter be home by twelve, young man. I no want her to go. She say she go anyway. I not approve." He glared at me with fatherly disapprobation.

I said, "Look, Mr. Valentin—" but was cut off.

He grabbed the newspaper under his arm with his other hand and waved it at us. "Go. Go. Home by twelve."

The door closed behind us.

Marlyn said, "He thinks you're a student."

"I'm beginning to feel like one."

It didn't seem to make much sense, sitting there on top of Chicago, near a floor-to-ceiling window in the 95th. There must have been some kind of weather inversion over the city. The haze was so thick you could have jumped into it and never hit bottom. Marlyn didn't seem to mind. She was developing a kind of ease in new surroundings. She knew when to unfold her napkin. She was less jittery when she reached for her wineglass. If I'd had a quarter for every stare she got that night, it would have paid for the waiter's tip. Almost.

"Do you like it?" I asked. She was trying to see the ground from the window.

"You're never taking me to Burger King again."

"I've never taken you to a Burger King."

"Well," she said, "now you'll never have the chance."

"Wait till you see the bill. After that, Burger King will be out of our league."

Sometime after the main course, someone slapped me on the back. It shot a nifty little pain all along my shoulder and I felt as if I'd been plugged into a wall socket.

"Mr. Johnny Spector, I presume."

I turned around. Randy and Janet Glick. Well, she'd got him out of the office at last.

Randy asked our waiter if he and Janet could use the table next to ours for a drink until their table came available. I ordered martinis and had them put on our bill.

"Randy, Janet, I'd like you to meet Marlyn Valentin," I said. Randy shook her hand. We were being so proper tonight.

"I knew there was a reason I hadn't seen much of Johnny lately," Randy said to Marlyn. "I thought he was working on a new book. Now I know what he's been working on."

I said, "Randy, you're such an animal."

"No, he isn't," Janet said. "I should know."

Randy's and Janet's drinks came and I was a little saddened that our twosome had been interrupted. With the Glicks at the table, some of the niceness had gone. It was like having someone dig up my past and dump the remnants into seats next to us.

"So—*Mar*lyn, is it?" Randy asked.

Marlyn said, "Yes, Randy."

"So what is it you do?"

"I go to school."

Randy took a sip from his martini and nursed the glass in his hands. "That's a good thing to do. What are you majoring in?"

"Lots of things, at the moment."

Randy thought that was an intriguing answer. His eyebrow shot up.

Janet was warming to the conversation. "What school are you going to?"

That's when I went for my drink.

Marlyn said, "Freddie Prinze High."

"Oh, you're a teacher," Randy deduced, incorrectly.

"No. I'm a senior."

Janet coughed on her drink and set the glass down on the table. I couldn't swear to it, but I think she kicked Randy under their table. I felt a breeze go by my sock. Randy smiled idiotically until enough time had elapsed so that they could make a gracious exit.

"Look. You two obviously meant this to be a—a personal dinner. Janet and I are going to see if our table is ready yet," Randy said, standing up and taking his drink with him. "Marlyn, is it *Marlyn*?"

"Yes."

"Marlyn, nice to meet you. Catch you later, Johnny."

No, you won't, I thought.

Marlyn leaned over the table to me and said quietly, "Did I say something wrong?"

"If they left, I think you said something right."

After dinner I felt lighter. It was probably just my wallet. We took a ride on one of those carriages that are forever blocking the flow of traffic down Michigan Avenue. The horse's hooves were clock-ety-clocking on the pavement and the sun was down and cars raced past us in the night. Marlyn had her head on my shoulder. This was part three of our continuing evening topic.

"What if I'm not accepted to Loyola?"

I said, "They'll accept you. Give it time. Your application just went in a few weeks ago. One thing you'll find out about colleges, if there's a slow way to do something, they'll find it."

"If you want to marry me, and if you love me and everything, then how come we can't get married first and *then* I can go to school?"

I remember taking a cigarette from the inside pocket of my suit. It came out crumpled and I straightened it in my hands before I put it in my mouth and lighted it.

"A lot of reasons. First, I just got divorced and you shouldn't make a track runner begin a new race after he's just come in dead last from the previous one. The guy might keel over."

"Sometimes I think I'm being strung along."

"You're right. I'm stringing you into yourself before I string you into marriage."

Marlyn sat up more rigidly in the carriage and said, "Whatever that means."

"I said there were a lot of reasons. That was the first. Now, in the second place, take Wanda, for instance. That girl I drove to the church?"

"What about her?"

"Marriage was like the last chance for her. She's no scholar. She has no ambition. It was her only out, the wedding. *You've* got options. But you want to forget about the options and run from one home to the next. I know it. I see it with kids all the time."

Marlyn stiffened again. "I'm not a kid."

"You're right. You're an adult. All I'm trying to do is get you to realize it. Go to college for one year. Feel independent. Live in a dorm. If you still love me next year, then fine. We'll get married. I'll make an honest woman of you."

"I could just punch you sometimes, Johnny."

"That's a good sign," I said. I put my arm around her and drew her over against my side.

Yellow streetlamps glowed in the park near Lake Shore Drive, and if you looked at the co-ops above you, every once in a while you could see some rich person walk in front of a window and peer down at the street life below. You had to wonder how they'd made it up there.

Marlyn leaned her face on mine when our horse stopped for a red light. "Can I stay with you some nights?"

"Weekends."

"Just weekends?"

"Wednesdays."

"Just weekends and Wednesdays?"

"Yes. You have to study sometime, you know."

She said, "We can study together."

I flicked my cigarette butt over the top of the carriage and out into the street. "They don't give you grades for that kind of studying."

I wondered how much engagement rings cost.

That night, back at my apartment, Marlyn and I were curled up in each other's arms under some new sheets I'd bought for the occasion. They were gray with white piping. I'd had a rush of domestication and had even bought a new lamp. I was half asleep and dreaming of the two of us on a beach in southern California in the sunshine. Big rolling waves washing ashore. It was the first time I'd felt at peace with the world in quite some time and I was enjoying it, just lying there, just breathing.

What interrupted all this was a click in the lock of my apartment door. It made me jerk my spine. I heard the door open. My first thought was that I was under arrest for lewd behavior with a girl too beautiful for me. Then I slowly developed a picture of a home invader in my mind. I sat up in bed, ready to confront the prowler, when the light clicked on.

Shelly.

She stared at the two of us from the bedroom doorway. Marlyn had just awakened and saw me sitting up. She looked toward the doorway, spotted Shelly, and drew the sheets up to her neck. She said, "What the hell is going on here?"

It was a little like being caught in the act by a chaperon.

I said, "How in God's name did you get in here?"

Shelly just looked embarrassedly back and forth between us.

"Can I talk to you in the kitchen?" she said. Then she walked out of the bedroom and was evidently waiting for me to get decent and make my explanation to Marlyn.

"Who is she?" Marlyn demanded, in a whisper. There was something in her eyes I had never seen there until now.

Castration.

I got out of bed and stepped into my suit pants.

"I'll bet you wouldn't believe me if I said she was a friendly burglar."

"It's your ex. It's her, isn't it?"

"Yes."

"That's the limit."

Marlyn climbed out of bed and began immediately to get dressed.

"Just relax. I'll go get rid of her. You stay here."

Marlyn did not look satisfied with that idea. "It's nice to know your ex-wife has a key to your apartment. *I* don't even have a key to your apartment."

I said, "She doesn't have a key."

"Then how did she get in?"

I threw on my shirt and left the bedroom while I was buttoning it. I closed the door behind me. Someone had a lot of explaining to do.

Shelly was leaning against the refrigerator in a tan polo coat. She had her hand up to her face as though she had a terrible headache. She had terrible headaches frequently. I thought of an instant remedy for her, but they would have given me life for it.

There didn't seem to be much reason to beat around the shrubbery.

"How the fuck did you get into my apartment?"

With one hand still up to her face, she extended the other and dangled a spare set of keys in front of me.

"Where did you get those?"

The demands of a half-dressed man always sound anemic.

"That day. That day I was here with Carl. You had them on your dresser."

"Oh. And so you figured I left them there so you could steal them."

Shelly was wiping her eyes. Crying, for God's sake. I didn't know any longer how her mind worked. Maybe she thought people got divorced so they could become monks or something.

"I took the keys because I was worried about you. I thought someone should be able to check up on you. I tried calling for two nights in a row and there was no answer. You're not the most *stable* person in the world, and I was worried. Boy, I guess my worrying is over—judging from the little honey you have packed away in there. What is she, anyway? A model? A stewardess?"

That sunny beach Marlyn and I had been on a few minutes before was vanishing rapidly. I saw it in my mind as if through a zoom-out lens. Going, going, gone.

"What she *is* doesn't happen to be of any concern to you. And don't give me any shit about stability. At least I don't go around breaking into your house when you're with Carl what's-his-name. Carl Boring. Carl Normal."

Shelly walked to the front door and opened it. "Don't you talk about Carl, *you*. Carl doesn't lock himself in a little room and disappear for months at a time, pounding on a typewriter."

"It's a good thing," I said, following her like a jerk, "because nobody would be able to read it."

Bam! She slammed the door.

Fuck, I thought. Dinner at the 95th, a carriage ride, and my ex-wife. If they ever make a movie of my life they're going to have to exhume Alfred Hitchcock to do the screenplay.

Marlyn was fully dressed when I went back to the bedroom. She was straightening out her dress in the mirror and brushing her hair back quickly with her fingers. I stood there in my bare feet as she started loading things into her purse.

"I never gave her a spare key," I said. I felt ridiculous apologizing, even though it was the truth. The truth was stupid.

She said nothing. With deep breaths and suppressed sounds moving around in her throat, she was trying to slip back into her dignity.

"Shelly's got some idea that she has to mother me. I don't know what it is. I think some married people have a hard time realizing when it's over, even after it's over. You know?"

She walked icily out of the bedroom to the hallway. She stopped to take something out of her purse at the front door.

I said, "If you give me a second, I'll finish dressing and drive you—"

"I'm taking a cab."

"No, don't do that. It's late. Wait for—"

The door slammed for the second time in as many minutes. I stood in the hallway by myself. I tried to catch up with the events of the night. Then I sat down, right on the tile floor, and leaned my back against the wall. *The Picture of Dorian Spector.*

I wondered what the heart attack statistics were on men close to thirty.

Thirteen

It was Monday and it was fourth period and I was sitting at my desk drinking a cup of coffee. I couldn't wake up. I'd spent the weekend staked out at the phone, but it never rang. On my desk was a memo asking for my homeroom students' notes of excuse for the month of April. I went about looking for them. I found one in my top desk drawer.

> *Please escuse Juan he not come yesterday to*
> *school account of his mother she in the hospital.*

I could not find the others. I took out some loose-leaf notebook paper and made the rest up myself, using Juan's note as a format. "Please escuse Miguel." "Please escuse Maria." *Please escuse my ass.* I made up two colds and one strep throat. I placed the notes in the little manila envelope the administration had supplied and signed my name on the front.

I had not seen Marlyn all morning.

I was about to go out and get another cup of coffee when my phone rang. It was Marco Gonzalez.

"Didn't see you at the prom on Friday," he said, instead of good morning.

"Yes, you did. We danced together three times. Jesus, you must've been loaded."

"That was *you*? I thought my wife was growing a beard."

"She is."

"Listen, I'll bet you're wondering why I called."

I said, "I'll bet it's not 'cause you were lonely."

"Carlos. He's not in school today. He called up to tell me he wouldn't be in. When I asked him if he was sick, he said no."

"Then why isn't he here?"

"I don't know. He sounded funny. He wouldn't tell me what the problem is."

"You want me to go over there?" I asked.

Marco blew a little breath into the receiver as if he were deciding. "It couldn't hurt. Unless you're busy."

"I'm not. I was just sitting here reminiscing about some of the great fire drills we've had this year."

"That bad, huh?"

"I'm very sensitive, you know."

"Look, Johnny," Marco said, in an altogether different tone of voice, "I think you should know something. I mean, we're friends, right?"

"You don't want to dance with me anymore?"

"Seriously. There was some talk up in the breakfast room this morning."

I said, "There's always talk in the breakfast room. The best idea is not to listen to it."

"I wasn't listening until your name came up, and then I thought I'd better eavesdrop for you."

I didn't have to guess what it was about.

Marco cleared his throat self-consciously. "According to one lady, you were seen at the symphony last week in the company of a female student."

"Maybe I could say it was a very small field trip."

"I don't think so. Another woman saw you driving this girl down Fullerton in your Jeep. Different night."

I said, "Well, Marco. If you ever lose track of me, now you know who to go to."

"I just thought you should know."

"Thank you, Marco."

Teachers make good private detectives, I thought. It wasn't very comforting to think that you couldn't get lost in a city of 3,005,072 people.

I took a final gulp of my coffee, put on my sport coat, and left the school. I didn't bother to sign out.

My records on Carlos showed that he lived on North Avenue near Leavitt. I had never been up to his apartment. I parked the Jeep illegally in front of a currency exchange. It was a funny arrangement where he lived. Upstairs you could see open windows with dirty curtains flapping in the wind. But there were no buzzers, no names listed in the hallway. Inside, the wooden floors smelled of stale beer. I walked in and out the front door several times, trying to decide what to do. I finally resorted to calling his name loudly with my hands cupped around my mouth. Two little children came to the window directly overhead. They waved at me.

"Do you know Carlos?" I asked them.

They shook their heads.

I called him again. The kids waved again. I waved back. This was making me friends, but getting me nowhere. I entered the building and began to climb the stairs. There were bags of garbage at almost every landing and they smelled of rotten food and sour coffee grounds. I had to hold my hand over my mouth. I was beginning to understand how things were done here. Most of the doors had the last name of the family written on a piece of paper or stenciled on tape. On the third landing I found a rear-facing apartment with the name Villavaso stenciled on black tape. I knocked on the door and called out, "Carlos?"

I listened and heard some movement inside.

"Who it is?" It was Carlos's voice.

"It's Johnny, Carlos. Can I come in?"

"Yohnny?"

"*Sí.*"

"No."

I said, "No *what?*"

"You not come in."

"Why not?"

"Coz."

Brother. I looked at my watch and saw that I had fifteen minutes to make it to my study hall. At this rate I wouldn't get back until next week.

"Listen, Carlos. Buddy. Open the door. I'm running out of time."

"I ain't got no clothes."

He ain't got no clothes. Why ain't he got no clothes? I wondered.

"It's okay. Just open up. I won't look."

"Promeese?"

"On a stack of phone books. I promise. Open up."

I heard clicking sounds, like a lot of locks being opened, and finally a chain was removed. The door opened slowly. I could see a little bit of a room, and then a little more of a room, and then a lot of a room. What a mess. I walked in. No Carlos.

"Where are you?"

"Behind door."

I closed the door myself. Carlos stood there in his underwear. Behind him, covered with bags˙of flattened-out aluminum cans, was an old marred table of no particular type of wood. All over the apartment things were thrown discordantly. Clothes. Rags. A transistor radio. Crumpled up packages of cigarettes and candy. There was a poor excuse for a rug that looked as though it had been cut with a pair of shears by a drunk—it was an unproportionate attempt at a rectangle. Green.

I took all this in with one turn of my head and then looked back at Carlos. He shouted, "You say you no look!"

I put my hands on his shoulders. "Hey, what's the matter with you? Don't you think *I* wear underwear? Don't you think I've seen a lot of guys in just their underwear?"

Carlos rubbed one eye with his fist. I still had my hands on his shoulders as I looked around the room again. The plaster of the walls and ceiling was crumbling. In the corner was an old steam radiator that had once been painted silver and then flaked. All the paint flakes were strewn on the floor beneath it. I thought about all the layouts I'd seen of luxury palaces in *Better Homes and Gardens* and *Architectural Digest.* Had anybody who designed those pages ever seen a place like this, or even dreamed that it existed?

"How come you didn't come to school today, buddy? You sick?"

Carlos shook his head; he was looking at the floor. A roach weaved its way around the floor molding and then disappeared under the woodwork.

"What's the problem, then?"

He turned away and walked to another room. When he came back he was holding a pair of green pants I'd seen him wear frequently. He held them out to me. I took them. There was a big wet spot near the front and crotch. I smelled it.

Urine.

Carlos was looking at the floor again.

"Don't you have any others?"

"In the dirty clothes place. No washed."

I put my arm around him and led him over to a beaten couch

with torn corduroy upholstery. I sat him down and sat beside him.

"A lot of people wet their pants, Carlos. It happens to everybody once in a while. It's nothing to be ashamed of. You know that?"

"No."

I said, "Well, it's true. I've done it."

"You?" he asked, looking up, his eyes wide.

"Yeah."

"You too old to wet you pants, Yohnny."

"I suppose I am. I'm just a slob."

I took off my belt and put it around his waist. I wear a thirty-inch waist, and I figured his to be about a twenty-seven.

"If you wait here for me, I'm going to come back with some new pants for you, and then we'll go to school together. Okay?"

He nodded.

"Atta boy."

I was up to go, halfway to the door, when he called back to me. "Yohnny—get me *yeans,* like you."

That's exactly what I'd had in mind. *Blue yeans.* I waved goodbye to him and let myself out.

I've never considered myself a sentimentalist. I have a hard time taking most things seriously. But when I walked out of that building onto the filthy streets of West Town, I felt as though someone had pulled my heart out. Someone with a hell of a grip.

There was a jean boutique—it claimed to be a boutique; actually it was a grimy hole-in-the-wall—two blocks down on North Avenue. I ran there instead of taking the Jeep. There were no parking spaces on the street, and it was quicker that way. I bought two pairs of pants, one pair of blue jeans and a pair of khaki slacks. I was uncertain about the length and I had to hold the pants out in front of me and imagine Carlos in them. A chunky short lady behind the counter told me I couldn't pay by *cheque.* She didn't take *cheques.* She took MasterCard, though. I waited close to thirty minutes for her to complete a simple transaction. She kept tearing the carbon receipt in the machine. I was ready to kill her by the time I got out of there.

The jeans looked super on Carlos. They were a little long, so I turned the cuffs up. He looked like Sal Mineo in them. A short Sal Mineo. If I hadn't been in such a hurry to get back to school, I would have bought him a few shirts as well.

Before we left the apartment I stopped him and said, "Listen, kid. What do you do with the money you make selling papers? Do you give it to your uncle?"

"Some. Some I give my onkle." Then he led me to the bedroom. He lifted the mattress and took out an old dingy white sock. "Rest I poot here."

"Remind me to tell you about bank accounts, sometime."

"Onkle no like banks."

I said, "I'll bet he doesn't. Banks you can't find under the mattress."

We zipped back to Freddie Prinze. Someone had taken my space in the loading dock, so I had to park illegally near a fire hydrant. We never had real fires, just false alarms. I was thirty minutes late for my study hall. I grabbed my green attendance book from my office and told Carlos to report to his teacher right away, and that I'd explain the situation to Mr. Gonzalez as soon as I could. He flashed me the *okay* sign and dissolved in a river of kids riding up the escalator.

There was the familiar sound of a *bleep* that usually preceded an announcement over the intercom. The intercom was affectionately referred to as the bitch box.

"Mr. Spector, Mr. John Spector, please report to the main office at once."

The voice belonged to Fran Stakavoetch. The request belonged to McCaskey. I couldn't get a break in that place. McCaskey had spies all over the goddamn school. I wondered who had turned me in.

Inside the main office I found Fran sorting out an endless stack of government forms at her desk. She literally had boxes filled with the stupid things.

"If this is your desk," I said, "I'd hate to see your home."

"Dr. McCaskey wants to see you right away, Johnny."

I looked to see if there was any more information available on the subject. I looked into Fran's eyes for this. She said then, quietly, so the few teachers at their mailboxes wouldn't hear, "Janice Newman reported that you weren't in study hall."

"That's what I like about Janice," I said. "Burdened with work and she still has time to mind my business. That's a gift."

Fran winked at me and I went to get my head chewed off.

McCaskey's door was open. I stood just to the side of it thinking about how I'd handle the situation. But all I could concentrate on was Marlyn. I kept seeing her the way she'd looked when I first spotted her in the park. How would I ever be able to live alone without her? No more raspberry sherbet. No more dreams. No ocean whispers at night when I was half asleep. I did not want to talk to Dr. McCaskey. What I wanted was to find Marlyn, to explain things to her. How do you explain seven years of a bad marriage to an eighteen-year-old? How do you account for all the wreckage that washes ashore?

I wasn't in study hall, Dr. McCaskey, because one of my favorite students is emotionally handicapped and he wet his pants and I couldn't leave him at home alone in his underwear.

He'd never understand that.

No more lovemaking amid cardboard boxes of leftover pizza.

Maybe I could tell McCaskey that I'd gone out to get cold beers for my lit class. *That* he'd believe.

I rapped on the open door and went in. McCaskey was sitting at his desk and looked up, his ridiculous glasses a good distance down the bridge of his considerable-sized nose.

"Spector, you weren't in study hall."

"I know."

"You know. That's your explanation?"

I got the impression that I wasn't to sit down while we talked this over. No one had invited me to.

"Dr. McCaskey, there's this Special Ed student who had an emergency."

"I'm not interested, Spector," he said, looking at me over the tops of his lenses. "I don't care to hear where you were or what you were doing. I just want you to know that I know you weren't where you should have been."

How, I thought, was I supposed to respond to that? Okay. Good enough. I know that you know. Logic was never around when he was. He went back to reading something on his desk while I just stood there.

After a few moments he looked at me again, as though he had forgotten I was there. "On your way out, you may want to pick up a copy of your rating. It's in your mailbox."

"Is that all?"

McCaskey smiled—actually *smiled*—and then returned to whatever it was that had arrested his attention so completely.

I saw myself to the door.

True to his word, the rating envelope was sitting all alone in my mailbox. I picked it up, tapped it on a counter a few times, and then pulled it open. It was one of those self-contained jobs where you have to press your thumb on a tab and remove a copy from the inside.

Spector, John
Rating Code: E-1

It went on to say that I had a hearing scheduled for May 16. I could, at that time, give my side of the story to a so-called objective panel. This meant that I'd probably be transferred to a different school. Dumping-ground schools were ordinarily located in black neighborhoods. I'd just drop the *¿Qué pasa?* from my act and learn to say *y'all* a lot. I'm flexible.

It amazed me to think that some people managed to work their way *up* in a system. Sort of like salmon.

Marlyn did not call me that night. I tossed and turned in bed and thought of her. When there was no hope of sleep, I smoked a joint and watched an old black-and-white movie dubbed in Spanish. It made me feel at home.

I woke up at seven-thirty on Tuesday and did not feel like going to work. I called in sick. I had about fifty sick days to my credit and it seemed dumb to save them, so I splurged.

I took a shower and thought about getting my mail. Maybe Marlyn had written a letter to me. But on the television lobby monitor I could see a kid hanging around. He buzzed my buzzer every five minutes and a few times in between. I did not want to talk to him. He would have wanted to smoke a joint with me, or talk about writing, or ask if I had at one time been the kid in my book. It was getting to the point that I didn't know what to tell people anymore.

My next-door neighbor was a friendly guy who recruited for the army. I knew he was home because I could hear his TV. I knocked on his door and ran down the situation for him and he agreed to get my mail for me. When he returned a few minutes later he handed me my garage bill, a bill from Saks (the three-hundred-dollar dress), a bill from Visa, and a newsletter from my congressman that cited the milestones being reached in education.

Some milestones.

I had four Scotch and sodas in a row after that and sat at my desk overlooking Clark Street. The army guy next door was playing "Where or When" on his piano, and really doing a pretty good job with it. I switched to beer then and began feeling maudlin as hell. I remembered a girl I'd once kissed in eighth grade and wondered what had ever happened to her. I saw her in my mind. She was married and had three kids and lived in Northbrook and had gained twenty pounds and wore curlers to bed. She was probably a lawyer and voted Republican. It was a good thing I didn't keep a gun around.

At eight-fifteen the phone rang. *This could be it,* I told myself. I'd started talking to myself on the third Scotch.

"Hello?" I tried not to sound anxious. I bit my lip to accomplish this.

"Hello, Johnny."

It was Shelly.

"Look, don't hang up. I just called to tell you what was on my mind the other night. Remember the other night?"

"It's kind of hard to forget a home invasion, Shel."

"Well, it wasn't exactly a *home* invasion."

I said, "Okay. Apartment invasion. What is it? I've got a very impatient bottle to finish here."

"Are you depressed? You usually drink when you're depressed."

"Not anymore. Now I only drink when I'm ecstatic. I'm ecstatic."

"I hope I didn't louse things up for you when I barged in."

Like hell she did.

"I mean, when I found you in bed with your little stewardess."

She sure wanted to talk about her. "She's not a stewardess. And you didn't louse things up. As a matter of fact, she was hoping you could stick around for coffee so we could all get to know each other better."

"What is she, then, a model?"

"Nope."

"Well, what is she?"

"Student."

"A student? Not one of *your* students."

"Wanna bet?" I lighted a cigarette and lay down on the couch.

I felt around on the coffee table for my beer. I accidentally put my hand in the ashtray and retracted it. I wiped the ashes off on my jeans.

Shelly said, "Oh, Jesus, Johnny. Why?"

"Why what?"

"Why are you going to bed with one of your students?"

"I don't know. To get to the other side, I guess."

Then there was silence on her end that I attributed to confusion. *It's none of your business why I'm going to bed with a student. You and I are divorced. Get on with your life. Leave me alone.*

If there is such a thing as telepathy, I had just told her off.

"Well," she said, and then she cleared her throat, "that's too weird. The reason I called was to clear things up—and to tell you that Carl has asked me to marry him."

Weird must be in the eye of the beholder.

I said, "That's nice."

"I'm going to do it."

"I hope you two are very happy together."

"You could at least sound as though you mean it," she said, offended. "I was planning to invite you."

I sat up then. I did not know what this woman wanted from me. Maybe she wanted me to go insane with jealousy. Maybe she just wanted me to go insane.

I said, "Shel, no thanks. You don't need any ghosts hanging around your wedding. But I'm delighted for you, really."

She listened for a second. She always had trouble telling if I was sincere. "Thank you," she finally said.

"Yeah. You two can have little kids with overly developed chests and no sense of humor. If they get bored, they can learn how to sell real estate and find out what real boredom is all about."

There was a fraction of a second more silence before the phone went *click* in my ear.

I should start a business. Dial-an-Insult.

I slept on the couch because that was where I passed out. I woke up at noon. My back was killing me. The living room was littered with highball glasses and beer bottles. If I hadn't known better, I would have sworn someone had broken into the apartment and thrown a party while I'd slept. Elves or something. I hadn't called in sick.

Too late now. McCaskey was a clever guy. He'd get the idea.

When there was no word from Marlyn by five that afternoon, I couldn't take the suspense anymore. I showered and dressed and drove to Walgreen's. I didn't plan what I was going to say. I just drove over, found a parking space, and walked in through the turnstile. She wasn't at the checkout counter. She wasn't at the fountain. I turned down an aisle where they kept the deodorants and had to squeeze my way around an old woman who was examining a can of hair spray as though it might have been a valuable icon.

I noticed Marlyn behind the counter in the camera department. She was writing up a film-developing order for a guy who was all but drooling on her. I waited a good distance away. I didn't want to have to stand in line behind a moron. It would have taken all the drama out of my entrance.

"You *fine*, babe," the cretin said to her.

She just continued to write the order.

"What you doin' after work, huh? You wanna see the world with me, mama?"

She tore off the receipt for the film and handed it to him. I wondered what kind of pictures he took. He stood around and watched her for a while. When he got the message that he'd struck out, he walked away and shook his head and put the receipt into his wallet.

I approached the counter while Marlyn was busy sorting things out. She grabbed her pen and looked up, presumably expecting another half-wit customer. What she got was just another half-wit.

"Hi," I said.

She looked away, and then back. I don't think she was too happy to see me.

"Johnny, I'm busy at the moment."

"I miss you."

That's what happens when you trust your ability to ad-lib.

"I miss you, too. But I can't talk now."

"Then everything's all right?" I said. I couldn't get her to look me in the eyes. They were off limits.

"No. Everything is *not* all right."

"You're still mad?"

"No."

"Then what's the problem?"

She sighed, put her hands on the counter, and tilted her head.

"Look, there's a lot you don't know. About my situation at home and all. I tried to tell you about this, about Latin fathers and how they have their own way of doing things."

"And?" I asked.

A black woman walked up to the counter. She put a roll of film down and Marlyn took out an order sheet and asked for her name. The woman said, "Delhaney."

I said, "What about the way Latin fathers do things?"

Marlyn held up a finger to me. This meant I should shut up. I didn't feel like shutting up, though. I wanted to know about the situation at home.

Then Marlyn asked the woman for her phone number.

"Ain't got one."

"What about the way your father is doing things?" I asked.

Marlyn tore a little receipt from a film envelope and handed it to the woman. "Thank you," she said.

"Uh—I want some cullah film." She was scanning the shelves behind Marlyn now, looking for the type of film she wanted.

"What kind?"

"I forget what it's called."

I stepped behind the counter and took Marlyn by the forearm. Turning to the black woman, I said, "Why don't you look at the shelf until you see what kind of film you need and we'll be back in a minute." Then I pulled Marlyn into the aisle of deodorants, where I let her go. I should say, she pulled her arm from my grip.

"What do you think you're doing?"

"I want to know about the problem at home. Are you moving back to the island, or what?"

"This is my *job*. I can't just walk away from the counter, Johnny."

"Yes, you can. For two minutes you can. She doesn't even know what she wants. Are you moving or not?"

Marlyn dragged a hand through her hair and looked sideways and then looked at me. She could lend class even to a stupid Walgreen's smock.

"I have two choices."

"They are—"

"One, I can move back to Puerto Rico with my father on June first."

June first. That was just a few weeks away. "No, you can't. Graduation isn't till the seventh."

"The way my father figures it, they have mail in Puerto Rico. They can send me my diploma."

"What about number two?"

Marlyn shook her head. The woman at the counter was braying, now.

"Miss? Miss?"

I stuck my head out from around the corner and said, "She'll be right with you."

"Number two. All right. Do you remember the first time you came here to see me at work? Do you recall a little man with a dark complexion who talked to me in Spanish?"

In fact, I did remember him. He was the guy who'd given me the dirty look when he left. I said, "You mean the one with the burgundy polyester pants and the red socks? Kind of hard to forget that. Why?"

"He's the man who's buying my father's business. My second choice is to stay here and marry him. His name is Tutti."

"No, it's not."

Marlyn looked bewildered. "Of course it is. It's Tutti."

I said, "*Nobody's* name is Tutti. Come on."

She blew a little gust of wind between her lips and glanced at the film counter. The woman had gone. "Look. It's been arranged since I was fourteen or something. My father has been pushing this guy at me ever since I got to high school. I think that's why Tutti agreed to buy the business. I don't know which is the fringe benefit— me, or the store."

A Latin family of two toddlers, a thin bony woman with turquoise shoes, and a man with just a bit of hair isolated in the area where some men have a widow's peak, walked down our aisle. One of the children said, "*Papi. Papi. Papi.* Buy me candy."

I said, "I don't suppose anyone took the time to tell your father or this guy Tutti that it's 1985 and marriages just aren't arranged anymore."

"I don't tell them anything. I avoid the topic, whenever possible. Look, Johnny. I tried to tell you it was a waste of time thinking that I could go to college. He won't let me. For a while there I thought it would be different, kind of, if you and I—but then the other night happened. You're not ready for another—"

She stopped then. There was a little tear trickling down the side of her face, near her hairline. She did not appear conscious of it. I followed its progress all the way to her ear. A mini-river.

"Wipe your face," I told her.

She put her sleeve up to her temple and blotted the tear stream. All around us shoppers were reading labels and throwing merchandise into carts and arguing in Spanish about the merits of one product over another. I felt strangely suspended from the scene, from the store, from Marlyn.

Tutti. For Christ's sake.

I told Marlyn that she wasn't going to Puerto Rico with her father, and that she wasn't going to marry someone named after an ice cream flavor.

"What do you mean?" she said.

"You're going to college."

She asked me how, but I was already on my way out of the store by then.

When I got to Marlyn's house I knocked hard on the door and tried the doorbell for good measure. It was as I had expected. The doorbell didn't work. I could hear voices inside. They broke off, or trailed off, and steps approached and the door opened. Marlyn's father understood enough English to know that I wanted to talk to him about his daughter. He regarded me with his suspicious look that was half genuine skepticism and half sheer bluff, and invited me into the dining room.

It was an orderly house, but cramped. The carpet was worn, though clean, and on the walls were faded oil paintings of streams, of forests, and on the far wall of the living room there was an exceedingly graphic depiction of Christ immediately after his unfortunate accident.

The dining room was lighted by table lamps—their shades wrapped in plastic—that gave off a yellow fluorescence. There I found Tutti. He was wearing the same burgundy pants he'd worn when I first saw him. I was directed to a seat at the table. I had interrupted their dinner. I sat down. A plate was put before me and then loaded with some rice concoction from a bowl. Mr. Valentin apparently stood on ceremony and would not discuss anything on an empty stomach.

I had the strangest notion that they'd been expecting me.

Tutti was seated across from my place setting. He, also, had perfected the machismo glare. I kind of had a hunch he knew who I was, and *what* I was to Marlyn. There was the sneer of a rival around the corners of his mouth. He looked like he wanted to beat me up with his eyeballs.

No one said anything during dinner. Mr. Valentin went about eating as though it were his sole purpose in life. From time to time he held up a serving dish of rolls or some gooky stuff that was brown, but of indeterminate origin. It may have been very good, for all I knew. I was in no hurry to find out, though.

Two things added to the absurd atmosphere in the house. I found, by almost breaking one of my molars, that there was a soup bone of some sort that had made its way into my rice. I removed it from my mouth while I hoped no one was looking, stared at it, and then placed it discreetly on the rim of my plate. *Rice and bones*—an old Caribbean recipe. And then, something about the contour, the color, the expression of Tutti's face was familiar to me. What was it? I ate on in silence.

Twice I was offered the mystery plate, and twice I refused it politely. The only sounds in the house were the clinking of forks against plates and the muffled chewing of rice.

A chili bean. That's what it was. Tutti's face, his entire head, reminded me exactly of a chili bean.

"If my daughter was here," Mr. Valentin said, standing, "she clear the plates away. She is at work."

He reached out for our plates, first for Tutti's, and then for mine. He went to the kitchen and came back with a coffeepot and began to pour coffee into our cups. Both Mr. Valentin and Tutti took several teaspoons of sugar in their coffee and a lot of cream. They made a big business out of stirring. I wondered how three or four teaspoons of sugar were supposed to dissolve in a small cup. They probably didn't. The sugar probably sank to the bottom. When you got down to the last sip, you got diabetes.

Still without talking, a jar was produced from a dinette shelf. It contained what looked like a huge urine sample. This, too, was poured into each cup. Even mine.

"Uh—what is that?" I asked. I had a funny feeling they were playing Slip the Honky Some Piss.

"Tutti makes it," Mr. Valentin said, tilting his head toward Tutti's chair.

That didn't exactly put me at ease. What was it he made and how did he make it? I thought.

After he finished dosing the cups he held the open jar under my nose. Whiskey. Moonshine. Well, it was better to have asked. After seeing what was for dinner, I wasn't in the mood to take chances.

"We know who you are," Tutti said to me, stirring hell out of his coffee. "You are a teacher at Freddie Prinze."

"You are seeing my daughter," Mr. Valentin added.

Mi culpa, mi culpa, I thought. I faintly expected a firing squad to appear with a blindfold and my last cigarette.

"I like your daughter quite a lot," I said.

A lot more than your cooking.

Tutti said, "This is not right. A teacher should *teach*. A teacher, a *maestro*, should not keep the company of his students. Especially—" His voice faded out there, as though he had reconsidered what he had been about to say.

I asked, "Especially?"

"Especially a divorced teacher. One from outside the community. A white teacher."

I had some of my coffee. It was the strongest stuff I'd ever drunk—both the coffee and the booze. You could put a man on Mars with that stuff.

"You don't mince words, do you?"

"What?"

"I say, you don't mince words."

He had a gold filling that caught the flare of an overhanging lamp, and it distracted me.

I said, "What do you say, Mr.—uh . . ." I was not going to call him Tutti. It sounded like a form of endearment, and I had altogether different feelings about this guy.

"Rivera."

Tutti Rivera. Old chili-bean head.

I started over. "What do you say, Mr. Rivera, that we don't start telling people what they should or shouldn't do. You sell groceries any way you want, and I'll stay out of it, okay? And I'll do what I do. You know. Get divorced when I feel like it. Teach the way I want to teach. Deal?"

Mr. Valentin spoke up from the head of the table. "My daughter go to Puerto Rico with me. Or she stay here to marry Señor Rivera."

"I don't think you've talked to your daughter recently, Mr. Valentin. If you had, you'd know she plans to go to college here, in Chicago."

Mr. Valentin drank his coffee as his eyes consulted Tutti's. They both grinned. They seemed to be in on some terrific joke together.

"If my daughter wish, she go to school on the island. In San Juan. We have colleges on the island, señor."

I said, "Yeah. You have colleges on the island. But have you asked your daughter if she *wants* to go to college in Puerto Rico? Or for that matter—have you asked her how she feels about marrying Mr. Rivera?"

Tutti had just gulped down some coffee and began to laugh with his mouth full. He tapped his lips with a napkin—a gesture that was more affectation than anything else—and then said to me, "A man does not ask a young woman what she wants. Not a *real* man."

He was a Puerto Rican Norman Mailer.

"Well, I don't know," I said. "I think he does. Slavery is dated, buddy."

The *buddy* must have rubbed the grain wrong. Tutti flinched from where he was sitting and his eyes grew larger. His bottom lip became wet. Pavlov's chauvinist.

Mr. Valentin moved our little party to the living room where I found a comfortable but tattered chair to sit in. My legs were getting heavy and I almost tripped along the way. Every so often one of the two men would mumble something in Spanish to the other and laugh. A photo album that traced the early years of the Valentin family was circulated. Marlyn as a kid was instantly recognizable, even in faded color snapshots. Mature eyes. Stoic chin. Cheekbones. Still, there was a distant longing in her expression. She *looked* like a girl who had no mother. It showed.

I leafed through the pages and determined that she had been born an adult by some weird accident of fate. Someone owed her a childhood, and that same person could at least extend her the right to choose her own future. I pursued the topic again.

"She wants to be a nurse," I said, out of nowhere. The comment stopped Tutti and Mr. Valentin cold. They had been chatting together on the couch.

"A nurse?" Mr. Valentin. The moonshine had made him more

amiable, but the idea of his daughter becoming a nurse amused him. "Nurse—my Marlyn? Oh, *maestro*. You tell a good joke."

"I do?" My lips were out of sync with my thoughts and I was feeling sleepy. The smiling faces on the couch were blurred and fuzzy around the edges. Tutti took out a guitar from somewhere and began playing silly melodies while Mr. Valentin carried the conversation.

"My daughter, she nervous when she touch a Band-Aid. She see blood, she get sick. A headache—she lie in bed all day. A fine nurse."

Tutti stopped playing the guitar and reminisced about Marlyn's baptism. "She was just a few months old and I was there. My brother was her godfather. I was at her first communion, *también*. *Qué linda*, such a child! White veil, white dress. You see, *maestro*, some things are beyond your control. We have been a family for as many years as the days you have known her."

The room was tilted, now. It disturbed me that I couldn't lay down a snapshot or a memory to match Tutti point by point. I had no ammunition. What was worse, I was beginning to like them both— in an uncomfortable and qualified way. And I was drunk. Another shot of that stuff that they'd put in the coffee and I'd become a permanent fixture in the living room. Right under the picture of Christ. And we'd have the same look on our faces.

"Hey, listen." I looked around the room. My own voice came as a surprise to me and seemed to make the room sway. "Listen now, really. You guys. Let's not argue, okay?"

"There is no argument, *maestro*," Tutti said.

"Right. Listen. Marlyn's gonna go to Loyola. Be a nurse, you know? I just want you guys to know she isn't going to Puerto Rico."

"Then she will marry me." Tutti. Tutti chili bean, smiling with a guitar on his overstuffed burgundy-polyester lap.

"Nope. Not gonna marry you, Chili."

"Tutti."

"Right. Okay? Just so there's no argument."

Then the sound of Mr. Valentin's voice. He was talking about roads. Fucking roads? What's this about roads? I wondered.

"There are only two, and it is a father's duty he point them out. There are only ever two roads, *maestro*."

I said, "She'll build her own goddamn road."

Laughter.

"It swallow her up. It is enough to choose and follow, *maestro*."

Maestro. Maestro. It is enough, *maestro.*

The drink, the broken English, the light, the portrait of Christ, the food. When I got up unsteadily to excuse myself, I said what came to mind.

"Me go now."

At the front door I saw that I had been followed by both men. Tutti was saying, "And let's not hear that you are still seeing this girl. The school board would be very interested to learn this. If this should happen, we can tell them everything."

"No, you can't," I said, with a smile, swerving down the cement steps to the walk. "You sure can't tell them everything. Good night."

Tutti said, "What does that mean?"

"Think about it," I said.

I was in the Jeep when I heard him call something after me. But it was indistinct, and probably in Spanish. It was most likely not an invitation to join them again soon, though.

Fourteen

May 16 was a bright clear Thursday that woke me up before the alarm clock had a chance. Happy day. My hearing. I was always having a hearing of some sort.

I'd called in sick on Wednesday. Yesterday. Then I walked around Lincoln Park and wandered into the zoo and thought about my life. That made me want to get drunk. I started at a bar on Diversey, the one where Jack Henley and I had had a little talk a few weeks earlier. Then I stocked up on Heineken at a liquor store and took the show back to my apartment. Using long division, I tried to imagine what my financial forecast would be like if it consisted entirely of royalty checks. The proverbial rainy day came to mind.

Marlyn had called me when I was loaded on the couch. She said something about having a lot of decisions to make; I don't recall her exact words. I was listening to the sound of her voice again, and it left me thinking of palm trees and coconuts and brown lizards in the sand. I didn't know anymore where all this would take us. I'd lost my bearings. All I was certain of was the hearing, and that I'd be charcoal-broiled by the committee. They would probably assign me to a new school where I could make a clean start of things. Then I could bring the system down around me all over again. Sort of like Sisyphus.

I decided to wear a sport jacket and a tie and a pair of slacks to school. Better men than I had sold out. I always had trouble with Windsor knots. I tried to tie one, gave up, and settled for something that looked like a Boy Scout's square knot, just below the collar. The skinny end of the tie came out longer than the wide part. I tucked it into my pants. No one would ever know.

I drove to school with the top off the Jeep. The wind rushed around and blew ashes out of the ashtray and it smelled of Florida dampness. At a bottlenecked intersection I had a mental picture of Shelly in her wedding dress—a frightening little vision. It had been a lot of going to get nowhere.

Someone honked his horn from behind me. I was stopped at Ashland and Fullerton and hadn't seen the light turn green. I waved. I put the Jeep in first gear and returned to the present.

Right on North Avenue. A one-mile strip of *barrio* shops and a lot of cars on the side of the road, all missing a tire or two, a fender or a hood. Left onto the Humboldt concourse. Green grass and up the drive to Freddie Prinze. Something was odd about the look of the building. I pulled up to the front entrance and stopped. The lobby windows, which encompassed the width of the structure, had all been smashed. There was glass strewn around the walks and inside the school. A security guard with long sideburns and a bushy mustache walked in little circles, kicking glass and shaking his head.

There—at the cul-de-sac, surrounded by what used to be a green lawn that was now suffering because of negligence and the tromping of student feet—was a word spray-painted in yard-high Day-Glo letters of black, gold, orange, green, and white. It was a conglomerate of colors representing the Latin Kings, the Ghetto Brothers Organization, and the Unknowns. It occurred to me that the message was merely a euphemism.

PEOPLE

I parked the Jeep in the usual spot in the loading-dock area by the auto shop. Similar graffiti greeted me there. Medieval script. Bright colors. It was bound to happen sooner or later. A multimillion-dollar war zone.

Inside the building teachers were speaking softly. Some were holding Styrofoam cups of coffee. They were gathered into little clumps and reminded me of insects buzzing closely together. Whenever I passed one of these clumps I could feel eyes follow my progress into the main office, where I signed in. I must have been one of the hot topics. I questioned whether it was because of Marlyn, or if they'd heard about my new E-1 status. Who could tell? Maybe they thought I was the one who had broken the windows. I'd done just about everything else.

At eight o'clock the intercom blurted its obnoxious *bleep* and Fran announced that there would be a brief faculty meeting in the auditorium before classes began. We were all expected to attend.

I took the elevator to the sixth floor. In the cafeteria I bought a cup of coffee. More insects up there. I smiled each time I came up against a group of two or more faculty members. They always seemed to look the other way.

In the breakfast room the lobotomy table was in full swing. I could hear their voices rising stridently even before I entered. Raymond Donatucci was telling everyone in his big bass voice what should be done to the vandals who had attacked the school.

"Hang 'em upside down and shoot their goddamn brains out. That's what Mussolini would've done."

No one bothered to remind him where that had got Mussolini.

When I walked in, there was a gap in the conversation that lasted until I sat down. Everyone looked at me. The only other person at my table was Megan Croner. She sat and grinned at a fly on her coffee cup. I wondered what was going on in that mind of hers—and how she could be enchanted by the presence of a fly. When the fly took off, she watched it momentarily and shifted her gaze to the plate she had placed on the table in front of her.

I said, "Tell me about yourself, Megan."

She looked up, surprised, and said, "Oh! Hello, Mr.—uh. Mr.—"

"Spector."

"Yes. Spencer."

"No. *Spector.*"

She smiled at me in such a way that I guessed the fly had landed somewhere on my face. "Mr. Spector, yes," she said. She just sat there smiling.

"So tell me about yourself," I tried again. I felt an unusual affinity for her. Outcasts. Strangers in a weird land.

"Well, well, well! What would you like to know? You're a married man, aren't you?"

You couldn't even sit down and have a simple idiotic conversation with Megan. You could only have a *complicated* idiotic conversation with her. And then she assumed you were coming on to her—which verified the fact that she was out of her mind. Megan Croner must have been sixty years old if she was a day, and a dead ringer for Burl Ives.

"No. No, I'm not married, Megan. I used to be."

"Oh. I'm sorry. What happened, died?"

Talk about blunt. The word *died* impacted on me at the same instant she sipped her coffee from the rim where the fly had been sitting.

I said, "Yes. She's dead."

"How did she die?"

I sat there, looking directly into her blank eyes.

"Drowned."

"Oh! I'm so sorry. In the lake?"

"Nope. In a hot tub."

"Oh, for heaven's sake. What's a hot tub?"

"It's been nice talking to you, Megan."

"What's a hot tub?"

I picked up my coffee cup and headed for the auditorium.

I found a seat about ten rows from the back and sat down. There was some kind of electricity in the air this morning. Must have been the vandalism. All these nice people had just driven in from their nice suburban homes in their nice cars and suddenly realized that they could get their asses severely kicked in this neighborhood.

Dave Volmer appeared to my right. He stood in the aisle and looked down at me.

"Any room for a professional?"

I said, "A professional what?"

"Move over."

He climbed over the obstruction my legs had created and sat down beside me. He was carrying a white coffee mug that said in block letters DON'T THINK ABOUT ALIMONY.

Dave said, "Isn't it nice to meet like this in the morning and see all of our colleagues scared shitless about being shot?"

"We ought to do this more often."

"No, thank you."

McCaskey entered the auditorium from between the curtains. He had probably been back there the entire time. The school was ready to blow up and he was worried about his entrance. There was some polite applause from a mostly wary audience. I did not clap. It seemed pointless to clap for a man who was ready to send me packing.

He said something into the microphone, but it was dead. No sound. He tapped it a few times to see if it was working. It wasn't.

"So far, this is a good meeting," Dave said.

Stan Laughton, the drama teacher, played with the microphone connection. Then he hit it with his hand and suddenly the sound system purred into action and McCaskey was off.

"Good morning, ladies and gentlemen. I want to thank you for getting here promptly. This will be a short meeting."

Not short enough.

McCaskey walked back and forth across the stage as he went over a list of damage to the school, occasionally lifting his head to the audience, stopping, then bowing his head again and pacing. The stage lights gleamed off of his glasses, shooting light darts across the auditorium.

"We cannot have an academic atmosphere in a school where false alarms empty the building two, three, and four times a day. Our fifth-period classes are showing poor attendance. That is why I have assembled you here today."

The crowd, peering nearsightedly at him, hung on his every word. I was bored. But I sat. I listened. It was good preparation for my hearing. Sort of like walking on hot gravel before they bring on the glowing coals.

"The next time a false alarm goes off, I will announce school-wide over the intercom that everyone is to stay put. You are *not* to evacuate the building. I hope that is understood. You are *not* to leave the building."

First silence, then a growing murmur, the way crowds murmur. Then a question from the audience. Janice Newman.

"Dr. McCaskey, what about the students in the hallways? How do we stop them if they just automatically assume it's time to evacuate?"

McCaskey looked straight out into the crowd, undaunted. His response carried a note of improvisation. The bastard was winging it. "Those teachers without classes who happen to be in the hallways at the time will encourage students around them to stay where they are."

He didn't tell us how we were supposed to go about encouraging six-foot-tall gangsters not to leave the building.

Dave tapped my shoulder.

"Hmm?"

"Have you got a kid named Enrique Sanchez in one of your classes?"

I said, "Well, he sits in. You know. Whether or not he's all there is anybody's guess."

There were more innocuous questions from faculty members. Stuff about prosecuting offenders and the like.

Dave said, "The reason I ask is, you won't be seeing him there anymore."

"Oh?"

"That's right. Mary Esther Sheenan found him in her history class yesterday with his dick out." Dave reported this the way most people tell you if it's raining or not.

"Are you kidding?"

He held his hand out for divine sanction. "I shit you not, white man. From what I heard, he was hiding behind his Bible, whacking it. She came walking by, saw him, and nearly had a coronary. He's on suspension. When he gets back—*boom*. Right into sicko therapy. He can whack it all he wants, there."

"I can't tell you how you've made my day, Dave."

"Yeah? Wait till McCaskey gets through with you. Be sure you stop by my office so you can tell me which slum he's sending you to. I'll forward your mail."

There was one more question from the audience. Megan Croner. Someone must have woken her.

"Dr. McCaskey, what if it's *not* a false alarm and we all remain where we are? What if it's a real fire?"

Why then, Megan, we'll all burn to death. Don't worry. You won't know the difference.

I did not stay to hear the actual reply to her question. I got up, left the auditorium, took an escalator to the second floor, and walked to my office.

I sat down and had a cigarette. It would be nice, I thought, to end the year on a high note. If I had anything to say about it, Marlyn was not going to Puerto Rico. That was that. I wondered if I could beat up Tutti.

I began to alphabetize some computer grade cards that were due in the registrar's office by noon. Little manila cards with cryptic slots in them. Then I noticed that I had inadvertently mixed attendance cards with the grade cards. I put my cigarette on the saucer I used for a makeshift ashtray and tried to sort the cards out. It was pretty useless. They all had slots and names and one looked a lot like the other. I let the mess drop onto the desk and picked up the cigarette and found that it had gone out.

Good morning.

I took a good look at the upcoming summer. It stared back at me like a big curtain covered with question marks. I saw me moving Marlyn into a dorm, buying plants or something for a housewarming gift. Whatever you get for a young girl alone for the first time. Then the fantasy took a decided turn for the shitty. Marlyn disappeared and I was left alone in an ugly high-rise, with a bunch of homeless kids leaving me dope and ringing my doorbell.

Elsie popped in the office with really unique timing, interrupting my mental movie. Long black hair, three-inch fingernails. Tits the size of volleyballs. She looked like a healthy android.

"How's my favorite guy?"

"How should I know? Who's your favorite guy this week?"

She walked closer to my desk. She had tight jeans with pinstripes and zippers at the ankle. For easy access, I figured.

"Tony and the guys've been asking about you."

"Well. We've kind of had a parting of the ways. My gangster days are over."

"They still think you're the best, Johnny. Especially Tony."

"The best what?"

"Just the best. Tony said so last night." Elsie picked up a few grade cards from my desk and looked at them. "These're all fucked up. You got attendance cards mixed in with the grade ones."

Elsie was just what the Chicago Board of Education needed. She could tell the cards apart. She began sorting them into piles. Neat computer card piles on top of my desk.

"Why don't you go home sick today?" she asked, without looking up from what she was doing.

"No, thanks. Work is where I come when I'm sick. Whenever I feel well, I stay home."

"Why don't you go home anyway?"

Now, she was trying to tell me something. But with Elsie, everything sounded like a proposition. My first thought was that she wanted me to go home so she could drop by and initiate me as an honorary Cobra.

I said, "Why am I having trouble getting the hint?"

"I don't know. I thought you would've got the hint when you saw them windows out front."

So that was it. Gang wars, and Elsie was trying to save me again. I grabbed a cigarette but didn't light it.

"When is it going to happen?"

She had made some improvement with the cards and placed them down on my desk. "I'd be outa here by twelve, if I was you."

"If I *were* you," I corrected her.

"You know what I'm talking about."

I said, "Yes, I do. Thanks for the warning."

"You'll go home?"

"I have a meeting, but I'll be the first one out of here, okay?"

She kissed me on the cheek and patted my head. She made me feel like I had an older sister.

There was a copy of Marlyn's class schedule in my desk, somewhere. After Elsie left I began to open drawers and hunt for it. She would have to be told. Her lunch period was around noon, that much I knew. I thought that the two of us could grab a hot dog at Rocky's, a little stand on North Avenue. We had a lot to settle.

I found her schedule in a lower cabinet under some ungraded compositions entitled "My Values." They were very short essays. Marlyn was, at the moment, in Ray Donatucci's history class. I picked up my keys, put them in the pocket of my blazer, and headed for the sixth floor.

Outside of Ray's classroom his voice thundered through the door and the walls and made me hesitate before I knocked. He was reliving World War II—his favorite topic. I rapped on the door and opened it. I had stopped him at a point when he had balanced his right foot on the seat of an empty student desk, deep in some reminiscence of the Normandy invasion.

"Excuse me, Ray. Do you have a Marlyn Valentin here?" I held her pink schedule in my hand as if to imply that I had a program change I needed to talk to her about.

"Miss Valentin? Are you here today?"

Marlyn got up and acted very cool and made sure she did not look at me until we were in the hallway. I noticed that some kid in the second row hit a kid next to him with his elbow when we left the room together. The kids always knew.

When the door was closed and we were alone, we walked out of window range. "How are you?" I asked.

"I'm okay. How are you?"

Beige sweater. Brown skirt. Those eyes that knew more than they were supposed to.

"I don't have a program change for you."

"I didn't think you did." Her hand reached toward me and then dropped to her side, as though she had just remembered where we were.

"There's going to be trouble today, around noon. Just got the word from the Family."

"In school?" she said. Her hands were playing their old game again. She couldn't keep them still.

"That's what they say. I thought we could meet at Rocky's. It would be a good idea to be kind of far away from the scene of the crime."

"Okay."

"You have lunch at noon, right?"

"Yes. You've got the schedule right there."

I put a hand in my pants pocket and surveyed the hallway behind Marlyn. No one there. I could relax. When I looked back at her, there was something in her eyes. I don't know what, precisely. There was—space. Distance. They looked beyond me, through me. Little lasers.

"You know, we're going to have to talk," I said. "I mean, about us."

Her head went down when I said this. She was looking at her shoes. Little brown pumps. "Oh, God, Johnny. Not now. Not here." She looked for something and couldn't find it. "I left my purse in class. Do you have any Kleenex?"

I thought, This is not going to be easy.

"No, sorry. No Kleenex."

She stood there, trying to regain her composure, and then said, "You know what I'd like to do? I'd like to punch your goddamn ex-wife in the mouth."

"Yeah. I know the feeling."

"I'm serious, Johnny. Everything was so perfect. Now it's all happening too fast. I don't know where I'm going to *live*. I don't know what I'm going to *do*. I don't know about us."

"You thinking about staying?"

"That's what I mean. I don't know *what* I'm doing. I think I'm going crazy. I swear to God."

I put a hand on her shoulder and shook her a little. It was kind of a reassurance gesture, but once I touched her, it was more than that. If hands could speak.

I said, "Well, things were never really so perfect. I've got to learn to keep my pictures in the attic, and you've got to try to take one step at a time." I watched as she rubbed one of her eyes, leaving a brown mascara streak near her temple. Looked like war paint. "How is it at home?"

She made an involuntary noise that sounded like a laugh. "Home? Oh, home's terrific. Tutti was over last night. I kept trying to get my father alone, to talk to him. But everywhere I went, there was Tutti. I finally told both of them that I wanted to be a nurse, and they laughed. I said that I wasn't kidding. It was like they couldn't even hear me. I got so pissed I ended up locking myself in my room. My father keeps saying he'll come to school to get you fired if I decide to stay."

There was a whole bunch of people out there trying to make me unemployed. I said, "Let him."

"What if he does?"

"He won't," I said. I don't know what made me so sure of this. I guess threats were starting to lose their impact on me. What was one more threat?

A series of firecracker explosions sounded from a stairwell and made me jump. I could smell gunpowder. A security guard, a woman of about forty-five with dyed red hair, went running down the hall to see what the trouble was. Anything that sounded like an explosion in that school tended to push people over the edge.

Marlyn had become abstracted by the carpet. She was lost somewhere in tranceland and I wondered what it was she saw there. I snapped my fingers to retrieve her.

"Sorry. I was just thinking. I was just thinking maybe it would be easier if I just went to PR."

I said, "You want to do what's easy?"

"No. I don't know. Do you think I'm crazy?"

"Look who you're asking."

Her father was winning. I could see it in her face. He'd somehow undermined her system of belief—the little place where you keep your dreams locked up and hidden. The sonofabitch was kidding himself if he thought he'd finished his business with me.

The bell rang and classroom doors banged open against lockers and the hallway filled with students. More firecrackers went off. I was used to them by then.

"Rocky's, then?" Marlyn asked.

I nodded. In a little while we had got lost in the crowd and I remembered I had an English class to teach. I had no lesson planned. Fuck it. Who needed plans? I could teach first-year English with any of my various body parts tied behind my back.

My classroom was in its normal state of disrepair. Dusty scratched blackboard. Mounds of crumpled paper on the floor. A book cabinet with broken handles. A wastebasket with a two-inch layer of some kind of mold growing on the bottom. An academic environment.

Halfway into the period I'd managed to draw fifteen kids. They straggled in whenever they felt like it. I wasn't up to talking, so I went to my file cabinet and found dittoed vocabulary sheets and handed out dictionaries and let the kids work by themselves. They always seemed to prefer this, anyway.

I loosened my tie and unbuttoned my collar button and stared out the window at the treetops in Humboldt Park. I thought about Carl and Shelly. I supposed that no one wanted to live alone. Why else would anyone want to marry Shelly? Then I thought about Marlyn in the Caribbean. Hot nights. Ocean. Roughly half a million good-looking, young horny males.

Two roads, maestro.

Says who?

"Hey, Teach—"

Jasper. He was here to make up a class he'd missed and was standing in front of my desk with a pencil tucked behind his ear.

"What is it?"

"You want all the definitions, or just one?"

I took a copy of the worksheet in my hand and showed him the sequenced numbers. "Three for each word."

"What if there ain't three?"

"Well, then as many as there are. Which word doesn't have three?"

"*Stanza.*"

That sounded reasonable. A stanza was just a stanza.

"Okay," I said. "Just one, then."

Jasper said, "All of it?"

"Yes. All of it."

"Hey, Teach."

"What?"

"You look sick, Jack."

"Do I?"

"Shit. You look like yesterday's milk."

Good old Jasper. Good old honest, graphic Jasper.

I said, "You don't look so hot yourself. Now go back to your desk and finish that goddamn thing."

On his way back I heard him gripe, "You don't got to take it out on *me* just 'cause you look like shit today."

Of course he was right. I gazed back out over the park and tried to remember the last time I'd had nothing to worry about, whenever that was.

Throughout the morning I watched the clock, waiting for my hearing, waiting to see if the trouble would hit before it convened. There were some minor disturbances—fist fights and gangs representing. But other than that, the minute hand traveled around the dial like a magician daring you to spot the trick.

I decided it would be poor form to arrive at my own lynching on time. I waited until ten after eleven and strolled up to McCaskey's office. The door was open, but I knocked anyway. I just rapped a few times and looked at the new faces inside. Three official-looking people were sitting by the big mahogany desk. Strictly Board of Ed issue, with the exception of one. There was a short stocky man who wore a gold shirt and a brown suit and had a mustache that looked like a brush. There was a woman with bronze hair and a black hat and a black dress who could have won a chin contest. She had a lot of them. Then there was a young woman who was not at all unattractive. She wore a businessy suit and had long, very nice-looking, very *friendly*-looking legs. I hoped she'd be on my side.

"We've been waiting, Mr. Spector."

And there was McCaskey.

I said, "I'm sorry. The hallways were crowded."

Judging from the looks this remark fetched, I was guilty already.

There was one unoccupied chair and I gathered that it was reserved for me. I had the slight impression that it would be a smart thing to check it for electrical wires. Then all the guests were introduced, none of whose names I caught, except for the attractive young woman's. She was Miss Loring, from Field Services. I knew nothing of Field Services, but I was glad they had sent her. She was the only one in the bunch who smiled.

The man with the brush on his lip conducted the meeting. McCaskey just sat by, serving as a witness to verify the charges brought against me. My crimes were recited. At regular intervals I was reminded that this was just a hearing, and that the panel would simply make recommendations concerning my future assignment with the board. They were not here to formally accuse me of any kind of malfeasance. Yet they kept bringing up those infractions of mine. They questioned me about each individually. The lady with the chins went at me first.

"Mr. Spector, what I'm having difficulty understanding is why a teacher with seven years' experience—"

"Eight," I corrected her.

"—eight years of teaching experience would leave a potentially disruptive class of children, like yours, unattended. Could you explain why you chose to do so?"

The wall clock in McCaskey's office was moving at the same rate my classroom clock had. Everything seemed protracted, like more stuff was packed into every minute than it could hold. My palms were starting to sweat, and I remember that I wiped them on my slacks uneasily.

"I was called away to the phone by a colleague."

"I see. And it didn't occur to you to have the colleague take a message so that you could return the call?"

"I rarely get phone calls here at school. And the other teacher stopped by just quickly enough to deliver the news that I had the call. She didn't stick around for further orders, you know?"

She looked at me and then wrote something down on a clipboard of yellow legal-size paper. "I understand. And was the call of a professional nature?"

"Yes."

"May I ask you who it was from?"

"Yes, you may. It was Father Perry, from St. Aloysius Church."

"And Father Perry wished to discuss school business?"

Tick, tick, tick. I felt as though we were all sitting on a time bomb and I was the only one who knew. Miss Loring crossed her wonderful legs and I pretended to look at the carpet.

"Yes, he did."

"Could you be specific about the school business?"

I eyed each of their faces. McCaskey was regarding the far wall. The man with the mustache was examining me closely, the way you might examine a kid standing next to a broken cookie jar, until he confessed. Miss Loring was simply listening, her eyes darting from my questioner to me, and back again.

"Well, I don't know that this will be relevant or not—"

"Mr. Spector, why not let us determine that? Can you tell us what Father Perry discussed with you?"

"Yes." I took a deep breath here and wondered how much of the conversation it would be wise to repeat. Somewhere back in childhood I had learned honesty and learned to like it, though a bit too much for my own good. "Father Perry was calling about a female student of mine who was considered a battered child. Her father had beat her severely on several occasions."

They all jotted this down on respective legal tablets.

"Was this an emergency?" the chin lady asked. "You see, the reason we need to know that is, it may shed new light on your decision to leave the class unattended."

"Well—an emergency. What do you mean? Do you mean life and death?"

"What I mean is an *emergency*. Did it call for immediate attention?"

"I couldn't possibly have known that until I had got to the phone, could I?"

"Just tell us about the conversation," the woman instructed.

I did not know whether a panel of this sort was operating within its bounds by demanding to know what was said during a phone call. My guess was that it was not.

"I'd prefer not to answer that, if you don't mind."

McCaskey grinned a little grin to himself.

The man with the brush on his lip went next. "Were you knowledgeable that there was liquor present in your classroom before you left?"

Knowledgeable. I don't trust people who talk like that. I did not like the implication. And I hated his goddamn mustache.

"Of course I wasn't."

"Just yes or no will do," he said.

"Well then, emphatically *no*. Decidedly *no.*"

"Yes or no will do."

I said, "Not in this case it won't. As long as you're writing down everything I say, you might as well quote me accurately. The answer to that question is *emphatically no.* I want my response to read like that."

He challenged me to an eye contest. I wanted to kill him.

Miss Loring went next. What surprised me was that a lady of her appearance could sound so utterly unsympathetic. I felt let down when I heard her speak.

"You seem to be watching the clock very carefully, Mr. Spector. Is there somewhere you have to be?"

"No. It's just that—" What could I say? That I was waiting for the explosion?

She said, "Please, go ahead."

I cleared my throat. "To be perfectly honest, I think this hearing is unnecessary. I'd like it to end very soon."

The man with the mustache said, "I understand you have not turned in one set of lesson plans this year, Mr. Spector."

"That's more or less true."

"Would you mind explaining why you have been so negligent in class preparation?"

There was always the chance that Elsie had not known what she was talking about. It was now eleven thirty-five and all was well. About as well as could have been expected.

"I have never been negligent in class preparation."

"But you have no written plans."

"I have a few. I wrote a few, for a while, to keep Dr. McCaskey happy. The way I see it, you can either spend your time writing plans, or you can spend your time teaching."

"And you can't do both?"

"No. I can't."

"Yet other teachers manage to do both."

I said, "Do they? Just because you see their plans doesn't mean they're also teaching. It seems to me you'd have to go into every teacher's classroom with a copy of the plans in order to make a statement like that."

"That's a fallacious argument, Mr. Spector," the little man said.

"I don't think so."

I had obviously got to him. He touched his mustache several times, a nervous habit he'd picked up somewhere, and began writing furiously with a number two pencil. The point snapped off and he looked at it, brushed the lead from his tablet, placed the broken pencil on McCaskey's desk, and produced a ball-point pen from his shirt pocket.

Now it was Miss Loring's turn again. "Mr. Spector, perhaps you could recount for us the events on the day that you—"

She was cut short by the fire alarm. One of the sirens was located directly outside of McCaskey's office, and the wail was deafening. McCaskey stood up and headed for the main office proper.

"Is this scheduled?" the chin lady yelled.

I got up and peeked out the window. I could see two or three Cobras in their black-and-green battle colors. One of them was Tony. He was spray-painting a FOLKS logo on the concrete out front. Students began to pour out of the building—running, pushing each other. The frightened ones fled for whatever protection the surrounding park might offer. All this in spite of the fact that McCaskey was angrily announcing over intercom speakers that the alarm was false and that everyone should remain inside the building. A volley of eggs splattered against the windows and scared me so that I ducked out of reflex. I closed the door to the office to deaden the sound of the siren. At best, it was only slightly muffled.

I said, "We've got some real trouble out there."

The man with the mustache said, "Please, Mr. Spector. It's only a false alarm. Stay seated until Dr. McCaskey returns."

The idiot was so indoctrinated by procedure that he didn't know a crisis when he saw one. The downtown people get like that. Unless it's been written on a form, it doesn't exist.

"Look," I said, "this is the real thing. You've got a building full of kids here about to have a gang war."

They looked at me as though they hadn't heard, or weren't interested. Miss Loring got up and came over to the window. The other two gathered their coats, and, as quickly as they could, waddled into the main office, presumably looking for cover. Good luck, I thought.

Outside, the kids continued to flow out the doors, screaming, throwing rocks at the already shattered lobby windows. Tony was nearly finished adding the third color to his rainbow-inspired trademark.

He'd learned to work fast in the train yards under similarly dangerous conditions.

Miss Loring stood next to me, watching the madness out there with an uncommon degree of cool.

"Who is that boy?" she asked me.

"Wanna be a little more specific? I mean—there're a couple hundred of them out—"

"No, I mean the boy with the paints."

Tony was outlining the logo in glossy black when someone stepped on the fresh paint and smeared the green. He kicked the transgressor in the ass—one timely, well-aimed karate kick. The kid went sprawling on the cement.

"They call him Fast Kid."

"I can see why. He's really good."

I said, "You don't sound much like an administrator, Miss Loring."

"I've been through this before, Mr. Spector. I was a teacher at Kennedy for three years. Someone should do something for that boy."

"Someone's tried. Someone's busy getting crucified by a bunch of shortsighted Board of Ed people, right now."

McCaskey's voice came over the loudspeakers. He wanted to assure us that everything was under control. What a comfort.

Miss Loring moved away from the window. She gave me an odd once-over, a two-second appraisal. "Look, Mr. Spector. I don't approve of some of the things you've done here."

"Save it," I told her. "I've got a riot to attend."

She bridled. "I was going to offer you some help, if you really mean what you say about these kids." She crossed the office to where she'd been sitting earlier and picked up a tan trench coat. I didn't think she wanted to be helped on with it. I wasn't sure I wanted to help her on with it, for that matter. "I've seen teachers like you before," she said.

"Yeah?"

"You knock yourself out against the odds, get nowhere, and then you assume the system doesn't work."

"I don't assume that."

"No?"

I said, "Hell, no. I'm living *proof* that the system doesn't work."

She took a card from her purse, scribbled a number down, and handed it brusquely to me. "Give me a call in a day or two. I'll see what I can do to get that boy a job at some ad agency. Just part time. He'll have to learn that the walls there are to remain graffiti-free, though."

Of all the goddamned things, I thought. A bottle splintered against the office window and made me start. I looked at the little card in my hand. Beverly Loring, it said. She was on her way out the door of McCaskey's office.

"Miss Loring?" I said.

She turned around and straight-faced me as though she'd just won a chess game. "Yes?"

"Thanks," I said. She smiled a half-smile and continued out the door. I'd been about to say, *Has anyone ever told you you've got terrific legs?* but that would have been inappropriate, even for me. What I had to do was find Marlyn, before things got too out of hand.

When I got as far as the glass doors in the main office, I saw that it was too late. There were screaming mobs in the corridor. Black-and-gold-hooded kids. Kings. Black-and-blue shirts and sweaters. Disciples. Over and over McCaskey insisted that it was a false alarm, but his voice sounded puny and pathetic compared to the noise of the gangs and the drone of the sirens. An anomaly.

A hall monitor's desk flew through the doors and sprayed broken shards over the clerks, who shrieked, and—in panic—fell upon the floor. I could see a free-for-all near the stairwell on the second floor. Arms and heads whirled in the confusion. Above all the racket I could hear the chant "Folks love!" They had cornered the Kings on the stairs and were beating the shit out of them. I reasoned that as long as there was no gunfire, it was still just another day.

Dave Volmer fought his way through a group of kids and ran into the office. When he slammed the door, tiny glass fragments fell and tinkled on the bar handles. Dave had a gash on his head, right near his receding hairline.

"I hope you've got your life insurance paid up, Johnny."

"What the hell happened to you?"

Dave said, "Do you see what's going on out there? *That's* what happened to me."

"Have you seen Carlos?" I asked him. Carlos would not know what to do in a situation like this, I thought.

"Carlos? I think he's in adaptive gym. Those kids are on the field. That's the best place they could be. Don't worry about them—worry about us."

Dave looked around the main office, at the clerks hiding behind desks, the glass on the floor. He appeared dazed.

"Dave, what about—"

"I haven't seen her either," he said, reaching for the wound on his forehead. "Just don't go out there. Stay here and watch McCaskey shit in his pants."

Behind the counter, McCaskey was speaking into the intercom microphone and fooling with the dials, apparently to get more volume out of the thing. I'll always remember him like that, grasping onto the microphone, hunched over the controls. Shouting like a maniac. The ship was sinking and the captain had freaked.

I pushed my way into the crowd in the hallway. Everything was one big swelling wave and you had to avoid flailing arms. An industrial-size wastebasket went flying over the throng and landed on the heads of two or three students, who went straight to the floor. The escalators were jammed with bodies. They hurtled kids on top of each other at ground level, where there was no place left to go. Someone slapped me on the back, and I spun around to see if I had a fight on my hands. It was Pedro. His eyes resembled Ping-Pong balls and he was yelling something at me.

"What?"

I lowered my ear to his mouth. I could feel his breath on my skin. "People on the sixth floor. They got guns. They shot one guy in the head up there. His fucking eyes popped out of his head!"

I said, "No."

"Fucking yes. Guy named Shorty. He was a D, man."

A D was a Disciple, as if I cared about his affiliation. Once your head explodes, it kind of doesn't matter which gang you've been in.

Pedro was screaming something else now, but I couldn't hear him above the shouting and the sirens and McCaskey's amplified voice. Some kid's elbow caught me in the stomach. It knocked my wind out. I doubled over but was kept standing by the crush of students. There literally wasn't enough room to fall down. You could either fight the movement of the crowd and get nowhere, or you could let it push you and make some kind of headway toward the down escalator. I kept my arms securely around my middle to keep from getting hit again, and slowly my wind came back. Short little nauseating breaths. The sirens shut down abruptly. In their place, McCaskey persisted in demanding that everyone remain in the building. No one paid him a bit of attention.

There was a corner in the main hallway that was relatively empty. I moved with the flow until I could push my way to it. A smoke bomb came sliding down the aluminum side of the escalator from the third floor. A big sulfur cloud went up and made the mob even more hyper than it was. I saw a small girl with a long plaid dress go under the legs of the rioters and disappear. I had to change my course and fight to get near where she had gone down.

"Please return to your classrooms. That was a false alarm."

No sooner had McCaskey made his statement than the fire alarm was pulled once more. A series of students trampled the girl on the floor. I could see her face. She was trying to call for help. No one heard her.

I pushed back on the kid behind me, a kid with black curly hair and a little blond ponytail—a boy. "There's a girl getting crushed here. Push back."

The kid just shoved me from behind and yelled, "Fuck you, **man.**"

So I hit him. Square in the jaw. He fell back against a wave of students and was soon circulated around the bend to the escalator. I reached for the girl's arm, but she was knocked backward by a ripple effect of bodies. She somehow was able to stand up by herself in the short amount of time that a small space developed around her. In a second more she disappeared again among the limbs and heads of kids moving slowly toward the first floor.

There was no fighting the movement anymore. I had to let the pressure carry me along. The escalator had been shut off, and when I was pushed onto it, I held on to the black railing and tried to keep my balance. Some of the kids in the middle fell and rolled onto the backs of others. Dominoes.

Mike Bane and a cordon of cops were directing the rioters out of the building once they reached the ground floor. Sometimes the mob would attempt to break through them, and the cops would hit the kids over their heads with nightsticks. They weren't pulling punches, either. I heard a nightstick strike a skull as I got closer to the bottom and it sounded like a hammer on wood. Hollow wood.

Mike had his walkie-talkie up to his ear. Outside, someone threw a rock at the windows and shattered glass rained over everyone in sight. Two cops with riot helmets caught the offender and knocked him senseless; there was a blur of sticks as they came down on him from all sides. A paddy wagon backed up slowly to the entrance. The kid was thrown in like a side of beef.

When I reached ground level I cupped my hands around my mouth and shouted to Bane, "Let me stay here and help you."

He nodded. He motioned to the cop next to him to make room in the chain of bodies. You had to constantly push the kids back just to hold your ground. Someone caught my arm and tried to knock me out of the line. The cop next to me brought down his stick on the head of a tall kid who was wearing a football jersey. The kid fell and the cop kicked him in the chest and repeatedly clubbed him until he crawled out the doors on his hands and knees.

"Fuckin' spic," I heard the cop say.

I said, "That's not the right attitude."

"Don't give me that. We oughta load a boat full of these cockroaches and send 'em all back where they came from. Better yet, hope the fuckin' boat sinks."

One side in this affair was as bad as the other.

From the side door, a group of seven or eight more cops in riot gear entered and ran across the lobby to the elevator. They were carrying tear gas rifles. The elevator doors opened and they boarded and vanished.

I looked up at the kids descending the escalator. They were coming faster now. Some of the girls were crying. Gang members were covered with blood. Bane's walkie-talkie went off and I could hear McCaskey saying, "Unit two. Confirmed shootings on fifth and sixth floors. Where the hell are the cops? We need some goddamn cops."

I think it was the first time I'd ever heard McCaskey swear.

Mike said something back to him, but I couldn't make out what it was. I kept my eye on the escalator for some sign of Marlyn. I hoped she was already out of the building.

I saw something red on my shirt and discovered that my nose was bleeding. In all the jostling, I hadn't noticed that I'd been hit.

"You okay?" Bane asked.

"I think so," I said. "Just a little blood."

There was a dull thud and a crack to my left. A kid had either jumped or been pushed from the escalator and now was lying unconscious, face down on the floor. A cop ran over to him and turned his head to the side. I looked away.

More cop cars pulled up to the circular drive. I counted a total of thirteen. Two paddy wagons. The cops were having a hell of a time keeping the kids away from the building. They'd shoot out the door in droves, disperse, regroup, and storm back, throwing rocks and bottles. There was one cop on the ground behind a car, holding something up to his head. He'd been hit.

Back to the escalator. Flashes of faces, bobbing heads. Familiar kids, unfamiliar kids. More skirmishes as the endless waves tried to break through the police line. Nightsticks. My bloody nose. I touched it with my hand. Solid red. Most of my shirt was blood soaked and I began to feel a bit woozy. I wondered who had hit me.

On a chance glimpse I spotted Marlyn on the escalator, halfway down the steps. She didn't see me. She was trying to get a hold on the railing, but other kids were pushing past her, keeping her in the center of the surge. I forced my way through a wall of people when she reached the bottom and took her by the arm. She tugged back as we were pushed outside.

"It's me," I said. "It's okay."

She put an arm around my waist and I hurried her around a struggle between some cops and some punks with broken bottles clenched in their hands. We were cut off again by a charging group of about five orange-and-green-clad kids. Ghetto Brothers. I pushed her close to the brick walls of the building and looked for a way out. To my left was a walkway that led to the eastern side of the school. There was a hill there and a few trees, where the park met the campus. I tilted my head in that direction. "C'mon. I'll race you," I said, pulling her by the hand. Once we were well out of the commotion we slowed down and walked the rest of the way. Marlyn leaned her back against one of the trees and held her hand out to my face.

"You're bleeding."

"I know."

There was a crash and then another. Desks were being pushed out of a sixth-floor window. I watched one fall and hit the patio below. It broke into two pieces. Up above, where there had once been a windowpane, a dark kid stuck his head out for air. Clouds of tear gas went streaming into the sky and hung over the walks.

Marlyn said, "What's happening here?"

"Nothing good."

"Are they crazy?"

"Yep."

Well, hell, I thought. At least we'd be getting rid of McCaskey. A fiasco like this was his ticket to a submerged office somewhere downtown where no one would ever hear his name again. Education politics in Chicago is a lot like major-league baseball. McCaskey was the manager of the home team and he'd just lost the series. Nobody was going to worry about Johnny Spector's lesson plans after the smoke cleared.

The sun was out and it created long shadows on the uneven ridges of the grass. Our silhouettes melted into the shadows of tree branches, and I was thinking what a nice day it was. Clean air. It must have blown in from the Rockies. If there hadn't been a riot, it would have been perfect weather for a picnic, or lunch at Jerome's, or any of those airy cafes on Clark Street.

Marlyn was looking back at the activity. She shook her head as an ambulance slowly rolled up the drive, its Mars lights twirling like little beacons.

I said, "I guess lunch is off."

"I wasn't hungry anyway."

She touched my shirt front. The blood was mostly dried by then. She made a futile little effort to straighten my tie. I remember thinking how beautiful she looked. She could take your mind right off a disaster.

"Do you love me?" she asked, making the question sound as light as an inquiry into my health. "I mean, *really* love me? No jokes, please."

"Fresh out of jokes."

"This wasn't just a spree?"

"I'm not into sprees."

I watched a Channel Five news-unit van approach the mess around the drive. Someone had set a police car on fire, and big whirling puffs of black smoke rose upward. Just like my old Buick. A cameraman jumped from the van and adjusted something on his video pack, which hung on a harness from his shoulder. When the kids spotted the camera, they gathered and stood in front of the lens and made gang symbols with their hands. The news director pushed a few of them out of the way and got punched and kicked for his trouble.

Marlyn took one of my hands in hers. She had nice hands. Adult hands.

"I don't want you to go to Puerto Rico," I said. "I want you to stay here. Be a nurse. Give shots. Do nurse things."

"That's what I want, too."

"Well then?"

She'd been about to lean her head on my chest, remembered the blood, and changed her mind. "Well then," she said, "there's a man at home who doesn't see it that way."

I thought about the first time I'd seen her, right there in the park. And then I thought about what our lives would have been like at that moment if she'd never asked me to sign the book. Funny.

I said, "We'll think of something. We're both smart, right?" Then she kissed my cheek. It took her a while to find a clean spot to do it. Some guys always have a handkerchief. I was the other kind of guy, who didn't. "You have to be your own man, sweetheart."

"You sure talk funny for a teacher," she said. She pinched my ear.

"Go straight home. I'll call you tomorrow."

She lingered a minute. "Going to stay here?"

I nodded. "I'm just going to think for a while. Go ahead. We'll talk."

She turned away and started down the path to the park. Her hips swayed back and forth—a little beige-and-brown metronome. Marlyn and her dreams. She melted into the colors and shadows, the moving forms along the walkways of the park, and I lost sight of her.

I took off my jacket and untied my tie and sat down on the wet ground under the tree. I could feel some dried blood on my chin and tried to rub it off. My nose was throbbing. A breeze made the leaves above me rustle. The wind smelled like spring. It was one of those winds that you smelled when you were a kid, and it seemed as though it should have had a name, that wind, but I couldn't think of what it was. It was gone—back there in a time when everything was simple and things made sense.

I tapped my shirt pocket, feeling for my cigarettes. Goddamn it. Down to my last one. I extracted it, straightened the rough edges, lighted it, and tossed the crumpled pack away. The brittle sound of windows breaking mixed with police radio calls. The crowd had dissipated, replaced by a few stragglers and an ocean of Snickers–Dr Pepper–Baby Ruth–Marlboro–Twinkies litter. A discarded newspaper page glided a few inches above the grass like a haunted thing. One kid wearing mirrored sunglasses wanted to know if I had a light. He looked like a metallic bee. I gave him my matches and waved them away. A little memento of the riot. A stretcher surrounded by police and paramedics was being carried out of the front door. I craned my neck to see better. The white sheet billowed in the wind and was pulled to cover the entirety of the body. Shorty.

Shorty was a D, man.

Fifteen

The next two weeks at Freddie Prinze High were like the aftermath of a peculiar and depressing nightmare. Teachers and kids walked around in a quiet daze. Some die-hard gangsters tried to get the momentum rolling again with fights and false fire alarms, but no one's heart was in it. When the sirens went off, the students climbed down the escalators at a drag-footed pace out to the park, past the boarded-up lobby windows, as though they might have been prisoners in a concentration camp with nothing better to do than obey the signals. It really had been quite a year.

I had to get used to the sight of cops in the hallways, cops in the office, cops in the lunchroom, and more of the same in the faculty lounge. Blue uniforms everywhere. Big smoky clouds from constant cigarette smoking in the prep room. And there were other things to get used to. McCaskey, as expected, had been sent indefinitely to the district office. Mike Bane and his ever-present walkie-talkie moved into the principal's office. He was in the driver's seat until they could find someone else who was capable of exercising bad judgment enough to alienate the students and staff. I started getting memorandums about washroom passes. Teachers were discouraged from writing any passes at all. The basic but specious logic here was, if we didn't write passes, then there would be no kids in the halls to start fights or inflict graffiti on clean surfaces. There would just be a lot of swollen bladders in classrooms. When Mike decided he hadn't gone far enough in imposing order on the school, he turned his attention to the student dress code. Girls were now forbidden to wear halter tops and shorts. They were a disruption, Mike claimed. With the advent of summerlike weather, it was my job to report the names of any students wearing shorts. Particularly brief shorts. In a faculty meeting one day, Mike held his hand at thigh level and showed everybody what constituted a *brief* pair of shorts. We just stared silently at him. Then he showed us what a halter top was. He actually held up a goddamn halter top. It sort of made me wonder where the hell he'd found it. Maybe he'd personally confiscated it. It wouldn't have surprised me.

I did not fight any of these new rules. They were all petty and fell short of what really mattered. Besides, everyone knew where I stood on these issues. My face gave it away.

My classes were smaller than usual. A lot of parents kept their kids home, afraid of a repeat performance. Shorty had become an unofficial legend. Someday, maybe they'll erect a statue of him in the courtyard. It would give the next couple of generations something to deface with spray paint, at least.

One bright light on the horizon was, surprisingly, Tony. Miss Loring, true to her word, had found the little bastard a job. Three times a week, Tony would gather up his art supplies and board an El and report for work at Anderson & Reese, an ad agency on Michigan Avenue. I kept my fingers crossed on those days that he wouldn't succumb to what I was sure was a burning desire to paint a mural on the president's Mercedes. So far, he hadn't. I went out and bought him an artist's portfolio so that he could take his storyboards to school and show them off. Who could tell? Maybe the other train-bombers would envy his position and try to break into the real world.

But most of my energy, most of my attention went to Marlyn during those weeks. She had been walking a fine line between grabbing her independence and sinking back into a submissive sleepwalk. She had tried talking to her father about the possibility of staying on in Chicago for her education, but every time she did so, he turned on his stoic mask and repeated the line about there being only two roads. He saw life as one long highway with a lone exit ramp. And then I'd be the one the next day who had to read between the lines, who had to decipher the looks on her face, the subtle traces of despair or hope.

She went out with me a few times—to the movies once, where she slept through the feature, and to the Chicago Public Library, where we gathered information about financial aid and state grants for undergraduates. On the way home from the library, she put her arm around me while I was driving and said, "If I get accepted, I mean to Loyola and everything, then I think I'll be able to stand up to him."

"You can stand up to him now," I said.

"It would be better then. I'd have something to show him."

That made me think of the night we'd gone to the 95th, and how Mr. Valentin had at first forbidden the date, and later given it his reluctant approval. I was banking on the same strategy working again. Get the acceptance, go to Miss Loring (who insisted I call her Bev—I had the faint inkling she was waiting for me to ask her out to dinner), have her give Marlyn a boost of confidence, and help her work out the details. After that, it was just a war of diplomacy. I didn't want to push Marlyn. Too many edges to fall over.

One afternoon, after a full day of telling kids no, they couldn't go take a piss no matter how bad they had to go, Dave Volmer slapped me on the back as I was on my way out of the building. A dim trace of pain raced around my gang wound—a little reminder of what teacher involvement could get you.

"Buy you a beer," he said.

"With your credit rating?" I said.

"You look like you could use a drink, Johnny."

"The way I look only tells one-tenth the true story."

"Fine. I'll buy the first round, and you pick up the other nine."

We ended up at Dave's favorite watering hole, the Ukrainian bar with the crazy jukebox and the old ladies with spaces between their teeth. It was hot inside and the lights were low and today you could smell the sour smell of cheap draft. I swished the first gulp of beer around in my mouth. It stung my taste buds and was like a slap in the face.

Dave and I just sat there, staring at the whiskey-lined mirror behind the bar. He said, "It feels like there's not a hell of a lot to say at the end of a day anymore."

I nodded. "I figure we can kill off the student population in no time with uremic poisoning. Hell, let's just get rid of the bathrooms altogether."

"Nope," he said, sipping his drink and saying, "Ahhhh," afterward. "Need the bathrooms. Gotta flush the memos somewhere."

I ordered the second round immediately. The bartender seemed to favor us over the regulars. Perhaps he knew how bad we needed to get drunk.

I said, "You know, I think I'm burning out."

Dave did not say anything.

"What do we do this for? Really. For what?"

"Because we didn't listen to our parents when they told us to become doctors."

I said, "My parents never told me to be a doctor."

"Then you were adopted."

The music started. Today, no one danced. They sat on stools at the bar, they looked out the window, or they tapped their knees with their hands.

Dave must have felt a rush of compassion. He put his arm around my shoulders. "Tell me, buddy. Do you love her, or what?"

I saw our reflections in the mirror, between a bottle of Jack Daniels and another bottle whose label I couldn't read.

"Yep."

"Then what the hell. Marry her."

"Can't."

"Why not?"

I gulped my beer. It was good to have someone to tell about this. Kind of like confession.

"Oh, I don't know. A lot of reasons. She's very young. How would I know she was marrying me for the right reasons? She's got to get on her own, first. You know."

He clicked his tongue a few times. Well, I thought. It had finally happened. The school had worn him down so much that he had no rejoinder—and after only two beers.

I left a ten on the bar, stood up, tapped him on the arm, and said, "Have the other eight without me."

Without waiting for an answer, I walked to the door and was ready to leave when Dave said, "Johnny, hey. I forgot to tell you. Marlyn's ACT scores came in today."

I closed the door and walked back over to his stool, which he straddled like an expert. "And?"

Dave said, "And *what?*"

"What are the scores?"

He looked up, apparently trying to read the scores on the embossed tin ceiling. "They were high for one of our kids. Twenty-nine, I think. Either twenty-eight or twenty-nine."

"Twenty-nine *composite?*"

"Yeah. Want me to tell her tomorrow?"

I thought about that. "No, it's okay. I'll get word to her." A new polka came from the jukebox. Sounded like the McGuire Sisters singing in Russian. "I wish you would have told me about this sooner, Dave."

He shrugged. "I was too busy looking for halter tops. I've got my priorities, you know."

Outside the wind was warm and smelled of tar and made me cough. I walked back to my Jeep and just sat in it for a while. I wondered how many teachers felt like I did. Beaten. Maybe if I kept my mouth shut and took the rules seriously and believed that strict obedience would save the day, I'd get somewhere.

Naw.

It was one of those days in Chicago when everybody who lived on the west side was out of doors, either playing conga drums, or hanging out in front of Laundromats, or getting high in the park. Every so often a group of Latin kids would stare at the honky and puzzle over what he was doing in their neighborhood. I started the Jeep, put it in first, and followed the winding parkway to North Avenue, under big leafy maples. Marlyn could use some good news, I reasoned, and the ACT score was as good as a college acceptance.

I parked a block away from Walgreen's in an illegal zone and hopped out of the front seat without opening the door. Vic Morrow used to do that on the old *Combat* series in the sixties. He wasn't doing it anymore, though.

Through the turnstile. People speaking rapid Spanish. I was the only guy without a beard. The only guy who wasn't wearing a pair of Pumas with fat shoelaces. Marlyn wasn't at the camera counter. There was a girl at the register—one with a very striking face—who could have been either beautiful or slightly funny looking. I couldn't decide which. I walked over to the fountain. No Marlyn there. Mary was there, though. She had a gallon of blush on each cheek and this week her hair was spiked. Every time I saw her hairdo I was tempted to offer it raw meat.

I said, " 'Scuse me, Mary?"

She had a blender going and was wiping her hands on a dish towel. She walked over to me, chewing gum the way a ballplayer does.

"Marlyn's not here today," she said, as though she could guess your thoughts.

"I thought she worked on Thursdays."

Mary nodded without losing a beat on her Wrigley's. "Yeah. She called in sick today. She pulled up from school and called in sick or sumpin'."

I'd seen Marlyn between the fourth and fifth periods and she hadn't said anything about being sick.

"Okay," I told Mary, tapping the counter absently with my keys. "Thanks."

"Wanna Coke?"

"No, really. Thanks, though." I turned around and had to wait behind a group of women buying lace gloves. Lace was big this year. Everyone thought she was Madonna.

Back in the Jeep. I sat and played with the gearshift, thinking about the worst thing that could happen if I drove over to Marlyn's house with the news. But her father probably didn't have a gun; he had a smoother approach than that. So then I thought about the second-to-the-worst thing that could happen. I'd just be told to leave, very unpleasantly. I started the engine, pulled a U-turn, and almost lost the transmission on the median strip.

I drove down Francisco kind of fast, past open fire hydrants where kids splashed in the water. Ghetto pools. If there was ever a fire in that part of town in the summer, the water pressure might sprinkle a lawn. It sure as hell wouldn't be any good at putting out a blaze.

I parked in front of Marlyn's house. It was too hot to light a cigarette. My mouth had gone dry. If Mr. Valentin could intimidate *me*, I supposed I could understand what it was he did to his own daughter. I wished suddenly that I'd taken Mary up on that Coke offer.

A group of guys stood on the corner. They were selling a different kind of coke. Pink shirts, black pants. Imperial Gangsters. I saw them leering at me as I walked up the steps to Marlyn's front door.

"Got that *toot*, white boy."

White boy. I think I liked *honky* better.

I rapped on the door and waited. A curtain moved in the door window and I saw Marlyn peeking out at me. Then the door opened. She was standing there in a pair of tennis shorts and white sneakers.

"Johnny, what are you doing here?"

The guys on the corner were giving me the razz now that Marlyn was there. One of them must have recognized me from school. He said, "Hey, Teach. Private lessons." Cute.

"Your father home?" I said.

She shook her head. Her eyes were swollen.

"Then invite me in. We have to talk."

She stepped out of the way and the door closed behind me. Inside, the house had that smell I remembered from Tony's place. There was a fan on in the corner. Marlyn said, "I don't know when he'll be back. You shouldn't be here."

"I had to come over. Look, you want to go for a ride?" I suggested. "This place gives me the creeps. No offense."

"Did you try to find me at work?"

"Yep. I hear you're sick."

She walked back to the dining room and sat in a chair by the table. On the table were a series of forms that had been crinkled and then straightened out. Marlyn pulled some Kleenex from a box and blew her nose. Kleenex was becoming a thing with her. She sat so that one foot was on the chair seat, her knee close up to her chin.

"This is never going to work," she said, nudging one of the forms. "I was washing the dishes before I was supposed to go to work. I found these in the garbage when I went to throw out the coffee grounds."

I read the letter on top. It was from Loyola. They were acting on her application, it said, but before financial aid could be granted, she needed her father's signature and a copy of his tax return. They might as well have asked for both of his arms and a few bricks of gold. Stumbling blocks. I was worried about how many more we could make it across.

Marlyn said, "Guess who's not going to sign these? He didn't even tell me they *came.* I had to find them in the goddamn *garbage.*"

"Let's not give up now, honey. Let's just be cool for a second."

"Cool," she said, and then snorted, and began the nose-blowing routine all over again.

I put my arms around her and she patted me on the back, as if *I* were the one who needed to be calmed down. I had a neat mental image of sticking some dynamite where it would do the most damage— but her father wasn't home.

I said, "Here's what we do. Can you find his tax return?"

Marlyn released the grip on her leg and sat silently. "I don't know where he keeps that stuff."

"Well, you can look, can't you? It couldn't hurt."

"He might be home any minute."

"So—just look in a hurry."

I walked over to the phone. No buttons. A dial. It was on a little table with bric-a-brac on a lower shelf.

"Who are you going to call?" she wanted to know.

"A friend."

She got up and walked into another room. I could hear drawers being opened and papers shoved around. I slipped Miss Loring's card from my wallet. I dialed her number and waited to go through the wild-goose chase that was a preliminary to any attempt at communication with the Board of Education. One operator connected me to the wrong department and I talked to a Mr. Logan. I hung up and tried again.

"Any luck?" I shouted to Marlyn, while I was put on hold for the second time.

"Not yet. I found my birth certificate, though."

I said, "Great. Now you've got proof that you're too young to drink in this state."

Then the prerecorded Muzak on the hold system was preempted by Miss Loring's businesslike tone. Just when I was sure that she had gone home early.

"Bev—it's Johnny. Johnny Spector."

There were typewriter noises in the background. Someone down there was actually working.

"Hello, Johnny. I wasn't expecting to hear from you. Listen, I'm kind of up to my neck at the moment."

"Me, too," I said. "Can you give me a second, though? I think I can make this quick."

"Just one. Is everything all right with Tony?"

"Tony's fine. Thanks a lot for that, by the way."

"You've already thanked me ten times."

"Who's counting? Bev—quick scenario. Eighteen-year-old girl, third in her class. A twenty-nine ACT. She wants to get into Loyola's nursing program. Her father won't sign the financial aid papers— wants to take her to Puerto Rico and keep her prisoner for a few

years. She's willing to stay here on her own. Career—no career. Know
what I mean?"

"A *Prinze* student?" she asked.

"Yes."

"A Prinze student with a twenty-nine composite?"

"Yeah, listen," I said. "We'll gasp and pass out later. I need to
know if she can stay here by herself and get financial aid without
the old man's cooperation."

She laughed to herself. Sounded exasperated. "What the hell is
wrong with parents these days?"

"I don't know. Maybe success is hard for some people to take.
What I need from you is some help."

"I'd like to meet this girl."

I said, "I'd like you to. You'd be impressed. Let's set up a time
early next week. I need an answer now."

She said, "Uh," thought for a second, rustled some papers, and
then said, "Hmm."

"You'll have to do better than that."

She asked for the student's name, and I gave it to her. Marlyn,
with a *y*. She said she would call up the financial aid director and
explain the circumstances. She was pretty sure that as long as a student
met the admissions requirements, the parent's signature on financial
papers could be waived at the discretion of the director. The tax
return was an absolute necessity, however.

"Kind of figured that."

She said, "Can you get it?"

"I'm working on that right now. Listen. Thanks."

"Bring that girl to me next week."

I said I would, and then she asked me to also bring her father's
head on a platter.

"Don't think it hasn't crossed my mind."

I had to hang up rather rudely. The front door opened. There
was no mystery as to who it was.

I stood next to the phone and waited as the footsteps approached
from the foyer. Marlyn was still in the back room. I had no way to
alert her. I heard the sound of a paper bag being carried, and in a
moment Mr. Valentin entered the dining room. He was holding a
brown shopping bag. Groceries. He stopped, looked at me, and put
the shopping bag down on the worn carpet.

"I was just leaving," I said, to break the ice.

He stood motionless, staring me down, until his eyes drifted to the dining table where the Loyola forms lay. Then back at me. Cold eyes. Screwdrivers.

"You no remember our little talk, *maestro*?"

I said, "Much better than I'd like to, Mr. Valentin. Like I said, I was just leaving."

In the next room I heard a final drawer close, and then Marlyn walked in, and the two of us exchanged quaky looks. It was the O.K. Corral.

Her father said something to her in Spanish, something I didn't catch. But his tone was openly hostile. She did not answer him. He made a move toward the dining table, a move that sent Marlyn there first, gathering up her application forms. She tucked them between her arms and her chest. Then he said something else to her that I didn't understand. She stood her ground. She spoke back to him in English.

"*Papi*, I need your signature on these forms."

Papi. It sounded incongruously affectionate in this situation.

Mr. Valentin looked away and said nothing. I was more or less holding my breath, wishing I could disappear or whisk Marlyn the hell out the door with me.

"Will you sign them?" she asked, extending the papers to him.

The answer came as a glare in his eyes.

"Not even if it means my future?"

Mr. Valentin said, "You have your future."

Well. English again, I thought.

"You call Tutti a *future*?" Marlyn screamed. Her voice pierced the quiet of the room and came as such a shock that I shuddered. I had never heard her scream before. It was not something that I would want to hear again.

A little gust of wind blew in through the open window near the fan and made the curtains swell and then retract. I felt as though we were all corners in an antagonistic triangle. Geometric tension.

"Johnny, let's get out of here." Marlyn went off to her room for a second, and I was left alone with Mr. Valentin.

"I have told you, *maestro*."

I said, "Two roads?"

"You would be wise to obey."

"I don't know," I said. "I don't see much wisdom going on here."

"We see," he said, with that way he had of making everything he said sound like a fully loaded threat. "We see."

"I suppose we will."

Marlyn walked back into the room, a purse slung over her shoulder. She looked at me and then continued to the front door.

"I forbid you to go—" Mr. Valentin called after her. Then he punctuated his demand by pounding the table firmly with his fist.

Marlyn turned back and said, "You can't tell me what to do anymore, señor."

On our way out, just before I closed the door, I heard Mr. Valentin shout his daughter's name, the way the Spanish do, with the accent on the second syllable. An old man and his anger. It made me sad, in a way. In nearly the same way I felt sad for Tony's mother.

It had been so dark in the Valentin house that the sun came as a blinding surprise. I skipped down the steps to the sidewalk. Marlyn was waiting for me. The guys on the corner gave their approval to her tennis shorts. They did this by whistling, clucking, and shouting suave compliments like *"Nice legs, mama!"*

I opened the passenger door of the Jeep and she hopped in. I preferred my jumping trick, but got my leg caught on the inside door handle. I played it off; I pretended I *hadn't* gouged my knee, by smiling a stupid smile.

"Do you have any sunglasses?" Marlyn asked me.

"Glove compartment."

She opened the glove compartment, which wasn't difficult. The door latch was broken and rarely stayed shut unless someone—usually me—kicked it vigorously ten or twelve times. Marlyn found the glasses, put them on, and then said, "Where are we going?"

"Any ideas?"

"No."

I started the Jeep and took off. The gangsters on the corner became tiny caricatures of themselves in the side-view mirror. Then I made a turn and the reflection of the sun wiped the mirror clean—a bright little shield that I couldn't look at anymore.

I said, "Did you find the tax papers?"

She slapped her purse without looking at me, indicating that she had.

I took North Avenue to Western, turned left, and rode until I hit a red light at Armitage. Carlos was working the intersection, running down the line of stopped cars. I took a quarter from my jeans pocket.

"*Hola*, Yohnny!"

I said, "Carlos—what's the Cubs score?"

He had just enough time to say, "Cubs win," before the light turned green and the traffic moved on. I flipped the paper over and glanced at the back page. The Cubs had lost, three to two. Carlos was learning.

I went east on Fullerton. I did not want to go back to my apartment. It seemed to me that the timing was rather poor to end up in a lovemaking clinch that would solve nothing and just delay the business at hand. When we were jammed in traffic under a railroad viaduct, I turned to Marlyn and said, "Are you okay?"

She did not answer me. Just stared straight ahead through the windshield as though she wanted to pick a fight with the bumper of a blue Chevy in front of us. The only barometer to her emotional state was effectively cut off by the shades I'd lent her. When you couldn't see her eyes, you had no idea what she was thinking, or feeling.

I turned on the radio of the Jeep—only AM—and the Beach Boys were singing "Little Deuce Coupe."

> *Well, I'm not braggin', babe, so don't put me down,*
> *But I've got the fastest set of wheels in town.*

Marlyn snapped off the song after the first chorus. "What the hell is a deuce coupe, anyway?"

I shrugged. "I don't know. I didn't take auto shop in high school. Some kind of revved-up car, I guess."

So much for the radio.

I had only seen her like this once or twice before, when I'd hinted by accident that I was the more mature one in the relationship, and therefore responsible for what had happened between us, and the night of Shelly's famous entrance. I debated whether I should try to put my arm around her as we sailed down Ashland, around trucks stopped for unloading and cars double-parked in a Mexican neighborhood. The hands-off tactic seemed best. We drove on silently, except for the click of the gears and the whoosh of the terminally ill muffler that I hadn't replaced. I tried to balance my checkbook in my mind to see if I could afford the replacement. With summer coming and no income for July and August, it made sense to get the most out of a noisy muffler.

I slowed down near Diversey and Pine Grove, by a liquor store I frequented. All of a sudden I wanted a cigar, something to help me mull things over during what I was sure was going to be a single-sided dialogue. I parked in front of a White Hen Pantry.

"Where are you going?" Marlyn demanded, from her position in the passenger seat.

"Gotta get something. I'll be right back."

The liquor store was cool and quiet and only the insulated sounds of buses made their way inside. I stood in front of a cigar rack and picked a couple of thin ones. Fat cigars made me look ridiculous. As I was paying the clerk, I spotted a display of white Zinfandel on sale for four bucks a bottle. My kind of price. I selected a bottle, set it on the counter, and picked up a cheap corkscrew, almost as an afterthought. I asked the guy if he had any plastic cups.

"Gotta buy the whole bag," he said, pointing to a dusty shelf with rows of plastic-covered cups. Twenty to a bag.

"I only need two, you know?"

"Sorry. Gotta buy the bag."

So I bought the goddamn bag. If the two of us got lonely, we could invite eighteen other people to join us.

When I got back to the Jeep, Marlyn was sitting there like Ray Charles, exactly as I'd left her. I put the bag of goodies in the backseat, save for one cigar that I unwrapped and stuck into my mouth. I did not know what it was about cigars that made me feel so good. I hoped to hell it wasn't Freudian. Marlyn took a sidelong look at me, and turned away again. Diversey was bumper to bumper and I had to inch my way into the traffic surreptitiously, while a guy behind me was daydreaming.

"Where are we headed?" Marlyn asked, watching me light the cigar.

The first few puffs reminded me why I didn't smoke the damn things more often. "I thought it would be kind of nice to sit at Belmont Harbor. Watch the boats." Since she didn't disapprove, vocally, at least, I continued on course.

There are some nice places in Chicago. Unfortunately, you have to go through the places that aren't so nice to get to them. Belmont Harbor sits off the drive like a serene pool unattached to the city proper. I found a parking space near a pier and glided the Jeep to a perfect stop between a Firebird and a Honda. I pulled up the emergency brake. I sat and looked at the bicyclers on the path and the joggers who never seemed to get anywhere.

"Take a walk?" I said, opening my door. I grabbed the bag with the wine and the cups inside. Marlyn nodded and got out. We were separated until we made our way around a row of cars. When I was beside her, I took her hand in mine and directed her to the most abandoned pier I could find. Wooden slats. Lake smells. There was a breeze off the lake that made the sun bearable. We sat down on a series of slats that hadn't yet decayed. I set the bag down and we dangled our legs above the water.

To my left, an old man with a sailor hat, rolled down to cover his forehead, sat patiently holding a fishing rod. He was statue-still, except for a hand that swatted flies away from his neck. Marlyn took off her shoes and socks and let her bare feet hang over the edge.

"I wouldn't do that, if I were you," I told her.

"Hmm? Why?"

"Sharks."

"Shut up, Johnny."

Well. At least we were talking.

I said, "Freshwater sharks are the worst kind."

I puffed on my cigar and watched as the clouds of smoke wafted and vanished in the clear air. Marlyn was looking at me, though I couldn't see her eyes. She slapped my arm and then grasped one of my hands in hers. We sat like that for a while.

"Always a joke," she said. "Always funny Johnny."

"I could get depressed, if you like."

"No, thanks. I'm handling the depression, at the moment."

I said, "And doing a very good job with it, too."

A speedboat, about a sixteen-footer, raced by the harbor and left a wake that rocked the moored boats. The old fisherman muttered, "Asshole," to himself and extended the rod outward, away from the pier.

Marlyn laughed to herself. "Did you hear what he said?"

I nodded.

"Do you think he'll catch anything?" she asked, looking at me with her hidden eyes.

"Take off the glasses, sweetheart."

She one-handed them off, blinking a few times to adjust to the light, which was coming off the lake in the form of an orange streak. It sparkled in the ripples.

"That's better." I held the cigar in my hand and twirled it around and shaped the ash on the wooden slat to my side. I was looking for words. I ended up watching her feet reflect in the water. "Why don't you give me the tax return. We can photocopy it on the way back and you can replace the original when you get a chance. He'll never know it was missing."

She unslung her purse from her shoulder and opened it, dug through it, and produced a few sheets of official-looking paper. She handed them to me and I folded them and stuck them in my shirt pocket.

"I'm so damn mad," she said, placing her hands on her knees and staring out at the water.

Don't push, I thought. Most important not to push. Not now.

I said, "Tell me about it."

"You were there, for God's sake. He threw out my mail. He wouldn't even listen to me. It doesn't matter to him if I become a nurse. Can you imagine not wanting your own daughter to go to college? It makes me so mad."

A sailboat slid by in the harbor, the waves lapping the hull gently, slurk-slurking just under the bow.

"Well," I said. "It's temporary. When he sees your grades for the first semester, he'll change his mind. This will all blow over."

I took out the bottle of Zinfandel, lay the corkscrew next to it, and tore open the bag of plastic cups.

"You make it sound like all my worries are over."

I set a cup on either side of the bottle. It looked nice. A little place setting out on the lake. I wished we had done this before. It made everything else seem so far away.

"I found out your ACT score. Mr. Volmer told me today."

Marlyn said, "What?"

"You got a twenty-nine composite. Congratulations."

The fisherman raised his rod slightly, let out some more line, and settled down to some more serious fly swatting.

"You *knew*? You knew and you didn't tell me?"

I inserted the corkscrew and began to twist it slowly. My history with corks was a pathetic one, and the last thing I needed to do now was break the goddamn thing in the bottle.

"Johnny, I don't understand you at all. I swear to God. You mean to tell me that all this time you knew and you let me—"

The cork popped and I drew a relieved breath. "Easy, kiddo. Easy. I just found out today. You had a lot to take care of first. A lot to think over on the ride. You *did* think things over, didn't you?"

She watched as I poured the wine, first into her glass, then into mine. I threw the extra cups back in the bag.

"Yes, I thought things over." She brushed some hair back, behind her ear. And then, as if she'd just heard me, she said, "Twenty-nine is pretty good, right?"

I took a sip of the wine. Not bad. Not great—but not bad, either.

"Twenty-nine?" I said. "Twenty-nine is spectacular, is what it is. You're in."

I watched her as she slid her hand on the wood beneath us, back and forth. Her eyes seemed to be mentally tabulating the chips as they fell on her side. She shivered a little shiver; the wind was coming off the lake, and the sun was mostly hidden by the buildings to the west.

She looked up suddenly and asked, "What about the papers? I'm still stuck with no signature."

"Drink your drink," I said.

She raised the glass and sipped and made a funny face. "It could use a little ice."

"You don't put ice in this stuff. Geez. Some people are awfully fussy."

She drank some more, put the glass down, and said, "I still need his signature."

I leaned back on my elbows, and for once I knew what it felt like to be a messenger with good news. I told her about Miss Loring and her plan to talk to the financial aid director. The remarkable Miss Beverly Loring. (I did not mention her legs.) I puffed some really fine smoke rings—sent them up like miniature helicopters all around me—and noticed the expression on Marlyn's face out of the corners of my eyes. Her smile got off to a slow start, but developed nicely. I got hugged. Lots of "You're kidding's" and "No, I'm not's." Girlish laughs. Marlyn's hair in the wind, made orange by the light